PEARS ON A WILLOW TREE

LESLIE PIETRZYK

Granta Books
London

Granta Publications, 2/3 Hanover Yard, London N1 8BE

First published in Great Britain by Granta Books 1998

The following chapters have been previously published (in
somewhat different form): "No Last Names" (*TriQuarterly*);
"Things Women Know" (*Shenandoah* – awarded Jeanne
Charpiot Goodheart Prize for Fiction); "I Want You to Have
This Now" (*New England Review*); "Braiding Bread"
(*Massachusetts Review*); "Cravings" (*River Styx*); "Blue
Beads" – under the title "My Grandmother's Rosary"
(*Willow Springs*); "Shortcuts" (*Explorations*); "Stories from
America" (*Janus*); "Best Friends" (*Fodderwing*).

A CIP catalogue record for this book is
available from the British Library.

1 3 5 7 9 10 8 6 4 2

ISBN 1 86207 220 5

Printed and bound in Great Britain by
Mackays of Chatham PLC

This book is dedicated to Robb:
husband, lover, friend, true believer & keeper of faith

Robert K. Rauth, Jr.
1960–1997

A C K N O W L E D G M E N T S

Heartfelt thanks to:

- Kate Hengerer and Howard Morhaim, David Hamilton, the editors who chose to publish some of these chapters in their journals (especially Rod Smith and Lynn Leech at *Shenandoah* and Stephen Donadio and Jessica Dineen at *New England Review*), my parents, Susan (who patiently answered every single question about Thailand), Bob and Marilyn, Rick Peabody, Jennifer Hershey and Chris Condry, everyone at the Arlington Chamber of Commerce for giving me time to write by letting me set my own work schedule, the Bread Loaf and Sewanee Writers' Conferences, Jack, and Donna.
- The four grand ladies who made the dinners and told the stories around the table: Grandma, Aunt Sylvia, Aunt Doris, and Cynthia. And in honor of a Polish lady I never met, Robb's *Bushia*, and the one I met but never really knew until now, Rose Lendo, the original Marchewka woman.
- Susan, Lisa, Paul, Susie, Jim, Chris and Kathy, Todd, Dan, Kate, Dana, Diana, and the countless others who were there when I really, really needed them.
- Robb.

CONTENTS

THE DAUGHTERS

Rose
Wanda
Joane
Helen
Marie
June
Ginger
Theresa
Marge
Amy

Shortcuts

AMY — 1988

After I moved to Thailand to teach English to rich schoolchildren, my mother took up letter writing, and often she enclosed old photographs with her letters. "Remember when we took this picture?" she'd write. Sometimes I did and sometimes I didn't.

Of all the photos she sent, I kept only one, a picture of my mother, my grandmother, my great-grandmother, and me, six or seven years old, lined up in front of my great-grandmother's stove, taken maybe twenty years ago.

It was my great-grandfather's camera. Just before he pushed the button, I remember him saying, "Four generations of Krawczyk women. Will you look at that."

My great-grandmother said, "These are Marchewka women," using her maiden name. "That's who we are, Marchewkas. Marchewka women." As she spoke, she squeezed my shoulder hard, pressing almost down to the bone, and I wasn't used to thinking of myself as part of this tiny, tightly made woman I saw only once a year.

My great-grandfather took the picture, and the four of us

stepped apart, shaking back our hair, plucking at our clothing, bending away smiles. Someone checked on my sleeping baby brother, maybe the phone rang.

We were at my great-grandmother's house because she was surprised my mother had never learned how to make *pierogi*, Polish dumplings. "There's no secret," my great-grandmother said as she opened and closed kitchen cupboards, barely glancing in them to set her hands on exactly what she wanted. "Don't all the time be looking first for shortcuts." I loved how she talked, her thick words like blocks stacking into a story.

"There must be a secret," my mother said. "Some special trick you can show me."

"No," my great-grandmother said. "No secrets. Everything is here in front of you. Just watch. That's the secret, for you who must have one. Watch and listen."

My mother tied an apron around her waist. "I'm watching," she said. But I saw her face turn to the window. She didn't care that she'd never made *pierogi*.

My mother didn't like Detroit, and as soon as she could, she'd left for the farthest place she thought of, which happened to be Phoenix. She loved the flat, wide city, the desert enclosing it like a moat. When she said, "Valley of the Sun," you could almost see it the way she saw it, waves of sunlight rolling down the mountains to collect in a warm shimmering pool.

But once a year she went back to Detroit.

Everyone in my mother's family lived in Detroit or its close-in suburbs: aunts, uncles, cousins, second cousins, great-aunts, great-uncles. Any relation you could think of. Our stay in Detroit was a string of visits to houses that smelled and looked identical, musty dollhouses left behind after the little girl grew up. You could count on finding the same things inside each: A glass dish with cellophane-wrapped candies on the coffee table. One or two lamp shades still shrink-wrapped in plastic. The freezer packed with Tupperware and old bread bags holding enough food to last two winters.

Conversation in these houses moved around and around in loops, but it never tightened into a knot. Or maybe we were the ones who didn't fit. After all, their news was shared over cups of coffee in the kitchen instead of through mimeographed Christmas letters jammed last-minute into a card. We were always "Ginger's kids, way out west," and no one from the family came to visit us.

Many times I asked my mother why she left Detroit, and sometimes she said "always that same gray sky overhead" and other times she said "too much bustle"—but once she told me she had to escape the clock on the fireplace mantel. My great-grandmother had given it to my grandmother as a wedding present, and it struck every quarter hour, the chimes stretching themselves longer and longer as the quarters passed, and my mother said there was never a moment that she was not aware that time was slipping by, and that every chime meant something had been lost. I remembered that clock on my grandmother's mantel, but I liked following its steady march through day and night.

My great-grandmother rolled up the sleeves of her dress and smiled as she gave me a small knife and a mound of mushrooms to slice. "Do you cook, Amy? When I was a girl, my mother took sick one winter, so it was me and my sisters working to feed a family of eight three meals a day."

"Amy bakes cookies," my mother said.

My great-grandmother said, "Cookies won't feed a family. You pay attention now, learn yourself some good cooking."

"We can be thankful she doesn't have to feed a family," my grandmother said.

"There was no choice for me, Helen," my great-grandmother said. "If I didn't cook, we didn't eat. Life was simple that way. There were two choices only, cook and eat, don't cook and go hungry. No, like this," and she took the knife from me and turned the mushrooms into tiny pieces with a quick tick-tick-tick.

I watched my mother and grandmother pass a look between them, each blaming the other for what my great-grandmother had said.

"Those are the old ways, Ma," my grandmother said. "Times have changed." They seemed to be words she'd spoken many times.

But my great-grandmother continued: "No one said so, but we all knew. There was no shame in only two choices, living or dying."

My mother stroked my hair. "But things are different for us," she said. "We have choices." She was almost talking to herself, not to me, not to my great-grandmother, who moved around her kitchen, finding a frying pan, unwrapping a stick of butter; no pauses to stop and think what to do next.

My grandmother said, "Are we here for *pierogi* or nonsense chatter?"

Then my great-grandmother dropped handfuls of flour onto a wooden slab, sending up a white cloud that made my mother twist and sneeze into her shoulder.

"How many cups?" she asked. "I can't get this recipe down if you don't measure." She was cranky, her voice lined up on that edge you didn't want to see her cross.

"Cups?" My great-grandmother looked as if she'd never heard of such a thing. She held out her palms. "Use your hands to introduce yourself to the dough. Four handfuls, five, six. Enough to give a good greeting. We did not need measuring cups. We used our hands; we *felt* what we were doing instead of always thinking it."

My mother wrote on her notebook, and I peeked over her shoulder. She'd written "4 C flour."

Meanwhile, my grandmother pulled a big pot from under the sink and began running water into it; the clatter filled the small kitchen. As she turned off the faucet, she said, "I saw they've got ready-made *pierogi* at Kroger—in the freezer case yet."

My mother said, "Are they good?"

My grandmother shrugged. "Who would buy them?"

"Maybe they're easier than all this." My mother gestured around the kitchen, at the bowls and spoons and the film of flour coating the counter and the dishtowels and the mushrooms I was chopping into tiny bits and the sauerkraut soaking in water and my grandmother lighting the stove with a match.

"Like a TV dinner is good," my great-grandmother said.

"Amy likes TV dinners," my mother said.

As a child, I didn't lie often, but this one unwound quick as thread off a spool: "I tell you I like them, but I don't." Probably my mother knew I was lying; I felt her looking hard at me, so instead I watched my great-grandmother burrow a hole into the mound of flour and then with one hand crack eggs into it, setting aside the shells to dig into her garden.

"Write this, four eggs," she said to my mother. "TV dinner, what kind of meal is that? Food served in compartments. What are we now, astronauts going into space?"

"They're nutritionally balanced," my mother said. "And they're fast and easy. It would be a snap to feed a family of eight with TV dinners."

There was a long pause as my great-grandmother stared down at the eggs nestled in the flour.

"That may be," she said finally. "A TV dinner may be simple, a 'snap.' But when I think of those days when every meal was a struggle, when I woke with the roosters to build the fire, I do not remember wishing that food was a snap. I worked for every meal, I thanked God for every potato and every shred of cabbage, every drop of soup, each crust of bread. You go to the market and everything is there in front of you, so how can you understand what is important to us? How do you know who we are? All you do is rush, rush, rush, shortcuts here, secrets there, hurry, hurry. Never stopping to listen." And she attacked the flour and eggs, squeezing again and again with her strong hands.

The butter in the frying pan caught onto the chopped onion and set it sizzling. My grandmother rustled through the refrigerator searching for the cheese.

Was this why women had daughters? When husbands and sons refused to listen, there was the daughter. I imagined my grandmother's ears filled with this talk, and then, like a waterfall downstream, my grandmother tipping it into my mother's ears. And then my mother leaving for somewhere dry, leaving behind this family and this talk for the stillness and emptiness of the desert.

"I'm sorry," my mother said. "I just meant maybe you would have saved yourself some time."

"What did I want with time?" my great-grandmother asked. "What happens to all this time you save? Where is it? Is it in the bank? Do you keep it under your bed?"

"I'm only trying to point out that—"

"I held a duck in my hands, its heart pushing against my skin, and I knew my family would feast on its blood in *czarnina* soup, and its body two days later with red cabbage. I knew I'd boil down the bones for broth. There would be moments I'd love that duck more than I could love any living creature." Her eyes circled the kitchen, as if pulling everything into a net. "Don't ask me now to love a TV dinner."

My mother tried again: "I'm only—"

My great-grandmother said, "This is what I did for my family, made their food with my hands. This is who I am, what I have— back then in the old country, when I first came to America, and still now, today. Never forget this."

There was a silence, but my mother did not try to speak.

My grandmother stirred the onions, slid my mushrooms from the cutting board into the frying pan, handed me the wooden spoon that I swirled around and around, watching the mushrooms darken as they soaked up butter.

My great-grandmother looked at the balled-up egg and flour she held in her hands. "Add water, salt, sour cream. That's the secret," she said to my mother. "I know you, Ginger Marchewka, you are always looking somewhere else for secrets. Here is what you want. Add some dabs of sour cream, two, three, whatever you have, whatever you can spare. One half cup, let's say. That is all I can tell you. Pears on a willow tree with you—always wanting what's impossible."

My mother wrote it all down—what was in the fillings, how much farmer's cheese, how much onion; she wrote that the fillings had to be cooled. She wrote down everything, every detail, and she even sketched a picture of the crimping pattern. But I knew she'd forget. She liked to cook fancy, flaming things that set a table of adults applauding. Those were the nights she allowed me to eat TV dinners in my bedroom while the guests oohed and aahed late into the night, their laughter seeping under the crack of my doorway, keeping me awake.

We all have reasons for wanting to go. Clocks are on mantels everywhere.

I left behind an empty desert to go to a school filled with students similar to the students I already knew, a country connected to my own by CNN, *Newsweek*, McDonald's, an airplane ride.

My great-grandmother had two choices, and so she came to America in 1919. She was seventeen, her husband twenty-four, and there was a baby on the way. To step into a future you couldn't picture, for the sake of children you could barely imagine; to pack up all you had so it could be carried in your own hands— that's what deciding to leave should mean.

I thought about all this many times, but until I was in Thailand and my mother started to write me letters and she happened to send this photograph of the "Marchewka women," I couldn't understand what it was I needed to know, what was missing.

When I looked at that picture, I remembered how delicious those *pierogi* were when they were finally finished, how the drift of their aroma reached my great-grandfather and pulled him out of his nap on the easy chair and brought him into the kitchen, and he looked at all of us, all of us Marchewka women, and he said, "Never have I seen anything so beautiful," and as he went to get his camera a second time, I felt a knot wrap round my throat, and my great-grandmother pulled me tight into the strong circle of her arm and whispered, "Save as much time as you want, but when you go looking for it, nothing's there."

We posed for a second picture, the four of us in the kitchen, smudged with flour, sweat beading our faces, the *pierogi* steaming on the platter in front of us, and we smiled and linked arms. "Beautiful!" my great-grandfather said. "Do you see how beautiful?"

Who knows why, but that second picture didn't come out, though of course we didn't know that until the film came back from the developer, long after we'd cleaned up the kitchen and all the *pierogi* had been eaten by the family.

Stories from America

ROSE—1919

August 28, 1919
Detroit, Michigan
America

Dearest *Matka*,

You will not understand this easily, so best I tell you quickly. Now my name is Rose. Do you like it? I whisper this new name and summer surrounds me: flowers and larks and quiet breezes, and I forget the boat and the people crowded tight against me, squeezing the thoughts out of my head. A new name cannot make your daughter a different person, *Matka*, and all you taught me is mine forever. But now I'm in America, and my name is Rose. It is a happy name. A name Americans understand.

Stanislaus, reading this letter to *Matka*, ask her to say my new name. She should feel for one moment what it means to be in America, where everything is new and different, even something so little and so grand as a name.

The people we know don't have the names they had on the boat. *Matka*, forgive me, but when I got here they made me Rose, so this is who I am now. You would be proud to see me.

I plan to become an American as soon as I can. I plan to learn English fast. One day I will have lots and lots of nice things, *Matka*, and you will have nice things too because I will send them to you.

Two days here, and already I see how there is so much in America: so much time, so much space. There is everything! Time to work hard and earn good money, time to tell stories and laugh.

My name is gone!

I am here! I am here!

With precious love always from your daughter . . .
(*trans. from Polish*)

November 16, 1919
Detroit, Michigan
America

Dearest *Matka*,

Late at night is the only time my thoughts of you aren't hidden. Overlook my crooked lettering because I'm writing in the dark as everyone sleeps; only the light from the moon peeks in where the curtain doesn't pull shut. It's never quiet here in America: Across the hall the Jasinski's baby girl cries, boot steps clump to the washroom, a harmonica plays the same song every night, then stops too suddenly.

Daylight hours are not ours anyway; they belong to the factory, the landlord, the hallways I can't scrub clean of muddy footprints, the peddler whose prices are too high, the butcher with the meat cut ways I don't understand, the teacher at night school and his long sighs and bad complex-ion, the babies who whimper to be held. Nights have always been for dreaming, so that is when I dream of you, *Matka*, and everything behind me.

When I went to say good-bye, you were surrounded by chickens; you were tossing out their feed. Neither of us spoke. Only the chickens squawked, as handfuls of food rained down upon them when it was supposed to be just one. These months later, I want to hear your voice, but it's chickens I remember.

It is like nothing you can think of, to live in America. Even the sun is bigger here, its light whiter. There are so many people, and they talk too fast; their language is twisted and gnarled, like trees growing in the wind. There are stories here, but I don't know them. I only know the stories you told me, *Matka*, and I repeat them to myself so I won't forget. The story about the day the rooster got its crow. The story about the wolves running through the snow and how their tracks filled with gold coins. I think of you telling me those stories, but I still can't hear your voice.

At night, I feel my American baby growing inside me. My body doesn't want to let go of this baby. This is not the right way to think because again and again this child will find new ways to leave me. There's no end to leaving. Not yet a mother and already I know this.

My husband learns English words at the factory school. "I am a good American," he can say and write. What he learns he teaches me. He is good this way. We learn together.

Stanislaus, reading this letter to *Matka*, please tell her we are fine here in America. Tell everyone we are fine. Tell them to remember us in their prayers. We remember them.

With precious love always from your daughter . . .
(*trans. from Polish*)

January 20, 1920
Detroit, Michigan
America

Dearest *Matka*,

With Stanislaus now in America, who is reading this letter to you? Perhaps the priest. He already knows the secrets of the heart and mind, so how revealing can this simple letter be?

The winds blow long and cold along the streets here. Every day there is more snow, more snow, until I am certain we will be buried under all this dark, sooty snow. Around us people are sick; there is no money for a doctor—if a doctor who will come here could be found. So many sick people. We can only pray our sweet baby stays safe. I hold her as close and warm as I can, and I whisper the songs you sang to me.

The stories, too. I remember the story about wolves running through the snow, their deep footprints filling with gold coins. How old are you before you forget the stories your mother told you? How far away? My sweet baby, I look in her eyes, and I see the story of the wolves. She doesn't understand it yet, but she knows it.

What more can I do? What are the things you did that kept me alive all those years, the years before the war, during the war? When the Russians came? What do you remember that I've forgotten, that I never knew?

Fever roams the halls here. Amid all this snow, people are fiery with fever. I hold my baby close, but it's not close enough. I whisper your words. Forgive me, Father, if it is you reading this letter, forgive that it is my mother's words I whisper, and not God's.

With precious love always from your daughter . . .
(*trans. from Polish*)

April 5, 1920
Detroit, Michigan
America

Dearest *Matka*,

The men now talk only of strikes and unions, and always my husband must be sure to say the right words to the right people or trouble will knot around him. Keeping silent is worst of all, because then you stand for nothing, you're a straw man. He turns in the bed all night, his fists clenched. What he wants is a job, fair wages for fair work. Maybe such a thing doesn't exist; paydays the foreman comes by for a tip; lately, this tip is bigger every week. There is no one to ask, Is this right?

When I dream at night, I hear English words in my sleep. They jangle me awake, and I don't understand. I *want* to know English, I want so hard to understand. But I'm ashamed to tell anyone except you how frightened I am when these English words come at me as I sleep.

But you shouldn't collect my worries along with your own, *Matka*. How sweet the baby is. She is the first American I can truly love. She holds my finger so tight I believe she will never let go. We are saving money for a photograph. Better to wait than buy on credit like some we know.

On Sunday after Mass we rode the streetcar to a park and watched the sun dance across the pond, bits of light small enough to scoop up and keep. There were many people like us at this park, filling our eyes with sunlight and green grass and flowers and pretty red birds and cool shade drifting down from the trees.

How long have I been away from home? Time in America is measured differently. Where you are, *Matka*, time is sharp-edged chunks; here, it is tiny droplets, like rain always there. Either way, it's nothing to hold on to tight.

You must have known. Or you never could've let me leave.

With precious love always from your daughter . . .
(trans. from Polish)

September 1, 1920
Detroit, Michigan
America

Dearest *Matka,*

We are strong and well, and I hope the same is true for you. The baby has so many different smiles that cross her face, as if she's preparing for a joyful life. She will look like you. If you can never see America, America will see you in the face of your granddaughter, and the children she has, and the children after that. Forgive me—I would never speak this (and still I hope for many sons)—but the men are wrong, I think, to want so much the boys when it is the girls who keep the family alive. The letters are daughter to mother, daughter-in-law to mother-in-law, sister to sister. No one (save God, perhaps) plans it this way, but this is how it happens.

I cooked a duck as a special dinner for our one-year anniversary in America. But an idea that started so well took a bad turn, because I wanted sauerkraut stuffing and my husband wanted chestnut. Everyone in the building heard our screaming and the baby crying and all the foot-stamping. But it was the first duck we'd had for so, so long, and we both knew it had to be perfect. It was supposed to be *your* duck, *Matka,* with the sauerkraut and onions in butter. To write the words is to have the taste overwhelm my mouth, my mind, to see you standing in front of the fire on Sunday dinner, to be there next to you wrapped tight in the smells of your cooking. I cried as I boiled the chestnuts to think of how long I've been away, how far I am.

We would've eaten in bitter silence—or worse, started screaming again—but his brother and his wife (a very nice lady) joined us for dinner, and the first words out of his brother's mouth were, "What? No apple stuffing?" and his wife said, "Apple? Don't you mean mushroom?" So we all laughed, and she and I put together a new stuffing that was everything: chestnuts, sauerkraut, apples, and mushrooms. It was delicious, like nothing I've ever eaten, and all of us were back in our own Poland for the afternoon, and at the same time the four of us were together in America. I will write out and send the recipe so with your next duck you can be standing at the cookstove with me, *Matka*, here in America, surrounded by the smells of *my* kitchen.

I am certain we will be having a photograph taken soon; there is a man everyone goes to, and he doesn't cheat people like us. I'm finishing a new dress for the baby, a beautiful embroidered thing that all the girls after her can wear. In the photograph you'll see.

With precious love always from your daughter . . .
(*trans. from Polish*)

December 4, 1920
Detroit, Michigan
America

Dearest *Matka*,

The priest wrote that you are sick, that you won't talk to anyone, that your eyes are snuffed out like short candles. Every day I'm in the church. I plead with the Virgin Mary to intercede and make you better. I sent what money I could spare to the priest to give to the doctor, and some to say Mass for you. Everything I can do, I am doing. Still I am too far away.

Think of the story of the wolves, *Matka*. How it was the coldest winter anyone anywhere could remember; so much wind blew through the village and across the farms that people were afraid the land itself would blow away and there would be nothing. It was mid-January, the night of the Full Wolf Moon, when the children were kept tight in the house for fear of the roaming packs of wolves. The howls started just as the last supper dish was cleared off the table—long and jagged, catching up with the wind, these howls wrapped the village in the darkest darkness, and again and again mothers counted their children sitting around the fire. As the moon rose brighter, the howls moved closer, and finally it was the men who couldn't bear sitting still; they flung wide the doors to see for themselves the fierce wildness that dared approach their families. The women stood near their husbands, looking out into the night, watching their husbands, watching for the wolves.

But there was nothing to see yet, only the empty howl like mist against your face, the moon rounder and brighter than anyone remembered, the glittering snow that stretched as far as anyone had been to and come back from. Children started to ask questions but were shushed by their mothers.

Then the wolves were all around, hundreds trotting through the soft snow, their yellow eyes sharp in the moonlight, the biggest wolves anyone remembered seeing anywhere. Not thin and knobby from the hard winter like the people in the village—these wolves were sleek as butter, their wide paws barely touching the snow as they glided under the moon. As they passed the open doors, their tracks filled with gold coins, so many you couldn't take your eyes away; gold coins lay on the snow, jumbled and tumbled inside those big footprints, enough for everyone in the village, enough for every debt anyone anywhere had ever owed.

There was a silence, so much stretched-thin silence that wives touched their husbands' sleeves, didn't let go. That's when the doors in the village closed; families gathered silently by the fire, feeling greed nip its tiny bites, but no one left to gather the gold coins, and the hungry wolves were forced to move on to the next village. Those people forgot their families and dashed through the snow grabbing coins; the wolves gobbled up every last person in that village until no one was left.

But back in your village, *Matka*, the sun rose the next morning, and there were no gold coins and no wolf tracks in the snow—but that didn't make anyone believe that it wasn't true, that it hadn't happened, that it wasn't the way they remembered it.

And just because I wasn't there, that doesn't mean I don't remember it too, *Matka*. You were there, or your mother, or her mother.

Hold on tightly. You will get well. Look at this photograph. See your American granddaughter? She will love you and love you, and I promise she will tell our stories, too; she will remember, and all the American granddaughters after her, too.

With precious love always from your daughter . . .

(*trans. from Polish*)

Cravings

HELEN—1940

I should hope and pray for a boy as my husband and mother do. A son is strong and able to take care of himself; a son will grow like a tree filling the sky and carry the family name across the future. My mother's words. My husband's name.

I tell no one I want a girl.

Around the kitchen table, two of my sisters flicked through baby names like boys trading baseball cards: Mary, Catherine, Theresa, Rebecca, Barbara, Cynthia. Only girls' names because the first boy was named after his father. There was no speculation to a boy. Between them, these sisters had two boys, one girl, and another child on the way.

"What are you craving?" Wanda asked. She was the oldest, the biggest, married to a baker. John and I were living in her house until we could buy our own, one bedroom for each of the couples, one crib in with Wanda and Henryk, the other in a corner of the dining room. "With me, I ate farmer's cheese in spoonfuls."

"Cravings aren't until the sixth month," Joane said. "Something's wrong if you're already craving in the fourth, Helen." She was pregnant with her second, afraid it would be twins because her husband was a twin.

"Farmer's cheese and *kielbasa*," Wanda said. "And sugar. I took sugar right out of the bowl. From the beginning it was sugar I wanted most."

"*Kielbasa* made me sick," Joane said. "Even the smell. Even to look at it. I won't eat it still."

The clock over the mantel in the other room chimed three, and I rose to take the cake from the oven. But it was still uncooked batter.

"She forgot to turn on the oven," Wanda said. She and Joane looked at each other, no smile, no laugh.

"Anyone could forget," I said.

They nodded too slowly, still not looking at me.

"It's just cake," I said.

They nodded again like they were a matched set of something.

"It doesn't mean anything." I dipped my finger in the cake batter and tasted it. Did I add vanilla?

Wanda said, "You're not like this, Helen."

Joane placed one hand on her rounding stomach. "You *can't* be like this. Not when you're a mother."

Wanda said, "You'll learn soon enough." She glanced at Joane, and they nodded again. What they looked like was our mother; she was the one who was always nodding, as if no sentence could be true without a nod of her head.

"Sure you will," Joane said, and without meaning to, I nodded.

Later my mother brought over a poppy seed cake. I was folding laundry I'd brought in from the clothesline. "Do you feel all right?" she asked.

"I just forgot to turn on the oven," I said as I held the middle of a bedsheet under my chin and brought the ends together. "That's all."

"And if it's the baby you forget next time?" she asked.

The sheet was folded, and I started on another. "But it was only a cake," I said.

"So you're lucky now," she said, nodding. "There is only so much luck to last one lifetime. And not much of that." She touched the sheet I'd just folded. "These pink sheets. Are they new? Or were they white?"

I shrugged. "A red bandanna fell in the wash by accident. So I have pink sheets now."

My mother cupped her hands around my face as my chin pressed an edge of the sheet tight against my neck. "There's no more time," she said. "You're already a mother."

I said, "There's nothing wrong with pink sheets."

"You're a mother now," she said. "What that means is—"

"I know what it means," I said.

She didn't seem as surprised by my outburst as I did; she simply said, "What does it mean?" When I didn't answer, she continued, "This child inside you feels your dreams at night now. It will be always like this; always the two of you knotted together so tight." She patted the folded sheets. "See? That is how I explain pink sheets. You feel what the child inside you dreams. He is strong-willed already."

I shook my head. "No doctor said anything like that."

"This a mother knows. Not a doctor."

I picked up the sheets, turned to carry them to the linen closet. Actually, I'd meant to iron them before folding, but that could wait until after my mother left.

"You're already a mother," she called as she followed me.

I set the sheets on a shelf in the closet, leaned against the door. "Stop saying that."

"Forever you are a different person," she said. "Forever tied to this baby." She nodded, tucked a loose piece of my hair behind my ear with one hand, tapped my stomach with the other. "Be always careful now what you think and do. Someone is here watching you, learning."

I shook my head.

She said, "That is the reason to want a boy."

I heard Wanda singing in the kitchen, then the icebox opening and closing, her murmuring to the baby.

As if I'd asked the question, my mother said, "Because a boy will not be you. You know that. But a girl you expect will be you. And then she isn't."

The kitchen door creaked open and slapped shut. It was my husband coming home from work as he always did just as the clock chimed six. He called, "Where's the afternoon paper?" and without waiting for an answer from me or Wanda, I heard him walk into the front room where the newspaper was on the side table.

Before going into the kitchen to help Wanda start supper, I said, "Ma, this isn't Poland. Things are different here."

"Some things are," she called after me. In the kitchen, Wanda nodded as she trimmed beans into a bowl.

When I couldn't sleep that night I sat by the open window in the bedroom and looked into the dark alley. My husband snored in the bed behind me, long and deep as if he were sucking up all the air in the room. There was no moonlight, and I couldn't think of when was the last time I'd seen moonlight.

The approaching autumn air was chipping away at the bit of summer that was left; the crickets we found in the house had grown fat and big, too slow to move out of the way of our swatting brooms, as if they, too, knew summer was nearly over. Every fifteen minutes the clock on the mantel in the front room chimed, each chime stretching longer and longer until it struck the hour, eleven, twelve—the hours that took the very most time to pass.

It was farmer's cheese or *kielbasa* or sugar I craved.

My husband sputtered, murmured, "There's only one way," the

first time I'd ever heard him talk in his sleep. But he didn't dream, never had; he didn't understand why I'd wake up screaming from a nightmare, or how I could push aside his nudging arm so I could linger in a place that wasn't here, that wasn't even real.

We got married before I knew John couldn't dream. Who would think to ask such a question? Who would think a man might not dream at night? What my mother asked was: "Is he Catholic? Is he Polish? Does he drink? Is he a hard worker?" What my sisters asked was: "Is he a good dancer? Does he have a car?" That's what I knew when I got married, the answers to those questions.

Oh, I also knew something about his brother Joe. Same height, same dark hair, same blue eyes. That same sideways smile like he had a private joke going with you. John and Joe were the type who wouldn't trust anyone who wasn't blood, who wouldn't all the way trust anyone who wasn't the other. They were born on the same day a year apart, but John grew so fast that soon they were the same size and that's how they stayed, like two shadows on one body.

When John and I started going together, it was always "my brother Joe this" and "my brother Joe that," until finally I asked, "Where is this wonderful brother of yours? I want to meet this Joe." We were at Luna Pier, finishing our picnic supper; the band was warming up; enough stars glittered overhead that the young men had something ready-made romantic to whisper to their girls.

I folded the napkins I'd brought, making sure to put my pretty embroidery on top so he'd see it. "What did you tell him about me?" I asked.

John shook his head, and I thought that meant his mouth was full, but he kept shaking until I said, "Nothing?"

He looked away.

"We're engaged," I said.

"Of course that." He brushed one finger across my knuckles.

"Didn't he ask about me? Who I am? What I look like?"

John said, "He asked if you were Catholic, Polish, and pretty. I told him yes."

"Did you tell him my name?"

"He didn't ask."

The band had finished warming up and started playing its first song. He said, "It's Saturday night, Helen. Let's dance. See how the stars are twinkling for you only?" and I tilted my head to follow his pointed finger. "The girl he was going with was run over by a streetcar the day he was going to ask her to marry him." He stood up, started leading me to the dance floor.

"How sad."

We glided together. He was such a good dancer I never felt clumsy. "She was a real nice girl," he said.

It was a simple thing to say, but he didn't say it simply, and when he sighed right after, I knew he'd been in love with this girl, too. He hummed in my ear, but not the song the band played.

Then it was the week before I was to be married. My mother insisted I wake up early every morning to light a candle and pray with her special rosary at the church, the same rosary she'd prayed with before she got married and her mother before her and her mother before her. My two older sisters had done the same thing the week before they were married; it was expected that my younger sister would do so too.

So every morning my mother woke me by jostling my shoulder, shaking away whatever dream I was having; she silently watched me dress, then gave me a penny to light a candle for the soul of my Polish grandmother I never knew, handed me the blue rosary beads, and hurried me out of the house, standing at the door until I turned the corner.

Because it was so early, usually I was the only one in the church, and I tiptoed to the altar for the Virgin Mary, trying not to look at the stained-glass windows, trying not to think how empty they felt with no sunlight behind them, like the eyes of a dead person. The penny clanked in the metal box no matter how softly I tried to drop it, and when I lit my candle, I was always surprised that the flame seemed so tiny since everything else in the church had become so huge. Even my yawns as I tried to pray grew bigger and bigger, swallowing all my thoughts, and the morning turned into a matter of simply staying awake until it was time to go back home and help my mother with the laundry she took in to add to my father's paycheck.

The day before my wedding, I lit a candle and knelt, watching its flicker shift and grow, slitting my eyes to widen, then shorten the flame. I held the rosary, but every time I began, something popped into my head, like whether or not my mother would finish the dress in time, or if Wanda, already huge as a house, would, in fact, have her baby at the church tomorrow as she'd teased she would. So the Virgin Mary and my mother would have to understand if the most I could manage today was sitting still and thinking good thoughts about how lucky I was to be marrying a man like John.

The wooden door in the back of the church creaked open; light stabbed in. I turned, expecting at four-thirty in the morning perhaps a repentant gambler or drinker, possibly the priest, maybe another girl about to be married whose mother was as old-fashioned and stubborn as mine. But it was a line of men carrying lunch pails and signs I couldn't read in the dim light, pulling their caps off as they filed through the door and clumped up the side aisle to the front altar. A few glanced at me as they passed, but I bent my head—just as a good Catholic girl deep in prayer. Nearly a hundred men clustered around the altar, some I recognized, many I did not. Someone said, "Where's Bill Grubowski?" and the words bounced through the whole church; several men went, "Shh," and that, too, became enormous. When one man dropped his lunch pail, the clatter set off laughter and normal conversation that quickly quieted as the man looked from one another to the crucifix hanging behind the altar.

Nobody spoke, nobody moved except to shift weight from foot

to foot. They seemed to be waiting, looking up at the ceiling, the crucifix, the darkened windows, back toward the door they'd come through.

He was in the back, and from where I was, I couldn't see him, only listen as he filled the church with his words: "Brothers. We're here today to humbly stand before God and ask for the strength to stay united, the strength to fight for what is just and right, the strength to make our lives better for our families, our wives, and our children. In the name of the Father, the Son, and the Holy Ghost."

"Amen," the men murmured, and they no longer looked awkward or surprised to be where they were, as they parted to let the speaker come forward, where he knelt before the altar, his back to me, and spoke slowly:

"I swear upon my soul, under the eyes of the Lord our God, that I will stand strong beside these men. I swear I will not scab out my brothers, I swear to do what is right and just." Though he didn't have a loud voice—and actually, now he seemed to be talking more to himself than to the other men—I could almost see his promise written in the air around him; it lingered, hung in the air like a mist.

He stood and stepped away, hat crumpled in his hands, his head still bowed. If we weren't in a church, there would've been clapping, shouting, men tossing their hats in the air. But this was better.

I thought that was it. But another man stepped forward, knelt, made the same vow, changing the words just a little. Then another. And another. They were all here to stand at the same spot I'd be standing tomorrow and swear before God their allegiance to one another. I didn't know men did this.

He walked toward the altar where I knelt, and I closed my eyes, moved my lips in mock prayer, fingered my mother's rosary beads as if I were actually mumbling the right words.

His breath came sharp and quick, like his heart was going faster than it had ever gone before. I figured he must be on the line at the Dodge Main plant, about to strike. That was one good thing about marrying a man like John who worked for the city government paving streets—no strikes, no walkouts, always a steady paycheck. Already John had nearly two hundred dollars saved up to buy our house.

I knew how it was for men on strike: bottles and stones flying; the goons hired to beat you up if you wouldn't work—the strikers who'd cut off your ears if you scabbed; police plunging into the crowd with their blackjacks and brass knuckles. The coldest days, the hottest, the rainiest, were when you're registered for picket duty.

Women tried to understand, but they hated when their fathers and husbands and brothers and sons were on strike. You never knew who might not come home at the end of the day. Women's faces twisted tight with worry during a strike; they said only what had to be said, using quick sentences in the kitchen, glances as they hung out the laundry and swept clean the front steps and sidewalk. All they could do was wait at home, wait, wait, wait, and hope, and wait. Be there when the men returned, wipe up the blood, set out supper that was harder and harder to get credit for in the shops.

Nobody liked it, but it had to be done. That's how you stood up for yourself and got what you wanted—we all knew that— higher wages, better conditions, shorter hours.

I slitted my eyes, but he wasn't even looking at me, so I watched him light candle after candle; though he'd already lit a great many, he kept going as the voices of the men kneeling and taking their vows continued like a chant, and morning light began to turn the stained glass red and blue and yellow, and more and more candles were lit, until they were all flickering, every last one, and my little candle had become part of theirs.

He turned and looked straight at me, as if he'd known I'd been watching him. I expected he'd be the most handsome man I'd ever seen, or one with an unusually powerful face, or someone with eyes that saw into the end of time, or whose future was mapped on the lines in his face—something unforgettable about this man with the quiet voice that filled a church—but there was nothing. He looked perfectly ordinary, like anyone else.

But I couldn't stop staring, like I'd seen him before, like maybe I'd had a dream where he was the hero, or I'd passed him on the street and we'd smiled at each other too long, each glancing back to see if the other was still looking, or a friend had been telling me about the wonderful new guy she was going with, and this is who I'd imagined as she spoke. Even though I was in church kneeling at the altar of the Virgin Mary, a girl about to be married, I smiled the way I knew so he'd smile back.

There was a pause. Then he sighed softly, put his hands in his pockets, whispered, "I hope you'll remember us in your prayers this morning, miss," and I stopped breathing, stopped smiling, I was so embarrassed. But he wouldn't look away from me either. He pulled his hands out of his pockets and put them on the rail, right next to my hands clasping the rosary, so close I wouldn't have to move to touch them, only breathe, only once.

So I smiled again, whispered, "You're very brave."

He shook his head. "It's not being brave when they leave you with no choice."

"Still."

"Still," he repeated.

He reached one hand toward my face—in the background the men spoke, the words going round and round, there were easily more than a hundred gathered now, the church was filled with men, more had joined the first group, men were standing all along the aisles, waiting their turn to kneel before the crucifix—and he set the palm of his hand against my cheek, left it there for a moment so I could feel how hard and rough and warm it was, slid his fingers down to my lips. He bent down because I was still kneeling, tilted up my chin and kissed me straight on the lips, where only John had kissed me, and only after I'd agreed to marry him, and I didn't close my eyes the way I did when John kissed me, so I never stopped looking at this man, at his ordinary unforgettable face, and how much time passed—or would've passed—but the rosary dropped out of my hands and the clatter of beads hitting the floor made him straighten, and I reached for the rosary, twisting it tight in my fist.

"You will remember me in your prayers?" he asked, backing away.

"Always," I said—a promise, not a word—and he strode down the aisle, out the front door, and men began to follow him until it was a steady tramp of their feet and the lingering words of their vows, and then the church was silent, then the priest, then some elderly parishioners arriving for sunrise Mass, and then me late for home, the rosary still bunched in my fist.

I dreamed about him that night: He was at my wedding. He was smiling. He was toasting the bride and groom. His cheek was bruised and one tooth had been knocked out during the first day of the strike, but when he lifted his glass and said, "To the bride and groom—may their future together be long and happy," his voice overflowed the room, until the whole world wasn't big enough to hold it. That's what I dreamed, again and again that night before my wedding, each dream one more flame snuffed out.

So when it happened that way, when it turned out that he *was* the best man, he *was* my brother-in-law Joe—I never knew if my dream made it happen that way, if that's what I wanted—or if I knew what I wanted—or if I even had a choice.

Everyone said it was a lovely wedding; all my sisters assured me I was a beautiful bride; even my father blew his nose during the ceremony; my mother and mother-in-law filled table after table with delicious food, trying to outdo each other. John whispered to me, "I think my brother likes you, Helen. He's been watching you all day." It was what I wanted, who I was: the wife of a

Catholic, Polish, nondrinking, hardworking man who owned a car and danced better than I did.

So my life was the way it was supposed to be.

A week later we heard on the radio the Germans had invaded Poland. Right after that, my husband told me he didn't have dreams.

The clock chimed one, and I went back to bed, nudging John so he'd roll over and stop snoring. I didn't fall asleep until after the clock chimed two.

The next morning I said to John, "You talked in your sleep last night. You must've been dreaming." I poured coffee for him, for myself, for Wanda. "Don't you want to know what you said?" I asked. In the other room the baby started crying, and Wanda got up from the kitchen table, clamping a piece of toast between her teeth.

A moment later the baby was quiet, and John hadn't answered my question. I poured the rest of the coffee into his thermos.

He stood, picked up his thermos and lunch pail, kissed me good-bye on the cheek.

"Everyone dreams," I said.

"What does it matter?" and he was out the kitchen, out the side door.

Wanda came back, the baby snuggled in her arms, the toast gone.

I said, "Is it possible John doesn't dream at night? Is it even possible?"

Wanda looked at me, looked at the baby who was reaching up to grab her nose. She said, "Helen, you're having a baby five months from now. He's a good man."

"Of course he is," I said.

"Better he has a steady job than dreams at night," she said.

I nodded, began scraping the breakfast dishes over the garbage can. Wanda said, "Let me tell you this. Once you have the baby, you won't have time to think about things like whether John's dreaming at night or just snoring away."

I nodded again.

Joe never said anything to me about what had happened that morning in the church, and I never mentioned it to him or to anyone. The decision had been made.

My mother, Wanda, and I were canning applesauce for the winter; John and Joe had driven out to the country and brought back bushels of apples for the family, and for three weeks we'd been eating apple fritters and apple noodle pudding and apple soup and apple cake and baked apples, and now we were putting the last couple bushels into applesauce. Yet I couldn't get enough of these apples; in the middle of the night I'd wake, dreaming about apples, craving a nice crisp one—I knew just the one in the cellar, I'd set it aside for myself, big and red and juicy—I could feel the crunch in my mouth, the sweetness. But Wanda's baby had been fussy lately, and sneaking to the kitchen would've woken him, and once the baby was awake, the whole house was awake. So I sat at the window in the bedroom and thought about apples until I got sleepy.

I peeled apples while Wanda cored and quartered, and my mother diced and dropped the pieces into the pot on the stove. "Just like the factory line at Ford," Wanda said.

It was wonderful to be sitting in the warm kitchen, surrounded by the smell of apples and cinnamon and steam, but I was sorry there'd be no more apples this fall. Applesauce safe in jars would be nice come January, but that was a long way off, and it wasn't the same as grabbing an apple out of the cellar anytime you wanted.

"And you, Helen, you're not tired yet of these apples?" Wanda asked.

I shook my head, bit into one. It was delicious.

"You'll turn into an apple yourself eating so many," my mother said. "I never saw one person eat so many apples."

"I guess I have a craving," I said.

"With me it was farmer's cheese," Wanda said. "I ate big spoonfuls. And sugar from the bowl."

"What about you, Ma?" I asked.

She stirred the simmering mass of apple pieces, spooned up some of the mixture and pressed it with her finger. When it was soft enough, she dropped it into a big bowl. Next we'd put the softened pieces through a ricer, then add sugar and cinnamon before cooking the puree once more and then packing it into jars that we boiled again. By the end of the day, they wouldn't look anything like apples.

I repeated my question: "What about you, Ma? What did you crave?"

"A son," she said.

"No," I said. "What kind of food did you think about?" I set down my knife, shook out my wrists.

"I didn't think about food," she said. "I thought about the sons I would have. The boys who would grow into the men of my family. The beautiful girls they would marry and the children they would have. That is how you should be thinking now, Helen, so you will have a son."

Wanda and I looked at each other. She giggled, said, "Well that didn't work for you, did it, Ma?"

My mother said, "It works fine."

Wanda said, "Ma, you ended up with four daughters!"

My mother said, "It's my fault for thinking too much about those beautiful girls my sons would marry. So I have beautiful girls marrying other women's sons instead." She shrugged, stirred the simmering apples. "Well, what can you do now? But you, Helen, it's not too late for you. Think only of the son you'll have. Think of him looking like John, the kind of boy who has a nice steady job and visits his mother after church on Sunday. A boy who saves his money for a house for his wife and baby. You are so lucky to have such a man—and to have such a son, too."

I smiled, nodded, ate the rest of my apple and another while my mother and Wanda gossiped, and the beautiful apples cooked down into mush.

But no. No. I will have a girl. I will choose the name myself—Ginger, after the glamorous movie star, Ginger Rogers, because that name is not on any list anywhere. I will teach my daughter Ginger things like this, making applesauce and embroidery and why it's important to mop the kitchen on the same days each week, and she will listen to me and nod.

But there will be one part of her—maybe not a part I can see, maybe not a part I'll always like or understand—but that one part of her will be a girl who lets a rosary drop to the floor and lay there because she refuses to let go of a kiss.

I swear upon my soul.

Blue Beads

GINGER—1969

"The car overheated," was the first thing I said through the rolled-down window. My mother was standing at the top of the drive-way, waiting to greet us though it was late, much later than I'd told her long distance we'd get in. The kids were asleep in the backseat; the long drive from Arizona had worn them down. I could've been asleep with them except that I had to drive.

My mother said, "She died."

At the same time I repeated, "The car overheated." I wasn't even sure what that meant exactly, something about the radiator; it happened in the movies all the time, so it might as well have happened to my old station wagon. It seemed a solid, believable story.

"Did you hear what I said?" In the car headlights, my mother's arms were crossed tight against her chest, the fingernails of one hand pressing deep half moons into the flesh of her arm.

"I'm too late," I said.

"She died, and you weren't here," my mother said.

"It was the car," I said. "If it hadn't overheated."

33

"If you hadn't moved away," she said. "That's what if," and she kicked the front tire with her foot again and again, until the car was shaking the way it did going too fast on the highway. I closed my eyes, leaned my head against the steering wheel.

When she stopped kicking, I opened my eyes, turned off the headlights and got out of the car, setting the door shut softly so I wouldn't wake the kids. I walked over and touched my mother's arm where her fingernails dug in. "I'm really sorry," I said. The skin of her arm felt like a loose rubber band. It had been only three months since I last saw her, but she was older than I remembered. I said it again: "I'm really sorry, Mom."

She shook her head and turned her back. The porch light was on, and the summer's leftover insects swirled and dipped in its glow. It was nearly ten-thirty; most of the houses in the neighborhood were dark. Just her porch light and one across the street.

"I said I was sorry."

"The funeral is in two days," she said. "That's when to say you're sorry."

"Okay," I said. "I'll apologize to everyone then."

"Not everyone," she said. "Her. Your grandmother. Apologize and tell her how you wouldn't come home to be with her when she died."

"It's the car," I said. "There was steam everywhere. We needed a new hose or something. They had to order the part from another town. It wasn't my fault." But as I was speaking, she was opening the backseat door of the car, sliding in, gently hugging Amy and Cal awake, murmuring soft words, kissing their faces as they squinted under the light off the car ceiling. I stood apart from them in the dark and listened as my mother explained how their great-grandmother had left us to be in Heaven now, how it was all right to cry. It should've been me, I know, my arms, my words, but I felt like crap, had never believed in Heaven, was ashamed that what was still easiest was to lie, and I was so very, very glad to let my mother explain things her way, any way, just so they'd be explained, just so this first moment of coming back to Detroit would be over.

The light outside the window was pale gray, but what woke me was Amy sitting cross-legged on the end of my bed, humming, playing that game she liked, twisting string around her fingers to make various shapes. She tilted her hands toward me and whispered, "Look, Mom. Witch's broom."

The web of string entangling her hands looked as much like a broom as the sky outside looked like day, but I said, "Good," and yawned. "What are you doing up so early?" I asked. Amy pulled her hands apart, unraveling the witch's broom into a loop of string. "Do you need a drink of water?" I asked.

She shook her head, started curving and twisting her fingers through the string. "I'll never see Great-Grandma again, right?" she asked.

I closed my eyes but my grandmother's face didn't come to me; instead I saw a white-haired lady who was in a telephone company commercial. I opened my eyes. "She'll always be in our memories."

Amy disentangled her fingers from the string and started fresh her process of looping and pulling. A faint pink reached into the gray sky outside the open window, and birds chattered across the trees. Amy said, "What if I forget?"

"You won't."

Her face scrunched. "What if I do?"

"I'll tell you a story about her," I said. "And then you'll remember."

"What if you forget?"

"I promise I won't."

She held out the string for me, elaborately intertwined between her fingers. "Put your hand through this hole," she said.

I sat up, poked my hand through. She dipped one finger around and pulled so the string was no longer around my wrist. "See that?" Amy said. "It's magic."

Sunlight edged the window, made me squint and reach to pull the shade. Outside the newspaper thudded onto the porch, the paperboy's bike clicked down the street. It was a day like every day. Except it wasn't supposed to be when someone in your family has died.

Amy said, "Our car never broke down." She pulled the string off her fingers, rolled it into a little ball between her palms, kept rolling it around and around, then said, "You told Grandma it did." She looped the string over her head like a necklace, tucked it inside her nightgown, folded her hands together and watched me, blinking a couple times.

"I thought you were asleep," I said, but it sounded like the wrong thing to say.

"Only partway," she said.

She wouldn't stop looking at me. Finally I said, "I lied to make Grandma feel better."

"Isn't it wrong to tell lies?"

"Grandma was sad that we took so long to get here. So I made up a good reason why we were late. That's all." I patted the pillow on the bed beside me. "Lie down, Amy, huh? Or you'll be tired and cranky all day."

She crawled next to me, poked the pillow, and settled in. "Tell me a story about Great-Grandma."

I couldn't think of one thing to say; all I had in my head was the white-haired lady from the phone company commercial and the jingle she sang. Finally I said, "Remember the way she talked?"

"Her voice sounded furry," Amy said.

"Because she came from Poland," I said. "So she had an accent."

"She told good stories," Amy said. "With wolves and roosters. They always ended happy."

"She liked happy endings." That was easy—who didn't?

"When we were here last summer I prayed with her special necklace," Amy said.

"Rosary," I said.

"I prayed for a horse," Amy said. "I sat in the closet and said a different prayer on each bead, the way she did at church, but they were all because I wanted a horse. When she found me in the closet, she came right inside and prayed with me, but not with the necklace. She said the necklace was for something else. But then she told me she'd pray for me to get a horse for Christmas because she could see I wanted one so bad."

"You want a horse?" I said.

"It's a secret," she said. "Because I know I'll never get one. So will you remember that for me if I forget? How she prayed with me in the closet?"

I nodded.

Amy said, "And I remember when we were at her house and she did that funny dance from Poland where she stamped her feet. Remember that?"

I said, "You and Cal and Great-Grandma were stamping your feet so hard the vase fell off the shelf and broke."

Amy said, "Then she stamped her feet on top of the broken vase pieces. Remember? Grandma said she was crazy, but Great-Grandma kept dancing, and we all twirled around and around, even you, and I got dizzy and Cal threw up and then I threw up too, but she kept going, and we were all laughing, and she said, 'Work when you have to, but dance when you can.' Remember that also, okay?"

"Okay," I said.

"Promise?" The word was slow and sleepy.

"Promise," I said.

She closed her eyes as I tugged the sheet up over the two of us. I listened to her breathe, listened to Cal breathe in his bed across the attic room. My own breath felt tight, dragged out like rope.

I'd done nothing wrong. It was a matter of saying what had to be said. Like about the car, when the truth was I'd had a wish-I-were-dead hangover so the kids played in the pool at the Holiday

Inn one or two days we should've been driving. The truth was that grinding a broken vase into the carpet was pointless; I was the one who cleaned up, collecting glass shards with my fingers because the vacuum cleaner couldn't get them all, while Amy and Cal cried and my mother scrubbed the carpet with a damp towel. Where was the fun in that?

The daylight got brighter; I saw it with my eyes closed tight and my face burrowed into the pillow.

The truth was, let's say I'd been here all my life. There would be no difference. Even when I was here, I had nothing to say to them.

I was in the kitchen washing coffee cups and saucers. My mother seemed to be in charge of the arrangements for the funeral, so family had been by all morning; already there were five different coffee cakes spread out on the kitchen table, poppy seed cake, muffins, and several plates of cookies covered with wax paper. My cousin June sat at the table picking at the two gooiest coffee cakes.

I'd never liked June much, but because we were the same age, our birthdays so close, the family had grouped us together. She was bigger than I was, so I had to wear her hand-me-down clothes to school, even though everyone recognized them as hers. "That yellow blouse was my favorite," she'd announce, loud enough so my friends could hear. "Of course, yellow is really *my* color, not yours." In high school, she was known for French-kissing after only a soda date and then giving critiques in the girls' bathroom the Monday morning after. "You know how a pot roast feels out of the refrigerator?" she'd say. "Flabby and cold? That rim of fat around the edge? It was like kissing one of those for half an hour." "Ee-yew," we all squealed, and later someone would say to me, "Your cousin's a case," and I'd say, "I was adopted." When I left Detroit after high school, June was the one to tell everybody I was going to a home for unwed mothers and that I'd be back in exactly six and a half months. "The skinny ones don't show," I heard she'd said, and there were plenty of people who believed her. She ended up marrying one of the brothers of my high school boyfriend, and damn if I didn't get her wedding veil UPS a week after her wedding.

June said, "Aunt Wanda's using margarine in her coffee cake, not butter."

"Probably cheaper."

"Tastes cheaper," she said.

"Plenty of other goodies to choose from," I said, rubbing Aunt Wanda's orangey lipstick off the rim of a coffee cup with the dishrag. "These people head to the kitchen the minute someone dies."

"You've got to do something." She plucked a raisin off the far coffee cake and popped it into her mouth before asking, "Where's Jimmy anyways? You'd think your husband'd be here. I mean with a death in the family and all."

I turned the faucet to full blast, let the hot water rush and pop over the soapy cups so it splattered the counter. "Business trip," I said.

"Sheesh, didn't you ask him to get out of it?" When I didn't respond, she continued, "If he'd come along, maybe you'd've gotten here before Grandma died. He could've shared the driving, right? I don't know how you drive all that way by yourself. You and two kids. How many miles is it from Arizona anyways?"

"About two thousand," I said.

"Wow," June said. "How long's a trip like that? How many days?"

Amy came into the kitchen through the side door. She said, "Our car broke down."

"Hi, precious," June said. "Isn't she adorable? She looks just like you did when you were her age, Ginger. Same skinny little stick with arms. Want some coffee cake, sweetie?"

"She's had enough," I said, but June cut a large wedge and put it on a plate. Amy came to the table and sat down, picked up her cake with her fingers like June was doing.

Amy said, "The car broke down when we were driving."

"It's not polite to talk with your mouth full," I said.

"She's a kid, what's polite?" June said. "If I had time to worry about my boys being polite, sheesh. Same old Ginger. Amy, your mom was always telling everyone what to do, what to say. Everything embarrassed her. Right, Ginger? Remember when you went around calling your mother 'Mama' with that phony accent? We all thought that was about the funniest thing, Ginger going around saying, 'Mama,' like she was queen of France or something."

"Mama," Amy said. "It doesn't sound right."

"Next it was your mom saying, 'An ant is an insect,' so she called them all 'ahnt.' Ahnt Marie. Ahnt Joane. Ahnt Wanda. We all thought she had the craziest ideas."

"Did she ever tell lies?"

"Amy!" I said. "Go outside and eat that coffee cake, you're making a mess. Look at those crumbs."

"That's my mess," June said. "Sit back down, precious."

"Did she?" Amy asked.

"In our family if they thought you were lying about something, they'd take you to Grandma's house—your Great-Grandma. Remember, Ginger? Grandma could look at anyone and know right on the spot if they were telling the truth. Remember that?"

I shook my head.

June said, "Sure you do. Say you came home with a candy bar that your mom thought you'd swiped from the corner store. 'We're going to Grandma's,' she'd say, 'and we'll see about this,' and she'd drag you over there, didn't matter what time it was, middle of the night or whenever, and you'd stand in the kitchen, and Grandma would hear the story from your mother and look you straight on for a long, long time. Then she'd clear her throat. That's when you started crying, right when she cleared her throat. That was all it took, that one little noise, and there you were, saying you were sorry you lied, begging them to forgive you, promising you'd be good, you'd do a hundred rosaries every day in church, anything. They'd stand there and watch you, Grandma and your mom, and you'd bawl and bawl—even the boys, can you believe that? That's what Grandma could do to us—but finally, when she'd decided you'd cried enough, Grandma would kiss the top of your head, whisper something in Polish, and that's when you knew it was okay, that no one really hated you. Remember that, Ginger, standing in that kitchen next to the table with the red-checkered tablecloth on it, the bakery breads wrapped in paper, the Virgin Mary on the windowsill. The way you always smelled bacon in that kitchen, no matter what time of day it was. Remember, Ginger?"

I said, "No one ever got dragged to Grandma's in the middle of the night."

June said, "That's what I remember."

"And it's not like Grandma really knew if you were telling the truth," I said. "She just knew you'd confess if she waited long enough."

"Grandma knew how to look into the deepest part of your soul," June said to Amy.

I tossed a dish towel to June. "How about drying?" and June stood up, wiped her hands on her skirt, reached for a wet saucer.

My mother brought in a stack of dirty plates and forks.

Amy asked, "Could Great-Grandma really look into the deepest part of your soul?"

My mother paused, then nodded. "That's what we all believed." She pressed hard with her fingers onto a couple crumbs on the table so they stuck, scraped them off into the trash can. "Everyone but Ginger."

I turned. "What's that supposed to mean?"

My mother looked straight and hard at me.

Soapy water dripped off my dishrag onto the floor, and I rubbed away the bubbles with my toe. Behind me June stacked each dish after she dried it.

Amy looked from me to my mother and back. I couldn't tell

what she was thinking. Not even guess, and is that the way it was when I lived here, people watching me with so many questions? So much surprise? Did Amy already know what I knew, that you can get used to it if you want to?

My mother cleared her throat, just the slightest of sounds combining with the clinking of dishes, the murmurs from the living room, the boys outside playing, a fly buzzing and banging against the screen window.

I kept my eyes on my mother. That was the trick, not to move. Eyes, still. Hands, still. Face, still. That's how you said what you wanted to say. That's how you kept your life your own here in Detroit.

My mother said, "Everyone else was here for her. Where were you?"

That stupid buzzing fly. I wanted to reach over and swat it, scream at the kids outside to shut up.

Amy said, "The car broke down, Grandma."

I let my breath out slowly, turned to explain to June: "Radiator hose. What a nightmare."

"I can imagine," June said.

There was a pause. Amy pushed her bangs off her forehead, and she really did look like me when I was her age.

My mother said, "The wake is tonight at six-thirty at Polzak's Funeral Home."

"I know."

"Don't you be late for that also," and she handed me Amy's empty plate.

"I won't," I said.

Amy said, "Grandma, look," and she pulled the string from around her neck and quickly laced it on her fingers, holding up the result. "Cup and saucer. See? Here's the cup, and here's the saucer."

"Isn't that something?" my mother said. "I did that same trick when I was a girl."

"Me too," June said. "Witch's broom, all that. Remember, Ginger?"

"You did this game, Mom?" Amy asked.

I shook my head. "Not me."

June said, "We all did it, Ginger. I remember. You and me and—"

"Okay, I did it," I said.

"Enough," my mother said. "All of you, come out front and visit. Amy show the family your cup and saucer."

"Let me just quick finish up in here," I said, and they left me alone in the kitchen, and I washed the last set of plates and wiped the counter. Even if I couldn't remember the tablecloth in my grandmother's kitchen or making a witch's broom out of string, there were things I remembered, things I knew that were mine. The drive between here and Phoenix. My car cutting apart the ribbon of empty road. How time and distance gather behind you until they're something physical you can almost touch.

The folding chairs at the funeral home were hard and cold, but standing for one more second was not an option; my shoes were too tight—I'd brought the wrong pair of heels from Arizona— which combined with the headache ringing my skull and the fact that the last gin and tonic I'd had was yesterday afternoon. The room overflowed with aimless, wandering voices that wouldn't shut up, voices that spiraled louder and louder as more and more family members arrived. No one seemed to leave, only arrive.

Amy climbed into the chair next to me. She still wore that stupid string around her neck even though I'd asked her to leave it back at my mother's house. I guess it didn't matter much; some of the other little girls weren't even wearing dresses. Amy said, "I looked at Great-Grandma. Me and Cal looked together."

I kicked my shoes off, stretched my toes. "I told you you didn't have to."

"Grandma said it was our duty."

"Well, I said you didn't have to."

Amy pulled the string off her neck, started fiddling with it, and I waited to see what she'd show me, cup and saucer or witch's broom. But she said, "I saw Grandma take the beads."

"What beads?"

"When Grandma thought no one was looking, she reached in and took the beads Great-Grandma prayed with."

"The rosary," I said. "Are you sure?"

She nodded and wouldn't look at me, just kept pulling at the string. "Witch's broom," she murmured.

"That's not something Grandma would do," I said.

Amy lifted her string creation above her face, stared hard at it, said, "She put it in her purse." A minute later, she said, "Mom! No lie—she stole it!"

I looked at Amy, but I wasn't my grandmother, I couldn't recognize the truth.

"Okay, let's go see," and I crammed on my shoes and stood up, started walking as Amy unwound the string and hurried after me into the room where my dead grandmother lay.

Aunt Wanda was praying at the kneeler in front of the casket, so Amy and I waited by the doorway. Candles flickered along the walls and in the corners, and the scent of flowers was as overwhelming as the sound of voices had been in the other room.

Aunt Wanda stood up and nodded as she passed, giving Amy a smile and a pat on the shoulder. I tiptoed forward and peered in at my grandmother. I hadn't wanted to do this, to see her dead and waxy-looking, still and stuffed like a piece of old furniture. So all I looked for was the rosary, which was draped across her folded hands, and I motioned Amy forward. "See?" I whispered. "Grandma must've been doing something else. Straightening her dress maybe."

Amy shook her head. "These beads are different," she said.

"It's a rosary," I said. "See the cross at the end?"

Amy shook her head harder. "It isn't the same. This isn't the one we prayed with in the closet. That one was blue beads. This is white."

"People like Great-Grandma have a bunch of different rosaries," I said. "How can you remember what color that one was?"

"Of course I remember," she said. "It was her most special rosary. She told me so right after we prayed in the closet for the horse."

"You're not getting a horse, Amy," I said.

"I know that," she said, tears edging her eyes, her voice. "But what about the rosary? Grandma took it. She stole it!"

"It's awfully dark in here. Are you sure it was the blue one you saw?"

"I'm a hundred percent sure. A hundred and fifty percent."

My feet hurt so bad that I sat down on the kneeler and pulled off my shoes.

"Do something," Amy said.

"Let's just forget it," I said.

Amy shook her head hard. "You don't even care!" she cried. "That's why we were late, you don't care!"

"Stop screaming like that," I said. "Everyone will hear."

She was sobbing so hard her body shook, and I reached to touch her arm, but she jerked away, and as she did, my mother said from the doorway, "Poor baby," and she walked in, putting out her arms for a hug. Amy turned her back. "Poor thing," my mother said as if accusing me of doing or not doing something.

"You shouldn't've told her to look at Grandma," I said. "She's not your daughter."

There was a pause, then my mother said, "Your uncle Joe and aunt Carolyn are about to leave, and he says he never got a chance to see you and the kids. That's all I came in for."

I nodded, shoved my shoes back on, and tried to stand, but I had to grab Amy's shoulder to steady myself because the pain in my feet bit through me.

"Mom!" Amy's tears hadn't slowed any.

"Amy's just a little tired right now," and I limped toward the other room, yanking her with me.

"Ginger!" my mother called. "What are you doing to that poor child? Why is she crying like that?"

I stopped in the doorway, looked back at my mother in the dim room, felt the crush of voices and family ahead of me, all those people who liked to think they knew me, all those people who thought I belonged to them. So I said, "Amy says you stole Grandma's rosary."

My mother didn't move her face; only the candles flickered shadows across her. Amy squirmed out of my grasp. I bent and took off my shoes, cradled them in my arms. The carpet was soft under my sore feet, almost like sand. "She says she saw you," but the words were awkward, like a tongue twister you can't get right.

We both looked at Amy, who had finally stopped crying. "Well?" I said.

Amy bit her bottom lip. "I'm sorry," she said.

"Don't be sorry," I said. "Just tell the truth."

My mother crossed her arms, pressed them tight into her body, her hands tucked away from view. In the other room, a woman screamed out, "You didn't!" almost as if we were at someone's cocktail party.

"Why are you upsetting this poor child?" my mother asked.

Amy looked at me.

"What did you see?" I asked.

"Mo-om," and she drew the word out long.

"Go ahead," I said. "Tell us what happened."

She started to cry again. "Grandma took the rosary out of the coffin and put it in her purse."

"Why would I do a thing like that?" my mother asked.

Amy cried harder. "I'm sorry," she said. "I'm sorry."

My mother said, "For pity's sakes, I've never stolen anything in my life. You know that, Ginger."

There was a long pause, and I couldn't look at either of them, so I closed my eyes. The organ music that had been playing all along moved into music I remembered hearing a long time ago in church, what the organist played Saturday afternoons when we went to confess our sins to the priest, my mother and her sisters and their mother and all the kids who were around the house and could be dragged off to church. We went every Saturday at four, and if you weren't old enough to go to confession, you sat in the church pew and watched the tiny candles slide big shadows along the walls, and listened to the women pray on their rosaries, beads clicking together like soft voices. The organist was there practicing, playing music you didn't hear on Sundays, songs that weren't in the hymnal. My grandmother praying on the blue beads. I remember whispering to her, "What are you asking God for?" I was maybe seven, eight, already thinking how I could ask for the things I didn't dare say, to leave Detroit, to have a different family; I was thinking that maybe what I needed were blue beads like hers. She shook her head, whispered, "The rosary is not for things. The rosary is for who, why, how. Life is questions, God is questions." She looked at me until I nodded, then she said, "Some questions are more important than answers," and I nodded again though I couldn't imagine how that could be true.

When I was old enough to know that being away from the house Saturdays at four meant not having to go to confession, I was also old enough to know that when they thought I was lying and my grandmother looked at me to see into the deepest part of my soul, she cleared her throat not because she knew I was lying, but because she didn't know. Either there was no truth in me, or it was where she couldn't see it. That's how alone I felt, how alone I was.

I opened my eyes. "Amy, stop upsetting Grandma. She has enough to worry about," and I reached for my mother's arm to walk with her into the other room, to talk to Uncle Joe and his wife; behind me I heard Amy, "What about me?" and after that, a quiet voice sucked up with the rest of the noise in the outer room,

"You know, our car didn't really break down," and I felt like crap, everything was crap, dying was crap, and why I did this, I don't know—I guess because I knew I wasn't really one of them—but a few minutes later I went through my mother's purse, pretending I needed a tissue, and there was the rosary.

The blue beads felt cool crumpled tight in my hand, like ice chips about to melt, and I thought of my grandmother holding on to this rosary as if she could keep questions safe in her hand, and maybe I could've held on, too, but there was Amy sitting on one of the hard chairs, there was my mother half listening to Aunt Wanda. Both of them watching, both of them looking for that something in me that never had been there.

I dropped the rosary back into the purse, the beads trickling between my fingers, and walked out of the funeral home, waving away offers of assistance, words of condolence, saying that what I needed was fresh air but knowing there was that part of me that had seen the bar on the corner across the street.

It had that smell that city bars have, a sticky darkness of spilled beer mingled with sweat. The bartender didn't take his eyes off the Tigers game on the TV as he said, "Yeah?"

I asked for a gin and tonic, and any other time I'd've told him to skip the tonic. But he practically did.

No one spoke to me or barely looked. It was the kind of place where you simply went to drink, where everything dissolved behind you like smoke you saw a long time ago. I settled into a wooden stool, shoes dangling off my feet, and let the TV and the gin drift.

About an hour later the door opened, and I was surprised to see that the streetlight outside was on. In the mirror along the bar I watched June and my mother come up behind me. I didn't turn around, not even when my mother put her hand on my shoulder; I just kept looking at her in the mirror. Her teeth seemed too big for her face, or maybe her face too small for her teeth. Something.

June said, "I was right."

I nodded at the bartender for another drink, which he brought over, sloshing it a bit on the bar. I ran my sleeve through the spill, sopping it up. In the mirror, June turned away, probably deciding exactly how she'd tell this story to everyone, how to start, what details to give, the expression on her face. I said, "You guys go without me. I'll be fine." On the TV the Tigers finally scored, but no one in the bar roused themselves.

My mother shook her head. "This isn't really you."

I laughed. "You never had any idea who I was."

In the mirror June and my mother looked at each other, seemed to say something without saying anything—that way they had. The way they all had. I blinked away tears, gulped at my gin, said, "Know why I wasn't with her when she died? I had a hangover. I'm a goddamn drunk, that's who I am. A lousy stinking drunk with a crappy marriage and kids on their way to being screwed up. That's who I am exactly."

"No," my mother said, reaching over to set the rosary on the bar. The bartender glared at the pile of blue beads as he filled a couple beer glasses at the tap. "This rosary is for you," my mother said.

"She doesn't know the prayers," June said.

"When she lived here she did," my mother said. "Whether she remembers or not, she knows them."

I shook my head. "Give it to someone else. Give it to June. I wasn't even close to Grandma."

June said, "Of course you were close to her, you're family."

"What does that mean?" I asked, sucking on an ice cube and spitting it back in the glass.

A moment later my mother said, "You're here in Detroit too late maybe, but aren't you here?"

There was no more gin and tonic in my glass, so I nodded for another.

June sighed sharply, and my mother said, "Just a minute," and she leaned in close to me, spoke softly in my ear, "You're family even when you don't want to be, Ginger." She scooped the rosary off the bar, slipped it over my head. "Don't forget to take this with you," she said. "It's yours now."

I watched in the mirror as she walked out, June following, the door slapping shut behind them. There was only the baseball game then, someone getting a third strike called in a September game that didn't matter.

When I asked for another drink, the bartender said, "Don't you think you ought to be getting home, lady?"

"I am home," I said, and he got me the drink.

I woke up early the next morning, the day of the funeral, the sky gray and unfinished-looking through the open window. Amy and Cal were asleep across the room on their beds; I listened to their breathing, inhale, inhale, exhale, exhale—never quite matching rhythms.

The rosary was still looped around my neck. It was wrong to wear it, so I pulled it off, fingered the blue beads one after another. June was right, I couldn't remember the prayers that went with it, just what my grandmother had said: Never ask for things on a rosary, some questions are more important than answers. I still couldn't remember her face, the way the bridge of her nose crinkled when she smiled, the blue of her eyes just like my own, how before she spoke she held her mouth open for just a moment as if thinking how to say the words before saying them. How her kitchen smelled like bacon.

My mother had stolen and lied to get this rosary. But with me, it would end up lost, broken, dropped into a drawer, forgotten. Didn't she know that about me?

But here it was.

Probably I should've returned the rosary to my mother, snuck it in her purse or left it on my pillow for her to find after the kids and I drove away. Instead I tiptoed to Amy's bed, sat on the edge, the rosary cupped in one hand as if to keep it from spilling.

Amy's eyes opened, and she looked straight at me. "What's wrong?" she said.

"Shh," I said. "I'm right here," and I slipped the rosary around her neck. "I'm sorry." Then I added, "This is for you."

She didn't thank me or ask why I was sorry; she fell right back asleep, breathing in unison with her brother as I watched and listened as the sun rose all around us like it was something that had never really left.

Later, when we were at the cemetery, they asked me if I wanted to drop a flower into the grave, and I shook my head, walked away. I couldn't. Amy went up with them, only it wasn't a flower she dropped but something I couldn't see. I figured it was the rosary. I should have known to do that.

But when we were driving back, I saw the rosary around Amy's neck, her hand fingering the beads through her blouse, and it was the string that wasn't there anymore. So that was really the question with no answer: How did someone like me have a daughter who knew with such certainty what to do, how to do it, why it had to be done that way?

Wedding Day

Rose: The Gift

Mine was the biggest, wrapped in ironed pages of *Dziennik Polski* newspaper, tied tight with sturdy string; two boys carried it in for me from Wanda's Ford station wagon, filling half the gift table when they plopped it down—"Careful!" I cried—and one of the bridesmaids had to hunt up another table for the rest of the gifts.

"Ma, what's all that?" Helen called. She was talking to her sister Joane, and they looked at each other as if to say, You go over— No, *you*, and it was Helen suddenly in front of me, her face trying hard to keep its smile, hands on her hips. Plenty of times I'd told her she only looks wider when she stands that way.

"Twelve quarts of pickles," I said. "And Theresa gets to keep the jars."

There went the smile. "Oh, Ma," she said. "That's not what brides want these days. Jars of pickles. What were you thinking?"

"I'm thinking no one doesn't like a good pickle." I set my hand on the corner of the box. It had been a very good summer for cucumbers. And twelve quart jars was certainly something. In the old country, what we would do to start a marriage with twelve quart jars.

"This isn't the old country," she said, and had I spoken or thought? Too many times now I said what I meant to think. Or thought what I meant to say.

"If you added a spoonful of horseradish, your pickles would taste better," I said. Something else I'd told her again and again.

"Girls like Theresa buy their pickles at Kroger," she said. "Then they throw out the jars when there's no more pickles."

"Well, maybe this husband of hers likes good pickles," I said. But he was almost a real doctor (one more year, Theresa said), and he wasn't Polish. Brad, he was called, not even a saint's name. What would he know about pickles?

Helen shook her head. "Maybe." Her voice had that cut-off sound that meant she thought she knew better. But I was still the mother, so she smiled, touched my arm, said, "Who wouldn't like your pickles?" then turned sideways to talk to someone from the other family, letting herself be led away to be introduced to someone else.

It wasn't that I didn't know what my granddaughter Theresa wanted. My daughter Wanda drove me to Hudson's downtown where a lady dressed up enough for Sunday Mass gave us a piece of paper with the presents Theresa had picked out—this teapot and that toaster and those plates and these forks. Front and back was that paper. "Let us know if you need help finding anything," the lady said, keeping a smile flat like glass across her face. Wanda and I walked along the aisles, admiring the pretty plates propped on the shelves, a separate little light shining bright on each plate. "Look how much they cost," Wanda whispered, and for that price, you could order a whole tableful from the Sears catalog. Or better to collect a nice matched set free with green stamps or from the gas station like everyone else. In this country you didn't need to use money for things like plates.

The plates Theresa wrote down that she wanted were smooth

white with a deep blue border like the top part of the sky just before night and a ring of gold all along the rim; "Twenty-two karat," Wanda whispered, reading off the card that said "Biltmore" in curvy writing. She kept whispering like we were in church, "I'd be too afraid to put food on something like this." She looked at Theresa's list. "Maybe a nice steam iron instead," and she started to walk away. I took the plate off its little stand on the shelf; it felt cool and thin and precious, the way I imagined a seashell in the sand would feel. But the only time I'd seen the ocean was on the boat ride to America, and then the ocean was endless waves crashing up against the walls, something groaning and clutching at the ship, trying to drag us all under, the worst days I lived through. So I didn't know seashells, the same way I didn't know a person might eat supper off a dish with real gold on it. That's when the plate slipped through my fingers and fell to the floor, knocking the counter and breaking into five or six pieces. Wanda came back, and the dressed-up lady hurried over, her smile stiffer than before.

"Oh dear," and she bent to pick up the pieces, stacking them in her hand one on top of the other so they made a crooked little tower.

Wanda grabbed my arm, like she thought she had to hold me back from breaking more plates. "What happened?" she whispered.

"Can we glue it together?" I asked.

"Ma!" Wanda said, her hand tightening. "She's sorry," she said to the lady, who stood up. The plate pieces were big, easy to glue. "She didn't know better," Wanda said. "We don't have to pay for it, do we?"

" 'Biltmore' is a very expensive pattern," she said. "Maybe you shouldn't be looking at things you can't afford to buy."

Wanda took a hard breath and tucked in her lips. "She's very sorry. She didn't mean to break it. Did you, Ma?"

Did I? I'd been holding plates since I was four years old—washing them, drying them, spooning food for other people onto them—in those days if you broke one, you got the back of someone's hand on the side of your head or worse. Plates didn't have names then—they were where you put your supper before you ate it, that's all.

"Well, that dinner plate was a demonstration model," the lady said, stretching that tight smile across her face. "Of course Hudson's wouldn't actually sell it." She looked at the pieces in her hand. "It's a pretty setting, isn't it? Quite elegant and refined."

"My niece picked it out," Wanda said. "She's marrying a doctor."

"Isn't that lovely?" the lady said. "I'm sure she'll be very happy." She set the pieces of the plate next to her cash register. "Hudson's has done bridal registry for a number of doctors' wives and daughters. Just yesterday the daughter of Detroit General's chief of surgery came in. Lovely girl. She's marrying into the Ford family, you know."

Wanda talked with the lady, the lady saying all sorts of things about "formal service" and "casualware" and "translucency" and other words that meant "plates," and I knew it would end with poor Wanda spending more money than she should on one of those plates for Theresa and later bullying one of her sisters to go in on it with her.

I imagined those plates lined up on Theresa's table; twelve, that piece of paper said she wanted. Did *kielbasa* and sauerkraut taste better off a gold plate? Or maybe that's not what you ate when you put twelve gold plates on your dinner table.

I picked up one of the broken pieces. "Can I have these?" I asked the lady.

Wanda said, "Ma! Why do you want a broken plate?" She rolled her eyes at her new best friend, the smiling lady, who tilted her head and gave Wanda a little wink she thought I wouldn't see.

"I was about to throw it away," and she flicked her hand at me, "take it."

I didn't want the pieces for the reasons they were thinking (though it would be easy enough to glue them back into a nice plate, hanging high enough on the wall where no one would see the cracks). I needed Theresa to remember that a plate is a present that can break, that there are other things to want on your wedding day that maybe can't be typed out on a piece of paper at Hudson's.

Helen returned to the gift table, now with Wanda. "I thought you took Ma shopping," she said, pointing to my big box. "She's giving Theresa pickles!"

"Oh, Ma!" Wanda turned to Helen. "I begged her to go in with me on a place setting for Theresa, but she said no. What will Brad's family think when they see all those pickles?"

Their eyes pushed into me, expecting answers. Were they so far from me that they couldn't see what I saw, hear what I heard? Those dill pickles lined up on Theresa's kitchen shelf, the soft pop when she opened the first jar and set a couple on a dish, the crunch as her husband bit down, that married-people smile they'd share—what a strange present that smile might mean at first, but then he'd take another bite, chew, swallow, smile a different way, ask, "How does someone make pickles this good?" and that's when Theresa would say without thinking, "Just add a little horseradish to the brine."

Helen: The Dress

Theresa called me at the end of June to say now the dress had to be ready for August 1, not October, so suddenly it needed to be an August kind of dress, not an October kind of dress. I didn't ask how come. In a family, there are some things you don't need to hear in words. I ripped out the long sleeves I'd just basted in, let the weeds go in the garden to find more time for finishing the lacework. With John passed on in the spring, I wanted to feel busy, so this was fine.

By the time my daughter Ginger came to visit from Arizona with Amy and little Cal, it was just hemming left, trimwork with my appliques, crocheting the lace to line the petticoat underneath, another foot or so of the bobbin lace for the dress and to edge the handkerchief Theresa would tuck into her purse, then turn into a cap for the first baby. The afternoon Ginger came, there was so much to talk about and family stopping by, so it was after supper before we finally came to Theresa. Ginger put down the *Free Press*, said, "I didn't bring anything to wear to a wedding. What'm I supposed to do?" But she didn't wait for my answer. "I guess Jimmy could send up my good dress," she said. "Or I could buy something new. Anyway, I thought the wedding wasn't until October. What happened?"

"She moved it."

"What a hassle. Why?"

I shook my head. Amy was lying on the floor, coloring in a book I'd picked up free from the bank, pretending she wasn't listening to us. But she was always listening, so of course you couldn't talk about these kinds of things when she was around. I pretended I had to count some stitches and shook my head again, held up a finger. Ginger didn't understand anything about the lace bobbins in my lap, so I could say what I wanted—I could tell her the next step to making lace was standing on my head in the corner and she wouldn't know.

Ginger said, "Well, I have absolutely nothing to wear."

"She asked if Amy could be the flower girl," I said. "Since Debbie's leg won't be out of the cast until September, Theresa said it seemed easiest."

"Do you want to be a flower girl, Amy? You get to wear a fancy dress."

Amy tilted her coloring book to get a better angle, nodded. "Okay. If Debbie's not mad."

"Are you making the flower girl dress, too?" Ginger asked, lifting the long stretch of lace off my lap, rubbing it between her fingers (which I hoped weren't smudgy from the newspaper; it was hard to wash lace: soap flakes with a minimum ten rinses in clear water, and it wasn't ever as pretty afterward. For a wedding dress you wear one time, every bride wants lace of her very own that hasn't been washed.).

I nodded.

"And the bridesmaids' dresses?"

"Wanda cut them out, and she said she'd do the hemming."

"But you're sewing them all? How many dresses is that?"

I nodded. Ginger wouldn't ask these questions if she still lived here because she would know. In fact, she should remember how a wedding went. I was the one who made the dresses. Joane made the cake; it used to be Ma, but now it was Joane, sometimes Marie. Wanda filled in—she could organize people to make the dinner if it was that kind of wedding or call up the Polish-American Century Club to get the best deal if it was the other kind of wedding; she could cut the dresses and hem them; she took people in her station wagon where they needed to be taken; she told photographers what kind of shots were best, who had to have a picture with the bride, who didn't. Marie always wrote the invitations because her handwriting was the prettiest. I don't know how it came out that way, who decided all this, but it's the way it was, how our family did weddings. My wedding, my sisters' weddings, their daughters'. Everyone's wedding but Ginger's.

"Hey, Mom, who was your flower girl?" Amy asked. She set down her crayon and rolled onto her back.

Ginger didn't look at either of us. "I didn't have a flower girl."

"Why not?" Amy asked.

"Shh, Grandma's trying to count," Ginger said. She picked up the newspaper again; Amy flipped to her stomach, turned to a new page in her coloring book.

It wasn't that Ginger's wedding was all the way down in Phoenix or that it happened so suddenly that none of us could go or that it wasn't in a church (though of course all of these things were difficult to explain to my mother and sisters). It wasn't that Jimmy wasn't Polish or Catholic. Or that dear, sweet Amy came along premature seven and a half months later. Or that no one remembered to take pictures. It was the dress. "I bought it at Goldwater's, the nicest department store in town," Ginger told me long distance after the wedding, "over my lunch hour." "Finding a wedding dress over lunch hour?" I started to ask; "Not a dumb poufy wedding dress, just a nice dress to get married in," she said. "Jimmy and I got married two days after we decided, so there wasn't lots of time. But it's a beautiful dress; in fact, I'm wearing it next week to a dinner party with one of the partners in Jimmy's firm," and I saw exactly the kind of dress—straight, severe, a long quick zipper up the back, no lace. "Sounds nice," I told her, "but why didn't—?" She cut me off: "The dress was perfect, exactly what I wanted."

Later that night, after Amy and Cal had their baths and went to bed, Ginger came into the kitchen where I was still working on the bobbin lace. It was my favorite pattern, True Lovers' Knot; my mother had put it on my own wedding dress, telling us that when she was a girl they sometimes used chicken bones for bobbins and when it was too dark to work, they filled a bowl with water to reflect the candlelight and brighten the room. My eyes ached and my fingers felt twisted together and I still wasn't finished with this most difficult part yet. How many more wedding dresses would I make? After Theresa, all the nieces would be married now, but they were having daughters who would grow up to get married. I leaned my neck hard to the right, then to the left to loosen the knot at the top of my back, in the place John always knew to rub.

Ginger kneaded my neck. "This feel good?" Her fingers were cool, as if she'd just let ice cubes melt through them.

"Thank you," I said, though she was too rigid or too rough or too far left or something that wasn't quite the way John had done it. But a daughter is different than a husband.

She said, "There's that lace packed away in the box in the closet upstairs." I didn't say anything, so she added, "Do you know the box I mean?"

"That lace is no good," I said. "It turned yellow."

"Amy found it," she said. Her fingers were in an even rhythm now, squeezing the soreness out of me. "It's beautiful."

"It's old," I said. "I thought I threw that out already."

"You could finish Theresa's dress with that," she said. "Save yourself some time."

"There's plenty of time," I said, picking up my pillow and lace pattern. The bobbins clattered gently, sounding like people talking in another room.

"Why's that lace packed up anyway?" she asked, still standing behind me. "How come you never used it?"

I worked quickly, twisting and lifting my bobbins. "Guess I forgot about it."

She sat down. "So put it on Theresa's dress," and she reached for my *Family Circle* that she flipped page by page without reading. The kitchen was very quiet, only the drip of the faucet that had started leaking the day after John passed. I looked forward to its whisper late at night when I worked alone in the kitchen.

I'd made that other lace, also True Lovers' Knot, long ago—late at night like this, bit by bit, no one day it had to be done—and then I rolled it inside fresh tissue paper to keep it clean and packed it away upstairs in the attic room that John had built up so nice. Do you forget something you take such great care with?

The next week meant more late nights in the kitchen. Amy wanted to make lace so I gave her a pair of needles to knit with, and she started on some simple edging for her flower girl dress. I fixed it up a bit, added on, and tucked a strip along the neckline.

Two days before the wedding, Theresa came over for the last time to pick up the dresses, and four of the bridesmaids came along, and everyone told me the dresses were absolutely beautiful, perfect, gorgeous—all the words there are that you use when you're talking about brides. They agreed that Amy in her dress was adorable, and she showed off her flower girl walk that she'd been practicing up and down the sidewalk outside and along the hallway, and they said that was adorable, too. There was nothing that wasn't adorable that day, including the dress that Ginger had bought at Hudson's that morning to wear to the wedding, no lace anywhere that I could see.

Amy: The Ceremony

"Now, who are you?" It was the blondest bridesmaid asking, the one who looked just like Cinderella in the movie, who stood as if she were waiting for talking animals to snuggle on her shoulder and share their secrets. She smiled and tilted the hand mirror to see the back of her head in the big mirror on the wall, touched a petal in the ring of pink flowers in her hair. No one real could be more beautiful; when she looked at me, I felt my face turn ugly red, and I tucked my arms tight against my body, so she wouldn't see that I hadn't scrubbed my elbows the way my mother had told me to this morning. Looking at her was jumping inside a fluffy cloud where it was hard to breathe.

"I'm the flower girl," I whispered, showing her my basket. We were all getting ready in the church basement, Theresa, Aunt Marie, the bridesmaids, and me. My mother called it "the bridal party," but there were no balloons or cake or party stuff, just a bunch of ladies running around in their panty hose and slips, aiming hair spray at each other until they coughed and sneezed.

"No, cutie pie, what's your name?"

"Amy."

"Are you related to Theresa?"

The one who kept going on how she was "too fat for this dress" came over and grabbed tweezers off the table, and bent in close to the big mirror, squinting as she stared at her face. "Her mother is Theresa's cousin, meaning she's Theresa's second cousin. Or something."

"Doesn't that make her once-removed?"

Her mouth opened and her tongue curled upward as she quickly yanked a few hairs out of her eyebrows, wincing each time she pulled. "I can't keep all that straight," she said, staring closely at her face. She got two more hairs, then said, "Her mom and Theresa were good friends growing up. I wish I had some ice; this hurts like hell."

"You know what they say—you must suffer to be beautiful."

"So why do I look like this?" She set down the tweezers, and I could see a line of hairs stuck to the edges. "Will you do this hook at the top of the zipper?" She draped her long dark hair over one arm and lifted.

Cinderella fanned her hands, said, "My nails are wet. Amy, cutie pie, help us out here," and the fat one leaned backward so I could reach the hook. Her skin was damp and a little sticky; a couple strands of hair were pressed against her neck. Still, she was beautiful in a different way, not really fat at all.

"Thanks, sweetie," and she let her hair fall in a swish to her waist. "You're a quiet little thing, aren't you?" she said to me. "Isn't your mom like the family bad girl or something?"

"Really?" Cinderella asked. "Like how? Hey, wouldn't she be really cute with some blush?" She reached under a chair for her fringed shoulder bag and pulled out a silvery square, which she clicked open. "Want some blush, cutie pie?" and she put the little brush in my hand. "Which one's her mom again?"

"Ginger. You know, up from Arizona." The fat one tilted a tiny perfume bottle against two cotton balls, then pulled out the front of her dress and tucked the cotton balls down the top of her slip. "She was the only one who moved out of here. Told everyone she'd never come back. Like, took a bus to Phoenix the week after high school was over or something wild like that, Theresa said."

"Then what?" Cinderella picked up the perfume bottle, sniffed.

"Can I borrow this?" but she didn't wait for an answer, just took off the cap and pressed the bottle up against both wrists, behind her ears, on her ankles. "These shoes are killers. It's like they're biting my feet in half every time I walk."

I didn't know what to do with the make-up she'd given me, so I looked in the little mirror. My face filled up the tiny square, overflowed, and I quickly closed the case. They said all I had to do was walk down the aisle and drop flower petals on the floor; easy as pie, Theresa said. The only one prettier than you is the bride, my grandmother told me.

"Well, you'd think she'd do something wild, wouldn't you? I mean once you got out of this stink hole and everything."

"And?" Cinderella soaked a cotton ball and stuck it down the front of her dress, too. She took my wrist in her hand and dribbled perfume on it, first one wrist, then the other. But she put the cap back on, no cotton ball for me. I smelled like when my mother was having people over for dinner at our house, and my father kissed up and down her neck saying, "Is it dessert that smells so good?"

"It was like she ran out of gas or something. Alls she did was get a stupid job, get married a couple years later. I guess it was even more of a hurry-up wedding than this one."

"Really?"

"Don't you get it? It's exactly the same as if she'd stayed here. She went to Arizona, but she didn't get anywhere. Help her with that blush, Jackie," and she pointed at me. Her fingernails were bitten down to the pale pink skin, just like mine. Maybe I'd stop chewing them like my mother was always nagging.

Cinderella took the makeup brush and stroked it quick across the powdery blush. "Smile, cutie pie," and she tickled the brush across my cheeks. "Right on the apples, just like that. Aren't you pretty now?" She gave me the big hand mirror, and my face didn't fill it up. I still didn't look like them, I looked the same as before only pinker, but I said, "Thank you."

In the mirror I saw my great-grandmother behind me, more dressed up than I'd ever seen her—no housecoat, her hair puffy like my grandmother's. I turned to show her how the bridesmaids were making me pretty.

"What's this?" she said, reaching to rub hard at my cheeks. "Only married ladies wear makeup." She shook her head at the two bridesmaids. "Shame on you," and she walked away toward the stairs.

I looked in the mirror. Now my face was really pink.

"Oh, pooh," Cinderella said, "what does she know?" and she reached for the brush. I smiled so she could put the blush on my apples again.

The fat one said, "It's just like I was saying."

"What?"

"Her mother was right to try to get out. But she didn't go far enough."

"Arizona's pretty far."

I wanted to tell them it wasn't like they thought, that we came back every summer. But I was afraid they'd stop talking.

"You know what I mean," the fat one said. "Alls I'm saying is if I was ever lucky enough to get out of here, you can bet I'd do something big."

"Like what would you do, Ramona? Win yourself a Nobel Peace Prize?"

"Maybe I would," she said, shaking back her hair. "You don't know. Nobody knows."

"You should have this conversation with Mark. Maybe it's something a fiancé wants to know."

The fat one turned me around and looked straight at me. "Don't get married," she said. "Don't ever get married. Swear it here, and it will come true. Once you're married, you're where you'll be for the rest of your life."

"Ramona!"

"Swear it, Amy," and she held the mirror to my face. "Watch

yourself say the words. Then if you break your vow, the next time you look in a mirror, you'll see a hideous old witch with yellow teeth and a long hooked nose with a huge wart on the tip."

"You're scaring her!" and Cinderella gave me the kind of quick hug my mother did after she'd put on her lipstick already and she and my dad were going out at night and it was one of the bad baby-sitters watching us. I smelled the perfume from the cotton ball spiraling up at me too fast. "Poor thing, she thinks you're serious." She laughed dropped the blush back into her purse. "Besides, it could be different for her. It could be Prince Charming."

"There's no such thing as glass slippers," the fat one said. "At least your mom tried." She held her hand close to my face. "Take a look, Amy. They buy you off with a diamond and a pretty white dress."

Someone came clattering halfway down the stairs; "They're seating the mothers!"

Cinderella clutched for her lipstick, rubbed her pink lips together; she tugged at her dress and patted her hair. The fat one whispered in my ear, "Go far away, Amy, like your mother did, but don't stop once you're there. Do the things we were afraid of, do everything we couldn't." Her breath was warm and quick, tickly inside my ear.

"For pity's sake," Cinderella said, shoving the fat one with one arm and pulling me away with the other. "You look adorable, cutie pie," and she slashed some of her lipstick across my lips; it felt like jelly I was supposed to wipe off with a napkin, and I let her lead me to the stairs, where someone was holding a big mirror so all the girls could check themselves one last time as they lined up.

Behind the cloud of misty-white veil and the girls hovering too close, touching this, tucking there, asking questions, Theresa's face was tight and pinched close together, as if maybe she didn't want to be married either. But in every picture book I'd read, at the end of every story I'd heard, all the princesses there were—they all ended up happily ever after with a pretty white dress and a wedding. Is that why my mother left her family in Detroit, to look for a different way, a way that wasn't being stuck in the basement with all the lipstick and blush and uncomfortable shoes and feeling too fat? As I walked up the stairs holding my basket of flower petals, I heard someone murmur, "Isn't she cute?" and I turned to look in the mirror they held in front of me. Without knowing what I was going to think, I thought, I'll be the one to find something different, I swear it.

But walking down the aisle in front of Theresa and her father, going feet-together-wait-feet-together-wait, how I'd practiced in my grandmother's hallway, the rustle of women whispering from pew to pew, nudging each other, the smiles, I reached the end of the aisle too quickly, before I was ready. So I turned to watch Theresa, and she was walking feet-together-wait, one arm leaning into her father's elbow, and Aunt Marie in the front pew was crying, with my grandmother leaning forward with a handkerchief in her hand.

From the other side of the church, a woman's voice cut across the organ music: "Why's she wearing a white dress if she's pregnant?"

There were several gasps, like tiny explosions going off around the church. Someone screeched, "Mother! You promised . . . ," and quick heels tapped the floor, but I couldn't see who was being led through the creaking side door. The bridesmaids whispered behind me; the organist held on to the note too long and then moved ahead, and Theresa was at the front of the church, her body hard and straight, and her father reached to lift the veil and I almost screamed NO, because I was sure it would be a witch with a long, hooked nose, but it was only Theresa under the veil, her face pale and tight but so beautiful, beautiful like I'd never seen anyone before.

Ginger: The Reception

The band was rollicking away on polka number two hundred or two thousand or two zillion. I was sitting at one of the tables along the dance floor, where pink-faced dancers slapped me with whisks of damp air as they spun past. Cal was sleeping in his infant seat on two chairs pushed together; he could sleep through anything. My martini was two-thirds gone, but another one would've meant the line-up of stares, whispers, and murmurs, because women in our family just didn't drink martinis, let alone three of them in one night. So I'd stretched two about as far as they could go (which had already gotten me enough stares to remind me what it was like to live in a place where someone's eyes were forever pinned to your back), and drinking gin out of a water glass was sounding like a plan, but my mother waved as she and Aunt Joane twirled by on the dance floor, and I felt like a bad girl caught thinking naughty things. Never mind that I was old enough to drink, that it was a wedding, that this many polkas would send the Pope scrambling for a bottle. The only group of people who halfway might know what I was thinking was a crowded table of Brad's friends and family. Their faces looked like they were talking deliciously nasty about someone who was close enough to overhear. I'd talked to the brother Andrew at the bar; I'd heard he'd flown here from New York City in his own plane, which was true. He also told me he thought he'd live his whole life and never meet anyone actually from Detroit.

Amy came up to my table holding hands with Aunt Wanda, and they sat beside me. It must've been a Shirley Temple (with six cherries) in her other hand. When she yawned, I saw that her tongue was stained bright red. "How many of those have you had?" I asked, taking the drink from her hand and setting it on the table.

"Don't cut me off," she said, yawning again, slower, wider.

The music was loud enough that maybe Aunt Wanda hadn't heard, but she asked, "Where'd Amy hear talk like that?"

I spoke quickly, "I guess TV." I sipped through the straw; the drink was unbearably sugary, instantly erasing the gin bite of my martini.

"I polkaed," Amy said.

"She's quite the dancer," Aunt Wanda said. "Picked up the polka like that." She snapped her fingers. "We're glad to see there's some Polish left in her, even all the way down there in Arizona."

My face ached from endless smiling, but I managed one more. "I like Arizona."

"It's too hot," Aunt Wanda said.

If we hadn't been at Theresa's wedding, I would've asked if she'd ever been there, just to see how she'd find a way to say "Never," and make it sound like my fault.

"Mom, will you polka with me?" Amy asked as she reached for her drink, fished out two cherries with her fingers and popped them into her mouth.

I glanced at Aunt Wanda. "That's rude," I said to Amy. "Use a spoon."

"But it's exactly how you eat the olives in your drinks," Amy said; at the same time, I spoke more loudly, "I don't want to dance right now. Can you find someone else?"

"I danced slow with Great-Grandma," Amy said. "And I danced with Theresa's new husband. He stepped on my toes six times."

Aunt Wanda said, "That's because he's not Polish. Who could expect a decent polka from him?"

With the straw, I maneuvered an ice cube from Amy's drink into my mouth. Like being Polish meant anything more than a hard-to-spell last name.

"Mo-om, please?" Amy stood up, yanked my hand. "Please?"

"All right, all right," but just as I spoke, the band stopped. "Too bad," and I crossed my fingers that it was a long break.

Stan (as in Stan and the Polka Dots), a white-haired, pink-faced man with a belly shaped like a meatball, said "Okay, folks. Ev-ery-body on the dance floor! It's your favorite and mine . . . the hokey pokey!" The crowd murmured its approval; my mother waved from across the room.

"Come on!" she called, clapping her hands. "Amy! You know this one! Ginger! I haven't seen you out here all night!"

"Mom, let's go," and Amy pulled at my arm, "you said," and it was a toss-up between which was worse, a polka or the hokey pokey, but at least the hokey pokey meant no getting stepped on, no bodies crashing into me.

"Okay," and I walked onto the dance floor with Amy tugging my arm back and forth. Aunt Wanda went to gather up stragglers throughout the room, including the gossiping table of Brad's family, many of whom finished up their drinks before smiling and winking at each other and following Aunt Wanda to the dance floor.

Stan whispered into the microphone: "I see a few party poopers still out there . . . everyone on the dance floor, chop-chop!"

There were too many of us for a circle, so we lined up in rows; I stood between Amy and my mother. I couldn't remember the last time I had done the hokey pokey—maybe a childhood birthday party? Or maybe that party at one of our friends' houses in Phoenix when we'd polished off a couple pitchers of secret-recipe margaritas, and someone dug out their kid's 45 record, and we hokey pokeyed for hours because it was such a ridiculous idea, and the next day we told everyone what a blast they'd missed even though we could barely remember it ourselves.

"Everybody ready to hokey pokey?" Stan asked.

The bridesmaids lifted their long skirts like cancan girls, each trying to raise hers the highest, and they giggled amongst themselves. Theresa laughed and hugged her new doctor husband. The gossipers from the other family stood with their arms crossed tight against their bodies, heads tilted all at the same angle like birds.

"Ev-erybody!" Stan called. "Right foot!" The band vamped and

Stan waggled his right foot for us to see, in case there was any confusion about which was right, which was a foot.

"Ready, Mom?" Amy asked.

"You bet!" This would be a good story for Jimmy, for our friends in Phoenix. You doing the hokey pokey? they'd exclaim, for real?

Stan started singing, accompanying himself with exaggerated gesture, urging us to join in: "You put your right foot in, you take your right foot out; you put your right foot in and you shake it all about. You do the hokey pokey and you turn yourself around. That's what it's all about!"

"Mom! You're great at this!" Amy shouted as she slowly spun, lifting her dress like the bridesmaids. "This is so fun!"

My mother leaned in and gave Amy a quick kiss on the cheek. The twirling bridesmaids looked like pink cotton candy. Brad's brother Andrew had a drink in his hand as he stood on the edge of the dance floor, forehead wrinkled just a bit as if, like me, he wanted to memorize this story to tell his friends back in New York City. "Left foot!" Stan shouted. Everyone sang and put their left foot in and out, shaking it like they were supposed to. Even my grandmother who was sitting at a table shook her left foot.

"Right hand!" Stan shouted, and I realized there were a hell of a lot of body parts to go, meaning the hokey pokey could last for hours; it was worse than the polkas. Those gave me a headache, but at least you could spin and twirl any way you wanted, you could close your eyes and feel some sort of music; this was just long-feeling the way a line that snakes through a maze of ropes is long—"Left hand!"—and I looked around at all the body parts jutting out, all of us synchronized as Stan directed, and it was like everything in Detroit was; what someone else wanted, someone else's way; and I started to go back to the table to sit down, but Amy and my mother said, "Don't go!" at the same time, and it was too crowded, so when Stan shouted, "right arm!" and everyone took up the tune, I stuck in my left arm; and Amy stopped, looked at her hands, then said quietly, "Mom, I think you've got it wrong," and I just smiled, bumping into my cousin June when I "shook it all about"; she glared at me; "Wrong arm," she snapped, "pay attention."

"Right knee!" Stan shouted.

Out shot my right arm, shaking all over the place. I pranced around, making a big show, crashing into a couple people who looked at me, at each other, back at me.

"Ginger!" My mother put her hands on her hips. "What's the matter with you?"

Stan called, "Left knee!" and I started singing: "Put your right hip in, take your right hip out . . ."; that was a fun one to wiggle; Andrew was watching me now, and what was wrong with a little attention? People were laughing, starting to point at me, and I pushed my way up to the stage, right under where Stan stood, and I belted out my version, and kicked my legs high as Stan tried to get everyone to shake their necks all about, and it was stupid; I wasn't even drunk, but all around me people were shaking whatever they wanted to shake, putting in their feet or their hips or their hands, nobody was singing along with Stan—maybe a few people like my mother were still trying to do it the right way— but most everyone was following me and my not-following; even Andrew was singing, "Put your scotch-rocks in"; and finally Stan shouted, "Last time—whole body!" but the rest of us were screaming and stamping and shaking any damn thing we wanted, and the band finished with a flourish, and Stan said, "Okay! Very nice! Very, very nice!" as if he wasn't sure what he meant, and when I looked around at the crowd, most people were smiling, the people my age anyway, the table of gossipers from the groom's side, Andrew, the groom's guests. Not my mother, not my daughter, not my aunts. When I finally looked at Theresa, she was listening to something one of the bridesmaids was whispering in her ear.

Stan wiped his forehead with a big red handkerchief. "Wasn't that something, folks?" he said. "That was the gosh-darnedest hokey pokey I ever saw." Andrew applauded, and several others joined in. So see, what I did was fine. Stan said, "Remind me not to give you folks fire-drill directions." He kept going, but I stopped listening; he was turning into nothing more than a blah-blah drone that was easier to ignore than his stupid music.

I started to leave the dance floor; no one spoke as I pushed by, just stared so hard at me it was like rocks against my back. I was hoarse from singing so loud, and what was one more martini? Let them stare, let them talk until their tongues fell out into a little pile on the floor.

The bartender was in back getting more ice, so people had clotted up, waiting for their drinks, and Andrew came up next to me, touched my arm for a moment. "That was the gosh-darnedest hokey pokey I ever saw," he mimicked softly. His smile tilted more on one side than the other, sort of like Jimmy's.

"Stan and the Polka Dots still don't know what hit them," I said. I saw my mother standing at our table, looking at me. She frowned and gave her head a quick shake. I turned so my back was facing her, rolling my neck as if I needed to work out a kink.

Stan pierced through: "So everyone understands? A dollar to dance with the bride; just slip your dollar—or more!—in that special little purse she's got, and dance with our beautiful bride until someone else cuts in. Come on, folks, let's send this great couple off to married life with a little something in the bank!" The band started up and Stan added, "This is a super-looong song, folks. Plenty of time for seconds! Dollar a dance!"

"Good lord!" Andrew said. "I'm in a World War II dance hall."

I looked at the floor, at a new scuff on my shoes. "It's a Polish wedding thing," I said.

"What's next?" he asked. "Do we follow the couple to their boudoir and wait for the blood-soaked sheet to be flung out the window?"

I laughed though it wasn't as funny as he thought it was. "Guess this guy's filling the ice trays himself," I muttered, pointing to where the bartender should have been. The song was sickeningly sweet, like syrup spilling all over a table, but it was familiar, something I'd forgotten from all the weddings I'd been to growing up, and I turned to watch Theresa. She was dancing with her father, a lacy white cloth purse tied with a blue ribbon dangling from one wrist, and now my grandmother reached for the purse and slipped in a dollar, and she didn't get two steps before Aunt Wanda was there with a crumpled bill, and a long line of my family wound along the dance floor; they were opening wallets, shaking purses, folding bills so no one could see how much they were giving Theresa, and my mother and Amy were in the middle of the line, and my mother's purse was hanging open and she was counting out some money that she put in Amy's hand; and now Theresa was dancing with her mother, and next was Aunt Joane and Uncle Ted and my cousin June and her husband Bobby and Deborah and Phyllis and Rob and Uncle Henry and Marge and Peter and Cynthia and William and Paul and John Jr. and my mother and Amy—everyone was there, I could name each one, I knew things about them that you know only about family—and Theresa's purse was rounding out; I guess the bartender was back, because I heard Andrew ask what I was drinking, and I said, "Dry martini." When he gave it to me, he opened his mouth, but I cut him off: "Excuse me," and I handed him my drink and walked away.

Stan was right; it was a super-looong song, which meant I was the last one in my family to buy a dance with Theresa.

The Bouquet

Amy's head was flat on the table, but anytime Ginger asked, she said, "I am *not* tired, Mom." Even the spoons clinking glasses and the follow-up kiss, which had delighted her earlier, weren't enough to raise her head. Bridesmaids' pink shoes were scattered on the edges of the dance floor like scraps of a parade float, and the band leader had given up mopping his forehead, instead tying a bandanna around his head, making him look like a jolly pirate.

"She's throwing the bouquet!" someone said. "Hurry!"

"Whoever catches the bouquet gets married next," Ginger told Amy as they crowded with everyone else to the stairs in the hallway. Theresa stood backward on the first landing as a group of girls—the bridesmaids prominent in the front—jockeyed for position beneath her like waves fighting to crash first.

"Go on, Amy," Helen said, joining Ginger. "Go for the bouquet. You're not married."

"I don't want to be married," Amy said.

Helen laughed. "Not now, but someday. You'll see. We'll all polka at your wedding, and you'll wear a pretty white dress like Theresa's. Maybe we can get your mother to show off her polka." She hugged Amy, first quick with only one arm, then longer with both, as if there were more than Amy's body to hold on to.

Theresa waved the bouquet over her head. "On three, girls," she said. "One."

"No hokey pokey for Mom," Amy said.

"Very funny." Ginger took a guess at who would win: the tall bridesmaid with the pretty blonde hair. Not that it meant anything anyway. Look at her—she'd never fought for the bouquet in all the weddings she'd been to, and she ended up married anyway.

"Two!"

"Where's Ma?" Helen asked, sorting through the faces, looking for Rose. "Theresa! Wait! Your grandmother wants to see this!"

But it was too late; "three!" and the bouquet arced through the air, and Theresa whirled to see who would get it, who was next to be married, as the girls scrambled and tussled and laughed as they reached for the flowers.

No Last Names

What I didn't like about AA was how everyone drank all that coffee. And how it had to be black, like they were telling you, I'm a certain kind of person because I drink black coffee. It happened that I preferred my coffee black, but to show I wasn't one of them, I dumped in sugar, loaded my cup with powdered creamer, sipped slow to choke it down.

And I hated the room in the church basement where they met. The floor was the colorless tile of a high school classroom, so when they stared down at it, your stomach knotted the way it did when the teacher used to say, Pop quiz. The room was stuffy, and there was an old piano that someone was always pounding on before the meeting, thinking they were a better player than they were. Or maybe it needed tuning.

There were about a hundred things I hated about AA. I hated how everything had numbers, like twelve steps and one day at a time and ninety meetings in ninety days. How the parking lot was gravel, so I nicked up the heels of my shoes. How you never knew if the basement door was unlocked or if you had to go around to the side, and whichever way you guessed, you got a locked door. There were a million things. Maybe the worst was how it was like confession in church back when I lived in Detroit, the same dry silence lingering uselessly between words, the same weight, the time-moving-backward-never-ending trap I'd already escaped once.

I kept going to AA because I'd told my husband I would for three months, and when he didn't believe me, I decided to prove him wrong. Hi, my name is Beth and I'm an alcoholic.

Only my name is Ginger.

The morning the kids and I were packing up the car for the annual summer trip to visit my mother in Detroit, Jimmy got me alone and put a folded piece of paper in my hand. I smiled, thinking it was maybe a lovey-dovey note about how much he'd miss me—we were both trying that hard lately—but it was a phone number. I didn't have to ask; his words spilled like liquid, how great that I was finally getting help, how important it was to our future together, how he was proud of my new beginning. Finally I put my hand over his mouth and said real slow, "Whose phone number?" and in the pause my hand got warm from his breath so I took it away.

"It's the AA office in Detroit," he whispered so the kids wouldn't hear. His eyes moved far away, and I looked to what he saw but it was nothing. "So you can find a meeting," and that's when he looked straight at me, his face open like a book with a picture you don't want to see. He'd decided he couldn't ever trust me again; with his face that way, he didn't look like a husband anymore, just a man I once knew. But it was the sun, because when I stepped back and stopped squinting, he was the same Jimmy, just more worried looking.

"Vacation doesn't count," I said.

"It counts," he said.

"I'll be fine."

"You're not fine here," he said.

Amy walked by with two pillows that she tossed into the back-seat. She made that flippy noise with her thongs, slapping hard on the pavement, and Jimmy and I stopped talking. She paused, then said, "We're almost ready to go," as if she were the one driving, as if she were in charge.

I folded the piece of paper as small as it could go. "You're right," I said to Jimmy. "Vacation counts." Then I slipped the phone number into the zippered pocket of my purse.

"Okay." He knew the word was wrong but he didn't know any others. "Okay."

I kissed him on the cheek. "You need to shave."

"Ginger, this time I mean it," he said.

I nodded, patted my purse, nodded again.

"I love you," he said, like it was a reminder. I probably would've thought more about that, but I needed to get in the car and get moving. Never mind that it was only Detroit at the end.

Another thing I hated about AA was how there was one pipe that made this pinging when anyone ran water in the bathroom sink, exactly like ice clinking in a glass. A lot of us stopped washing our hands because of it, but there was nothing we could do about other people in the church, people at different meetings, and the more you tried not to notice that ping, the louder it was, and I mean *exactly* like ice.

The drive up from Phoenix was fine; we stayed in Holiday Inns, even though the kids begged for Howard Johnson. Amy said HoJo pools were better, but I knew it was because Holiday Inns had lounges, and I could just hear Jimmy telling her, No Holiday Inns. But I was good; I sat by the pool and flipped pages of magazines while Amy and Cal squabbled and dunked each other and begged me to come swimming with them.

I was so good. Before the kids went to sleep, I sent Amy with the ice bucket and she didn't want to go, but finally I screamed enough and she went, and as the kids slept, I sat at the funny little motel desk and watched the ice melt to water in the plastic bucket. And the next two nights were just like that first one, and then we were in Detroit and I was calling long distance to let Jimmy know we'd arrived safely. When he wanted to know how I was, I said, "Fine, good," and then he said, "Let me talk to Amy," only he asked for her too soon, too suddenly, so I knew exactly the questions he wanted to ask her. "She's asleep," I said, and what could he say then? Wake her up? And the conversation crumbled to pieces that didn't connect, and when I hung up the phone, Amy came out the kitchen door and said, "I wanted to say hi to Dad," and I just said, "Sorry." She opened her mouth like there was more, but I guess there wasn't, because she closed it and went back into the kitchen.

The next day was Sunday, and in Detroit, Sunday meant 10:15 Mass. My first-ever Sunday in Phoenix I woke at noon and wore pajamas all day just because I wanted to, and that's how I knew I'd left home. In Phoenix, when I heard church bells, I didn't also hear "Hurry-hurry, Ginger, you're so slow, are your feet stuck to the floor?" All I heard was ringing, and it wasn't long before I didn't even hear that.

So I woke the kids by apologizing that we had to go to church. Even worse was how early we had to get up so we'd be done with breakfast an hour before taking communion. The whole thing was a pain and a half. "We have to do this for Grandma," I explained. "Church is something she thinks is important," and I kept talking so the kids wouldn't grab up silence to fill with their fussing. Amy tried to butt in; I cut her off. "I don't want to hear any more; we're going to church and that's that," and I headed for the bathroom to put in my hot rollers.

"I *like* church," Amy called after me.

"You don't have to lie," I said hairpin clenched between my teeth. "I thought church was a waste of time when I was your age."

"I like when we're early and the boys are lighting candles with that long, skinny torch," Amy said. "And when they jingle those little bells that sound like wind."

"I like the chairs they sit in," Cal added.

"And pouring water over the priest's hand."

I came out of the bathroom, my hair half-rolled. "Did you ever wonder why there aren't any girls up there?" I asked Amy. "Why it's only boys?"

"Mo-om," she said, turning so I could button the back of her dress. "It just is."

"Don't you think you could ring those bells as easily as any boy?"

She looked at Cal who bent to tie his shoe. "I guess," she said.

"Well, doesn't that make you mad?" I asked.

She shrugged.

"It made me really mad when I was living here," I said.

"Don't you like the pictures of the people in the colored windows?" she asked. "Or when Grandma holds our hands during that one Father prayer?"

She meant the "Our Father" but I didn't correct her.

"Or anything, Mom?"

All my aunts and my mother said Amy and I looked alike, but it wasn't something I could see. She twisted a strand of hair between two fingers, put it in her mouth, let it slip back out.

"I'm hungry," Cal said.

"I bet Grandma has waffles for breakfast," and they went downstairs, Cal because waffles were his favorite food and Amy because, even though she was only eleven, all our conversations now were like two people who'd just met on a train and were trying to be nice because they saw a long trip ahead of them.

What else did I hate about AA? That I never knew what to wear to the meetings. Was I supposed to put on a skirt and heels—and look like some moronic housewife hooked on cooking wine?

Or patched jeans and a T-shirt with holes under the arms—like a bum stumbling in off the street? No one thought about those kinds of questions.

My mother glanced at her watch as I walked into the kitchen forty-five minutes later, but she kept drying the breakfast dishes. I was right about the waffles; she'd set aside a plate for me, but there was no time to eat—not that I wanted such a heavy breakfast—so I held the plate over the garbage and let the waffles slide in. My mother still didn't say anything. I dabbed maple syrup off Cal's cheek with my finger, pushed Amy's hair out of her eyes. Then I poured some coffee.

My mother hung up her dish towel over a cupboard door and looked at my feet, at the chipped polish of my toenails. "Sandals to church?"

I had been planning to get my shoebag out of the car, but I said, "Sandals were good enough for Jesus." When she didn't say anything, I added, "Don't you think God has better things to worry about than what I'm wearing to church?"

"Same old Ginger," she said, shaking her head. How many million times had I heard that?

"Do you want me to change shoes?" I asked.

"You do what you want," she said. "You always do. Go on outside kids, we'll be there in a minute." She took the plate out of my hand, washed and dried it quickly, then pushed through the side screen door, letting it slap behind her. Just a pair of stupid shoes. I blew on my coffee to cool it.

"Did Jesus really wear sandals?" I heard Cal ask.

"Flip-flops?" Amy asked.

My mother laughed. "Jesus lived in the desert, and I suppose desert people wore sandals."

"We're desert people so maybe Mom's sandals are okay," Amy said.

The church bell started clanging, startling me. "Hurry, Ginger, we'll be late!" my mother called.

"Just a sec," but they started walking without me.

So I dumped my coffee down the sink and filled the cup with water, leaving it on the counter. I hurried to catch up to them, and when I got there, Cal was saying, "Once Mom threw her shoes into a hotel fountain at a wedding. Then she danced in her underwear."

"Shut up," Amy said. "That was one time. And you weren't even there, so how do you know so much about what happened?"

"I saw the picture before Dad ripped it up," Cal said. "The police came."

"Everyone thought it was fun," I said. "All my friends thought it was hilarious."

"Weren't your shoes ruined?" my mother asked.

"It was one pair of shoes," I said. "We were having fun."

"Shoes cost money," my mother said.

"We were having fun!" and I couldn't raise my voice, so I kept it low and tight: "That's the point of the story; that's why I threw the shoes in the fountain!"

"I couldn't be so wasteful like that," my mother said, and I wanted to stand and scream until she understood, that of course *she* wouldn't but *I* would, and that I had, and I'd do it again, because the way I remember, it was fun; everyone laughed when the police came and I was standing in the fountain with the water bubbling like champagne, and we were all laughing, and I was somewhere all my own I'd never been before, a place I'd discovered.

Maybe my mother didn't want to hear what I was going to say, because she started telling me about the wonderful new priest, and how the women in his former parish in Ohio used to make him *kielbasa* and sauerkraut for Sunday dinner, but now he said Detroit women fixed the best *kielbasa*, and hearing every last detail about the *kielbasa* and the new priest filled up the rest of the walk to church.

I had to talk at AA, so I told them about what happened at the fountain, going to the police station with some cop's too-big sweater wrapped around my body and how my husband didn't remember it all funny the way I did, and how copies of those pictures kept coming in the mail with no return address, and how our friends started calling me Bubbles because they said champagne went to my head (guess they didn't know about the gin and tonics). I talked about the hangover the morning after and how I demanded that everyone leave the house because they were breathing too loud; as soon as they were gone, I cried for hours, missing them, sorry I'd been so mean. I decided to bake a cake and I tore through every kitchen cupboard looking for a mix, but there weren't any, so I thought I'd make one from scratch, but we didn't have any eggs, and all there was to make was oatmeal, and when they got back that night, Jimmy said, "Why's this cold oatmeal on the counter?" and I screamed at him because he should've known why.

I'd been to enough AA meetings to know I was supposed to be sorry about the whole thing, the fountain and the oatmeal and the shoes, but after I was finished, I felt a smile where one wasn't supposed to be, because, damn it, the fountain had been fun—my friends applauding and the cop car's red light spinning round, me spinning with it; as soon as I smiled, there were murmurs, frowns, glances exchanged, and the leader sighed. So I added, "I never found out which of my friends was sending those nasty pictures."

Then it was someone else's turn. "Hi, my name is Joleen, and I'm an alcoholic," she whispered. "I'm here because last Saturday night I set my baby on fire by accident, and he died yesterday."

That's something I hate about AA: all those pathetic, sad people, and how now all they've got going is trying to out-pathetic, out-sad each other, and me sitting there, afraid it might rub off on me, knowing that if it did, that's when they'd really listen to what I have to say.

The priest was younger than how I think of priests, and he even told a funny story in his sermon; he had a nice, embarrassed kind of laugh, like maybe he knew a dirty joke or two. He was just chubby enough that I could imagine him caring about a good *kielbasa*. But it was still church, still one man who thought he was God trying to tell me what to do, and when afterward my mother lingered to light candles for my grandmother and my father, I headed to the back of the church to wait.

The bulletin board was an inch-thick jumble of scraps of paper pinned on top of each other, and smack in the center was "AA Meeting Every-Day in You're Church Comunity Center 8 pm." I read the words over and over, correcting the spelling and punctuation in my mind, rewording it to make it more discreet, less abrupt, and when I finally looked away, Amy was standing beside me, her arms folded loosely against her chest, head cocked to one side.

Finally she said, "Grandma's ready," but she kept looking at me.

I pointed at the bulletin board. "Parish picnic sounds fun."

"You hate picnics," she said.

For a moment I couldn't remember if I did or didn't.

"Grandma's waiting outside," and she sounded like someone who wasn't a daughter.

Outside, my mother waved us over to meet Father Lipinski. "Ginger lives in Arizona," my mother said. "Where it's a hundred degrees in the summer."

"I'd like to visit the Grand Canyon someday," Father Lipinski said.

"It's absolutely beautiful," I said. He watched me as if he knew things about me that he wasn't supposed to know. I imagined my mother talking about me to him, my mother whispering secrets in the confessional booth. "I enjoyed your sermon."

"Thank you, Ginger," he said. "Often people mention they enjoyed the homily and then through our conversation, I realize they weren't listening to it. Very humbling."

All I remembered was the funny story. My smile tightened.

"I never want to reach that point where because I'm standing in front of a group of people I assume I have something to say that's worth listening to," he said.

"Very wise," my mother said, nodding that way she had, slowly and deeply.

"Is it really true that God is always watching us, like how you said?" Amy asked suddenly. "Is that like a spy?"

"Like a friend," he said. "Like someone who cares about you."

"Can I ask you something else?" Amy said.

"Of course, dear." He smiled at my grandmother as if he knew that these children didn't go to church and were living like sandal-wearing heathens in the desert.

"Could you pray for me to get a horse?" she asked, her voice dwindling into a whisper.

My grandmother and the priest laughed and looked at each other again, same story: This is what happens when you raise children who don't go to church every week.

I said, "Amy, we talked about the horse, and you understood why we can't get one for you."

"I know you and Dad can't," she said. "But maybe God can."

My mother laughed again, and winked at the priest, and I could just see this being the funny story in next week's sermon. He said to Amy, "God has his own reason for everything, Amy, and if you don't get a horse, I think maybe there's something he's trying to tell you. It's hard for you to understand now because you're so young, but someday you will. I'll pray for you, Amy, I'll pray that if you don't get your horse, you'll come to understand why not. And I imagine one day you'll see that sometimes it's better that God doesn't let us have everything we want."

"You listen to him, Amy," my mother said. "Father Lipinski is such a smart man."

Silence stretched so thin it had to snap. This is what I didn't like about church, Detroit, my mother. This is why I brought my children here only once a year. It wasn't so awful simply to want a stupid horse.

But Amy thanked him, her forehead wrinkled like she was actually thinking about what he'd said instead of dismissing it as crap. Someone else was tugging at the priest's sleeve, so we said goodbye, my mother promising to bring by some *pierogi* on Wednesday.

As we walked home, my mother said to Amy, "There's a new petting zoo at the park; we'll go see the ponies after Sunday dinner."

Amy nodded, keeping just a little bit ahead of us, her head bent low, and she walked the way I used to, stepping on the cracks, scuff-step, scuff-step, and back when I walked like that, what I was thinking was how one day I'd be somewhere so far away no one could ever find me and bring me back.

The next evening, Jimmy called from his office. I sat in the chair by the phone table and listened to him talk through static that sounded like wind blowing a long way away. "What have you been doing?" he asked. I told him about going to church and going to the pathetic petting zoo in the park down the street and how the animals were crammed inside too-small cement cages and a kid near us got bitten by a goat, about all the cousins and aunts and cousin's children who kept asking how hot was it *really* in Arizona. "What else?" he said, and before I could answer, he said, "You promised this time would be different," and his voice cracked apart like the shells off hard-boiled eggs, and maybe he started crying because he didn't say anything else, and all I could do was whisper that the church had a meeting tonight at eight and that I would go, and I kept whispering on and on—same words, same promises—and it was easier to talk to him without seeing his face, without seeing how he didn't believe me; it was the way confession should've been, over the phone, not you pressed deep in a dark booth, tight enough you could hear each wheezy breath the priest pulled in or pushed out. My sentences spun like cobwebs in the corner, and finally Jimmy interrupted: "Don't you understand that it has to change, Ginger, it has to be different now," and didn't he know *I* wanted things to be different, too? Back then it was the two of us dancing cheek-to-cheek in fountains while everyone laughed; it was me and Jimmy driving out to the desert to howl like coyotes at New Year's Eve midnight; it was us at a party that went from Friday night to Saturday night to Sunday morning. Was having fun so bad?

But I told him I'd go to the meeting, and then he wanted to talk to Amy, and there was a staticky pause where I felt him wondering if I'd have the nerve to say no. "Hang on a sec," and just before I set the receiver on the table, he exhaled a long, heavy breath, like someone had been holding him under water. "So far she's fine," was the first thing I heard Amy say, and whatever the rest was, she turned away so I couldn't hear.

All the women at AA brought those little packs of Kleenex. Before the meeting started, they rustled through their purses, arranging the tissue pack on top. When someone started to cry, it was a race to see who could get out the first tissue pack.

I thought about not going. But that's what he'd think I'd be thinking.

Getting out of the house felt the way it used to, when I lived here and too many people had to know where I was each minute of every day. When I mentioned taking a walk, Amy wanted us all to go. When I said I had to buy gas for the car, Amy remembered the station that gave out the free glasses was closed for vacation until Wednesday, and my mother nodded. The three of us watched the clock on the mantel chime for seven forty-five; of course the longer it took me to get out, the more it wasn't the stupid meeting. Finally I told them my cousin June had asked me to stop by some night to help her sort through old pictures and clippings to put together a scrapbook for the high school reunion committee.

"Want me to come with you?" Amy asked. "I like old pictures."

"I'll be out too late," I said, shaking my purse, listening for the rattle of car keys. "You can look at Grandma's pictures."

"What time will you be home?" Amy asked.

"Late," I said.

"How late?"

"I don't know, Amy, ten or eleven. Maybe later," and I shook my purse again and again. "Where are my car keys? Where the— where are they?"

Amy pointed to the end table by the couch. "Where you left them," she said, and I grabbed the keys, poked one finger through the key ring, and held hard.

"See you guys later," and it felt like I was running out the door, though I forced myself to walk slow, to think slow, to breathe in only slow, deep breaths, but once I was outside, once I was down the front steps, I ran to the car, forgetting that they'd hear my sandals slapping the pavement through the open windows, and all I did was run fast, faster, I didn't even bother with the car, I ran down the street until the blood pumped hard and wicked through my body, pounded into my brain and I heard it in my ears. Escape was how I remembered, letting go of everything at once.

When we craved alcohol we were supposed to pick up the phone. The idea was we'd talk apart our desire, hold it back, force it into conversation. The reality was they'd talk while I'd think about the last drink I'd had, how I didn't know then that it was going to be the last, and how if I could have it again, I'd sip it slow, I'd stretch it out for a week, two, longer; maybe I wouldn't take the final sip so I'd have it always waiting for me.

It could've been the church basement I usually went to; the

cigarette smoke was like columns in the room, and a woman with crooked teeth was brewing the second pot of coffee as I arrived. "We're just about to start," she said as she poured coffee into a foam cup for me. "You said black?"

I took the cup, used a plastic spoon to scrape crusted sugar out of the bowl; the creamer was solid so I gave up on that.

"How long have you—?" the woman started.

I cut off her question because they always sounded like an inspirational poster when they asked. "Twenty-seven days," I said.

"You'll want to sit over there, dear," she said, pointing to the far table. "Herb will be guiding the discussion. He's a wonderful man; in fact, back when I started coming, he was—"

"Thanks," and I flashed one of those smiles that feels fake but you hope doesn't look it and headed to the table; I sat in a chair between two empty seats so no one could talk to me, stared into my cup of coffee, watched the steam twist and rise until the coffee cooled.

Herb started the meeting, and it took about two seconds to figure out he was the blah-blah-blah type who thought he was more interesting than he was. He had a bad laugh, sort of a donkey-monkey combo, like the kind of high school teacher everyone in the class imitates as soon as he goes out in the hall. By the time we started introductions, I'd stopped paying attention, started thinking about Jimmy and what he was doing, whether he was home tonight or invited to someone's house for dinner because he'd been using that "poor old bachelor" routine, and how the wives we knew liked to show off their gourmet cooking when someone was over and there were always things that flamed or were jelled in aspic or were prepared in special cookware that was used only for that particular dish, like a fondue pot, and how our friends had grown up in places where people knew how to pick really good bottles of wine to serve with these kinds of meals, and how now I was supposed to say, "Just water, please," and the way their faces looked the first time they heard that, the looks that flashed from one to another across the table, across the room, Jimmy and me pretending not to see, and how the water tasted dull and empty, like what there is when you take away the scotch; and how at my mother's house when I said, "Just water, please," she said, "No milk? Your teeth will drop out. Your bones will break," and she wouldn't stop talking until she'd poured out a glass of milk for me and I'd gagged it down, imagining it was an endless, icy martini with two olives, like the kind Jimmy made that our friends raved over. He soaked the olives in gin in the refrigerator— that was the secret. If I brought olives home from the grocery store now, Jimmy ground them down the garbage disposal.

"My name is Paul, and I'm an alcoholic." Smile, clap, put that listening look on my face, think about standing at the refrigerator and eating those olives at three in the morning when everyone was asleep. But this voice wasn't like the others; it wouldn't let go, so I looked at the man speaking. It was Father Lipinski, sitting one chair over from me. His fingers fiddled with a crumpled napkin as he spoke, and he watched them as if he had no idea they were moving, no idea how to hold them still. "I'm continuing to learn," he said. "It's great comfort to know that you're watching out for me, that you understand where I've been." He had been watching his fingers so intently that when he looked up, I was too surprised to glance away. I wasn't sure he'd recognize me, but then he gave a tiny nod, like someone who doesn't want your secret but suddenly has it forever. He looked away, continued: "This last week has been more difficult than some. But isn't it the struggle that makes us stronger, better people? God gives us only as much as we can bear."

Someone murmured, "Amen, Father," and he flushed red, lifted one hand in protest.

"In this room I'm not a priest," he said. "I'm just a man learning how to live one day at a time, like the rest of you."

"Well put," Herb said, and I was next.

I cleared my throat. "My name is Beth, and I'm an alcoholic."

It's what I always said—first name, no last name—and it sounded fine, except that I was still looking at Father Lipinski, and as I spoke, I remembered that he knew exactly who I was.

"Hi, Beth," everyone chorused.

Father Lipinski wasn't any older than I was, but he was a priest, so he felt older; or maybe I felt younger, I felt fourteen, as if I were back in Detroit when Sunday meant 10:15 Mass and Saturday meant four o'clock confession and, despite the screen between us, our priest always knew who I was, even when I disguised my voice. He was old and wheezy, every breath scraped out seemed a struggle for him, and I thought about what would happen if he died while absolving someone; would that count? I'd make up sins to confess—giving him something interesting to listen to instead of the endless round of women like my mother and grandmother and aunts who maybe at worst let "sweet Jesus" slip when they lifted a roasting pan without a hot pad. I made up sins that were exotic and extraordinary, sins filled with biblical words like "coveting" and "adultery." I claimed I'd kissed my math teacher more than once in an adulterous way; or I said I incestuously coveted my cousin who wanted to be a priest. Other times my imaginary sins encompassed moral dilemmas: I'd stolen fifty dollars from a cash register but I gave it to a bum on the street; or I'd taken a convertible for a joyride but while I was driving around, I rescued a child from a burning building. The priest sighed and said, "Fifty 'Hail Marys' for your disrespect. Fifty, five hundred—you don't say them anyway, do you, Ginger? If your mother knew . . . ," but he couldn't tell her—confessions were bound to secrecy. It was something that made me laugh, a way to get through another Saturday—how many hundred more before I was out of Detroit forever?

I got big laughs with my friends in Arizona over those stories.

But I didn't tell them about walking out of the confessional booth and the light coming through the stained-glass windows like soft breath and the organist in for practice holding the notes too long and too slow; there was nowhere to look, no one to look at, only down at my feet, only the scuffed floor. "Hail Mary" was in my head, but I'd be damned before I'd whisper the words, not even "Hail Mary, full of grace," not even "the Lord is with thee," because I could give a shit; it was what I did to survive Detroit. I was on my way out as soon as there was somewhere to go. I wasn't these people, my mother kneeling, hands clasped together, her lips moving, eyes closed; I wasn't someone trapped into one way of being, one way of thinking.

I looked at the strangers sitting around the table, at Father Lipinski watching me, concern spread across his face. "You don't know me," and there was nothing more to say, so I repeated myself.

"Honey, we're here to help," a woman my mother's age said. She unzipped her purse. I didn't need her stupid tissues.

I stood up, pushed the chair back, pushing, pushing; it was something to hold on to, and it made a long, loud scrape against the floor. "I don't belong here," and I hurried toward the door.

"Beth!" Father Lipinski called after me. "Beth! Come back. Ginger! Please!"

It was like hearing another language from somewhere you'd been once. I wasn't going back; I knew exactly where I would go—and what I'd do once I got there and how I'd feel while I was doing it, and the sound of my feet tromping the stairs was the rhythm of a whispered prayer, so I started to run.

There was a bar on about every corner in Detroit, so it took me about two seconds to get to one. I'd been to this bar before, in fact, maybe on the last trip, or the trip before, or who the hell cared. Five or six men lined the stools inside, the kind of men whose fathers had spent out their lives sitting at this same bar. I took a stool along the far end, facing the mirror behind the bar, and the gin finally going down was like ice melting into a cold, hard stream, something that carves gullies down the face of mountains, and it was just that feeling, no more.

It was the kind of bar where they wouldn't talk to you until at least your third drink. Even then, no one had much to say; and what they said was spoken straight ahead into the mirror. Or staring at the TV that played some cop show with the volume all the way down, so all there was was silent shooting and long quiet car chases; it all seemed so peaceful, so far away. It was what I loved about bars, that silence—the only sound the whir of the revolving fan, the whoosh as the stirred-up air hit your face, then moved away—it was being in the one place where all anyone expected you to do was order yourself a drink.

When I was partway through my fourth gin and tonic, a boy came through the open door. He was about Amy's age, but he didn't have that shy, looking-all-around look that most kids have when they're in bars; he nodded at the bartender, lifted his hand in a general greeting. A couple men nodded at him in the mirror. "Hey T," the boy said to a fat man with each hand around a Stroh's. "You seen my dad?"

The man tilted his head. "In the can," and the boy hopped upon a stool. The bartender pushed over three chunks of lime on a napkin, and the boy sucked on them one after the other, scraping off the pulp with his front teeth. Someone should've told him that would eat away the enamel. Finally the fat man said to the mirror, "How's school going, Bobby?"

The boy said, "Summer vacation."

We all turned at the creak of the bathroom door. The father was fastening the last button on his jeans, shoving his hand down deep to tuck in the front of his T-shirt. When he saw the boy, he scowled and rolled his eyes, slapped the back of one hand into his palm. "You following me?"

The boy took the last lime out of his mouth, dropped the rind on the bar, spoke into the mirror. "Mom's waiting at home."

"She can French-kiss my mother-loving ass," and he laughed,

got the rest of them laughing, too, slow at first, then louder and harder.

The boy's face reddened. "Come on, Dad," and he slid off his stool, his feet thumping heavily on the floor, heavier than you'd think a kid would be.

" 'Come on, Dad,' " the man mimicked in a prissy voice. " 'Come on, Dad.' Don't you know nothing else to say?"

"Time to get home." The boy reached for the man's arm.

"Who the hell are you, telling *me* what to do!" he screamed. "I'm your goddamn father!" He shoved at the boy who stumbled backward, knocking into a stool. "Why're you always spying after me, you little piss ant?"

The boy rubbed his elbow, looked toward the bar. "Hey T, how's about giving me a hand?" A moment later, he added, "Please?" I looked down into my glass; the ice was about melted, and I lifted one finger for a refill. Someone had scratched the initials A.S. into the varnish on the bar.

The father said, "Get on home to your mommy."

"Please don't miss Mom's birthday," the boy said. "I got us a cake."

" 'I gotta cake.' "

"It's okay that you missed my birthday and Katie's, but not Mom's. Please?"

"I said get!" and he raised his arm and stepped toward the boy, who spun away sideways and ducked. "Go on! Mommy's calling!"

The boy's shoulders hunched as he walked along the bar, head down. I hadn't noticed the bruise under one eye, and how he kept his elbow tucked close to his body. No one looked at him or his father or even at the mirror, and there were just his footsteps, then his voice, "See you later, Dad," then more footsteps, then nothing.

"What?" the father said, stepping over the chair he'd knocked down. "Fill me up."

Someone shifted their weight and a stool squeaked; maybe it was me. The bartender turned up the volume on the TV, slipped through a couple channels; "Tigers won," he announced to no one in particular.

I hated the way people talked at AA, as if they were never-fail, 100 percent, all-the-way right. As if we were too stupid to remember the flip side to our stories. Jimmy turned that way, not remembering how we used to stay up all night with our friends and cram into someone's car and tear three hours down to Mexico to eat *chilaquiles* and drink tequila while the sun rose. We'd pick up a bottle cheap for the ride back, everyone screaming when I bit the worm in half between my front teeth, Jimmy—my boyfriend before he was my husband—kissing me hard and wet and tight as he whispered something I never remembered the next day.

Every time I glanced down the bar at that man, I saw the boy instead. He wasn't any older than Amy, but already he had that kind of face, the got-to-get-out look I knew. It was more than the awful father; it was Detroit, it was gray skies pressing you in, it was being worn down into someone you aren't. Just looking at that boy you knew he woke up nights sweating, terrified he'd lose the race of getting away before turning into his father.

Two more swallows of gin—by this time I'd stopped bothering with tonic—and I remembered somewhere else I'd seen that face. It wasn't like I was forgetting my kids' birthdays or anything like that, but maybe I should do something nice and extra-special. Something fun to get Amy's face looking more like a kid's and to give her something to talk to her father about besides the spy report on what I was doing.

I finished the last bit, jiggled my ice, thought about having another. The boy's father slumped low on his stool, one hand loose around a shot glass, a couple lime rinds scattered by his elbow. When he saw me watching him in the mirror, he toasted me, beckoned for a refill. The bartender set the bottle up on the bar, not taking his eyes off the TV. "Those bastards," someone said, too tired sounding to mean it.

"Lady, what're you staring at?" the boy's father asked.

"Sorry," I mumbled.

I put down some money for the bartender, then headed for the door. Even when I knocked into a table, no one turned. "I know my kids' birthdays," but I didn't say it loud enough that anyone could hear.

Outside, moths circled the streetlights, and the air was heavy and drippy, something you want to wring out and throw away. I walked faster, passing the church, its narrow windows looking like eyes that weren't all the way open but weren't all the way closed—like when you're fifteen and coming home after curfew, and you're not sure if your mother sitting on the couch is awake or asleep so you tiptoe and she doesn't move, but the next morning she glares at you over oatmeal and whispers, "Don't think I don't know about you; you're coming to confession with me this afternoon," and nothing you could tell her or a priest would explain where you were or why you were there—because you were downtown, sitting on the hood of a boy's car, counting the headlights crossing the bridge to Canada. Even the boy you were with was only along because he wanted to kiss you, not because he cared about bridges or highways or Canada or you.

I stood under a circle of light, swatted at a couple moths. I wasn't that father at the bar, but I wasn't my mother either. How could I make my kids understand what that meant? That your life could be more than praying to God and waiting and learning lessons. That maybe you just wanted a horse—or to watch the bridge, or to dance in a fountain—just because you did.

I decided Amy should get a horse.

I decided she should get one now.

I picked up my pace and headed toward the park and the new petting zoo and where the horses were; there were so many there, and they were crammed too many to a pen—what'd they think they were, sardines? and I thought that was pretty funny, so I laughed and walked faster. In fact there was a sign on the wall— Amy had noticed it: Adopt a horse, or something like that. The zoo had too many, obviously. The whole getting-a-horse thing would be easy: all I needed was a rope to tie around its neck, and I was clever enough to realize that the detachable strap from my shoulder bag would do fine.

There weren't many lights at the park, but the moon was big. Besides, I'd been coming to this park since it had opened—I knew it well, especially since things never changed here: where the hoods hung out to smoke, where the easy girls went with their boyfriends. The petting zoo was in the far corner, and though it was new, it was already as tired looking as the whole park, as if it had been designed that way.

The front gate was open, but of course it was more fun to climb the wire fence (certainly my mother had never climbed a fence); partway up, I pulled off my skirt and let it flutter to the ground. How much more comfortable—and cooler—and even more unlike my mother—to be wearing just a slip. Swinging my legs over the top, I jumped to the ground and landed soft like a cat.

I was right near the goats, and a couple came bleating over to the fence, following me as I walked, but my daughter didn't want a dumb old goat. She wanted a horse named Blaze; it was all she talked about since she was seven; she'd be surprised to wake up tomorrow and see a horse in the yard. I couldn't decide whether I should tell her to share Blaze with her brother or not.

After the goats was the duck pond, with the chicken house over on the side. Then rabbits, then the deer pen, and finally the yard where they kept the horses, next to the horse ride setup that Amy went on six times in a row, thanks to my mother buying a whole booklet of tickets for her. No more corny twice-around-the-ring horse rides for my daughter, a soon-to-be horse owner.

I climbed over the wire fence and started calling, "Here horsey, here horsey," whistling, "Here Blaze," and one horse actually turned its head. I closed my eyes and held out my hand, its lips pressed rubbery against my palm. "Okay, Blaze," I said, "come on with me," trying out that soft, soothing, I-know-what-to-do-around-animals voice that worked on *Wild Kingdom,* and Blaze made a chirpy noise and seemed happy enough to let me loop my purse strap around his neck.

The gate was hard to figure out in the dark, and I whispered as I fumbled with the latch. "You'll like Amy," I said. "She's been wanting a horse for I don't know how many years, and she's going to love you to pieces. We'll feed you apples and grass and what else do you guys eat? Sugar cubes? Carrots? Whatever you need. Tamales, if you want them! We've got a nice little yard for you down in Arizona . . ." I paused, thinking how was I going to get a horse to Arizona, but didn't U-Haul rent trailers? "Maybe when it's nice Amy can sleep outside with you in a sleeping bag and when it rains, you can go under the carport, or whatever. Anyway, I know you're going to like living with us," and it all sounded so nice and so wonderful—exactly what Amy wanted—and the gate swung open, and I led Blaze outside, past the deer, past the rabbits, the chickens, the duck pond—where the horse took a little drink and I almost fell in—and finally past the goats and to the front gate, and we were on our way, clomping along the cement path to the main sidewalk, and I'd forgotten my skirt, but I just couldn't wait to show the horse to Amy—I'd wake her up if she was asleep, because this was just too good, too exciting. Your own horse! That's what I'd say as I'd lead her down the stairs to the front door where she'd stand on the porch and see the horse nibbling grass in the moonlight, and I'd be so good that I wouldn't even look at my mother, wouldn't say or even think, How's that for answered prayers?

Most houses were dark as Blaze and I walked through the neighborhood. I tried to keep him on the grass so the clatter of his hooves on the sidewalk wouldn't wake people through their open windows. I felt like Santa Claus, except that Santa Claus never actually brought horses to little girls; how many times had I told Amy stories like Santa couldn't fit a horse in his sleigh or Santa thought a bike might be more practical? After she found out about Santa, I just said no.

The porch light was on at my mother's house, and so was the front room light, which was unusual this late, but maybe she'd left them on for me.

I led Blaze to the tiny front yard. "Look at this great grass," I said. "She waters it every Thursday," and sure enough the horse leaned over and started nibbling, and I couldn't wait: "Amy!" I screamed. "Amy!" Let the neighbors see what a wonderful mother I was! "Look!" and Amy was at the screen door in front, and as soon as she saw me, she came onto the porch, pulling shut the heavy wooden door. When she saw Blaze in the yard her mouth dropped open, and then she quick slapped it covered with one hand, then let her hand fall away.

"What happened to your skirt?"

"Look!" I said. "Your very own horse!"

"Where have you been all this time?" She was about one notch away from yelling.

I pointed to Blaze. "Your horse."

My mother yanked open the door. "Do you want the neighbors to hear?" she hissed.

"Do you like the horse?" I asked.

"It's a pony, not a horse," Amy said.

She was supposed to be hugging Blaze by now, climbing up on his back, thanking me again and again, but she was still on the porch, arms crossed. She was wearing the nightgown with the pink flowers, the one that was too small for her, and there were circles under her eyes that I hadn't noticed earlier.

"What have you done now?" my mother said though the screen door, her arms folded like Amy's except tighter against her body.

"I got a horse for Amy," I said.

"Why is this animal chewing up my front yard?"

"It's what Amy's always wanted," I said. "A horse." My words felt slow and heavy, like they were coming from somewhere far away. It was so clear to me. "This is what mothers are supposed to do. Right?" I opened my arms to Amy, letting my purse fall to the ground, dropping the strap that was around Blaze's neck. But Amy didn't move, so I came closer, to the first step. "Right, Amy? You wanted a horse, didn't you?"

She looked straight up into the awning, blinked real quick.

"What are you going to name him?" I asked. "I think it's a him. Maybe it's a her. Blaze is a good name for a him or a her. That's the name you like, right?" She didn't answer, so I asked again. "Right?" and I walked up the steps to where she stood, barefoot, crying. "Isn't Blaze a good name for a horse?" I asked.

"Oh, Mom," she said, rubbing her eyes with the back of one hand.

"Isn't it?"

She nodded, then pushed through the door, past my mother.

"What were you thinking?" my mother said. "Where did you get that thing?"

" 'That thing' has a name," I said.

"Where did it come from, Ginger?" She said each word slowly, distinctly, like she was afraid I wouldn't understand her question.

"The petting zoo," I said.

"You stole it?

"I'm adopting it," I said. "Amy wants a horse so bad." It was all so simple.

"Come inside," she said. "Everyone will see."

"See what?" I sat on the step. "A mother who wants her daughter to be happy."

"You didn't go to June's house like you said."

It took me a moment to remember. "I did too."

She shook her head. "We called."

"We?"

"I called. June hadn't seen you all night." My mother's voice turned soft. "In fact, she didn't know anything about a scrapbook or a high school reunion."

"Amy told you to call, didn't she?" but I didn't really have to ask the question to know the answer.

I watched Blaze eat grass, tear-chew, tear-chew. He looked happy to be out of that awful petting zoo, happy to have been adopted by people who appreciated him. Amy would ride Blaze on trails through the desert; they'd see the wild flowers bloom in spring and watch forks of lightning shatter distant mountains. She'd say to me, I can't imagine my life before you got me Blaze; she'd say, He's like part of the family now.

"That animal better not go near my rosebushes," my mother said.

I could've spoken the words for her, because I knew she'd say them. A horse had appeared in the front yard, and she was worried about rosebushes. It was my whole life in one sentence. I asked, "How long did Amy wait before she told you to call, ten minutes? Fifteen? She's worse than Jimmy."

My mother looked at the house across the street, where an upstairs light went on, then went off. "I didn't raise you to be like this, lying, sneaking around at night, stealing ponies from the park, going to bars. You should be ashamed of yourself, Ginger."

"Plenty of people have a few drinks," I said.

She shook her head. "Not people like us. Not this family."

"I got Amy her horse, didn't I?"

She shook her head again, longer, slower, like a machine just starting up, just getting its rhythm.

"Stop doing that!" I screamed. "Listen to me! I'm not one of those people; I'm not like that! I'm not what you think." I slapped my palm again and again on the pavement near where I sat until blood ribboned up through my torn skin. "I just want to be who I am." The words sounded stupid and lost.

"Who are you?" she scoffed. "Good people like us don't do that.

I'll tell you who you are, Ginger, you're nothing but a—" and she paused, leaving me just enough space to say the only thing that would keep her unspoken words dangling.

"So's your precious new priest, Mother; I saw him tonight at AA."

The horse neighed and shook his head back and forth. I watched my mother's face as she tried harder and harder not to let it move. Now, she wouldn't be able to stand near him without secretly sniffing his breath; any time he laughed too loud or too long, she'd wonder; fixing Sunday dinner in his kitchen, she'd poke one hand all the way to the back of each cupboard, feel around, pretending she was looking for baking soda. What she'd tell him in confession would be measured out differently because the man who judged the secrets wasn't perfect after all. She wouldn't want to think all this about him, but now she would.

Amy returned to stand behind the screen door. "The police are coming to get the pony."

"The police!" I said.

"I looked up the number in Grandma's phone book."

"But it's the horse you wanted!" I said. "It's Blaze!"

"Mom, that's Fred from the pony ride. He's like twenty years old."

My mother slid her arm around Amy's shoulder. "Thank you, honey." She sounded tired, like an old woman. "I'll wait for the police. You go on up to bed."

Amy opened the screen door, walked to where I sat, knelt next to me, and held out her hand. "Come on, Mom," she said. "Time to go to bed." She waited one minute, two minutes, maybe three, her hand steady. I listened to her breath move in and out, faster than my own, softer.

A goddamn pony. Not even a horse. Even now, already, she was too big for a pony.

But the bones in her hand felt tiny. My hand filled hers, overflowed. I didn't know how to say I was sorry and really mean it, so I didn't say anything, just let her lead me upstairs to my bed, where I belonged.

Back in Arizona, I told them my name was Ginger. "Hi, Ginger," they said, like somehow they'd known exactly who I was all along.

All I Know to Tell You

GINGER — 1974

"After supper," Cal said. "You know, when Grandma goes out to sit on the front porch."

Amy rolled up her backseat window. "Nah. I bet it's when they're alone in the kitchen doing dishes. Yeah. That's exactly when she'll tell Grandma." Amy slumped farther down, wedged her knees up against the back of my seat so her weight pressed into my spine like a hard shove. To get them to stop fighting about who'd sit with me in the front seat, I'd sent them both to the back and told Amy I'd pay her a dollar if she'd play magnetic checkers with her nine-year-old brother for forty-five minutes. The plan seemed to be working: At twelve, Amy was too young to know she could've bargained for more money; after three days in the car Cal was happy to play a game with anyone, even his sister. Up until now, I'd been happily suspended in that place you exist in when you take a long car trip, neither here nor there; you're simply on the road. Since I was back to not officially drinking these days, driving was second-best, the same feeling of no-whereness. But the kids' conversation kept pulling me out of that between place, back into the "what if" and "what will happen when" I was trying to avoid.

Cal said, "That's a stupid time to tell bad news. That's the worst."

"No, the worst is like when Mom told us," Amy said. "Taking us out for ice cream like we're babies. Talk about stupid."

I watched them in the rearview mirror, the checkerboard between them, Amy barely paying attention as she moved her black checker into place for kinging. Though the kids spoke quietly, it was easy to hear them. Amy caught my eye in the mirror. Maybe that's what she wanted.

So I stopped thinking, stopped listening. I drove faster, harder. It would be night soon. We'd get to Detroit, and there wasn't any right way to tell my mother I was divorced.

When we arrived, the house was dark, and my mother wasn't where she usually was when we were due in: waiting in a lawn chair on the porch, standing up at the first sign of my car coming too fast down the block, waving.

I pulled into the driveway, turned off the car and the headlights. Amy said, "Where's Grandma?"

"She must be asleep," I said.

"It's only nine o'clock," Amy said. "She always, always waits for us."

"Maybe she forgot we're coming," Cal said.

"Duh, numbnut, Mom called her this morning from the motel," Amy said.

"Mo-om, Amy's calling me names," Cal said, slapping her shoulder.

"Don't hit me, dipshit," she said, shoving him.

"Mo-om!"

I got out of the car and started walking to the front door. From the porch steps I looked back at Amy and Cal—they'd stopped squabbling, and in the light off the car ceiling their faces looked blurred, like something you see faraway under water, but when they

saw me watching, they started up again, "Mo-om!" I wouldn't like
these kids right now if they were someone else's.

"Come on, you guys," I said. "Do you want to wake the neighbors?" I pulled open the screen door and pushed on the front door,
but it was locked.

"Maybe Grandma moved," Cal said, climbing out of the
backseat.

"You're so stupid," Amy said. "I can't believe I'm related to you."

"Well, ha, ha, you are," Cal said.

"The door's locked," I said, twisting the knob back and forth,
knocking.

"Don't you have a key?" Amy asked.

"Why would I have a key?" I said. "It's not my house." I was
really banging the door now. "Mom!" I called.

"I just thought maybe—"

I cut her off: "Check the side door," and she got out of the car
and opened the old gate to the backyard. It slammed hard against
the house, then back into place. So she was angry. It wasn't my
house anymore. I wasn't expected to have a key. What I expected
was my mother to be home to let us in.

I rattled the knob and pounded on the door. "Mom! Are you
there?"

Cal plopped into one of the lawn chairs on the porch. "Where's
Grandma?" he asked. "I gotta go to the bathroom."

"I told you to go when we stopped at that gas station," I said.

The porch light came on and the door pulled open, but it was
Amy holding the door for us, not my mother. Amy said, "She
keeps a key to the kitchen door in that old milk box by the
garden. So you know for next time." She held the key between
her thumb and index finger.

I took the key from her, slipped it in my pocket. "Would you
please start unloading the car?" I said. "I'll look for a note," and
Amy passed by me, letting the screen door slap shut. "Cal, go to
the bathroom, then help your sister," I said.

"I don't have to go anymore," he said.

"Then bring in stuff from the car. I'll be there in a minute," and I stepped inside, through the entryway and the front hall, and pushed open the swinging door to the kitchen, my hand touching the place on the wall where the light switch was. On the table was a note written on the back of a junk mail letter: "Will be home soon." But no indication of when the note was written, how soon "soon" might be. Like Amy said, she always, always waited for us. "Well, I wonder where she is," I said, not meaning to speak out loud, but Amy had just walked through the front door and heard me.

"I'm sure she's fine," she said, coming into the kitchen with an armload of pillows and two tote bags hooked over her shoulders.

"I know she's fine." My voice had an edge on it that sharpened as I continued: "It's just that she knew we were getting in tonight. She knew that. So where is she?"

Amy shifted the pillows in her arms and one of the tote bags slid down her shoulder onto her elbow. "Well," Amy said. "I guess I'll take this stuff upstairs," and I nodded, followed her to the living room. Her footsteps thudded the stairs up to the big attic room where we slept every summer when we visited.

The clock on the mantel chimed the quarter hour. There was a strange smell in the stuffy room, like when someone has died, and my breath caught quick in my throat—but I realized I was smelling the lilies in the vase on the coffee table. I knew I should get out of the house, help the kids with the luggage—there was tons of stuff, there always was every year when the three of us drove up here—but I couldn't move, not yet, not when I was thinking about Jimmy, and what he'd said one morning before he left, which was "Someday you'll wake up from your goddamned hangover, and I won't be here anymore," and I was so angry that I threw my drink in his face. I'd never done that to anyone, never even thought it was a thing real people did, but there I was, slinging my good gin at him, and he stood there, blinking and wet, ice puddling on the table and linoleum, and he said, "Don't think I won't leave." "You can't!" I screamed, "You-can't-you-can't-you-can't!" There was a stretched-out moment where he didn't move, and neither did I, and if I would've said I was sorry or started to cry or even looked surprised at what I'd done, maybe it all would've been different. But what I did was sit perfectly still with a face hard like cement. When he said, "Yes, I can, Ginger," his voice almost wasn't there, but I still wouldn't cry.

"Hello!" and it was my mother bursting through the front door, Cal's hand in hers, and Amy thumping down the stairs from the attic screaming, "Grandma!" and everyone hugging everyone else, chattering about the drive, about going to the Polish bakery for *chrusciki*—angel's wings—tomorrow, whether the birds had returned to their nest by the garage this year, how big the kids were already, and on and on until my head ached from the number of words that passed by me, and finally I wedged in my own:

"Where *were* you, Mom?"

She pulled herself away from Amy and Cal. "Why, over at your aunt Joane's," she said.

"Did you forget we were coming in tonight?" I asked.

"I found the key," Amy said. "I remembered exactly where it was."

"Of course you did," my mother said. "I knew someone would, Ginger—you or Amy. Aunt Joane needed to speak with me about an important family matter."

I sucked in my breath, then let it out slow. She already knew. "What family matter?" I asked.

"Two of your cousins are caught up in some kind of fight over money, not talking to each other. Joane's tried everything, so now I'm supposed to talk to the girls. She thinks I have a way, ever since that time I patched up that fight between Wanda and her mother-in-law. Did you hear of anything so crazy as two sisters not speaking to each other?"

"Who?" I asked.

"June and Marge," she said. "But we're not going to worry about those two tonight. Look at you, Amy, you're a foot taller than last year. That's from your grandfather."

"Me, too," Cal said. "I grew."

"Of course you did, sweetie," and she leaned down and kissed the top of his head. "How I've missed you. Tell me why your mother has to live so far away in Arizona."

"Why didn't you leave a note?" I asked. "We were worried."

"In the kitchen," she said. "Didn't you see it?"

"It didn't say much," I said.

"Anyway, here I am," she said. "You guys want cookies? I've got chocolate chip, peanut butter, and oatmeal. How about one of each? Or there's cupcakes. Maybe you'd rather have cupcakes?" She started toward the kitchen, Amy and Cal hanging on her arms, chattering and smiling like someone else's kids you wish were yours.

"Mom!"

She turned her head. "Well, come on, Ginger. Plenty of cookies for you, too."

"I'm divorced," I said. "Jimmy and I are . . . divorced."

The kids stopped talking in mid-sentence. Amy sighed and looked up at the ceiling. Cal put his thumb in his mouth, something he'd recently started doing again. When my mother spoke, her voice was normal: "You kids go in the kitchen. The cookie jar's on the counter. I'll be there in a minute." Cal went straight through the swinging door, but Amy lingered with the door half-open.

"Go ahead," I said to Amy, and the door closed. I heard Cal start to ask a question and Amy's sharp, "Shut up, they're talking."

My mother said, "Now say that again."

"You heard me."

"Say it again." Her arms tightened around her body, as if holding pieces she was afraid would fall off—or perhaps that was the only way she could keep her voice that toneless.

I cleared my throat twice, but there was no choice. So I said, "Jimmy and I are divorced. It was finalized in May."

The clock chimed again, the half hour, and she glanced briefly at it, then walked over to the end table along the couch where she slid a blue vase a half inch to the left. "It's a sin against the church," she said, pushing the vase back the same half inch.

I nodded.

"No one else in this family is divorced," she said. "No one else would do such a bad thing, destroy a family on purpose. Only you."

Again I nodded. I was the only one who left Detroit, the only one who didn't marry in a church, whose husband wasn't Catholic; whatever it was that was bad, I was the only one in the family who did it. That was me.

My mother shook her head slowly, touched her fingers to her lips. "I don't want them to know."

"Who?"

"The family. They don't need to know this awful thing has happened," she said.

"Are you serious? Not tell them?"

"You don't understand," she said. "Two sisters not speaking to each other is a problem that can be solved. A girl leaving her husband. A sin. What are we supposed to do about that?"

"How do you know he didn't leave me?" I spit the words out.

"Thank goodness your grandmother isn't alive to hear this," she said. It almost sounded like she was crying, and she turned her back to me.

"Why won't you let me explain?"

"Because it's something I can't understand. But do this one thing for me, and you can explain all you want tomorrow and the next day and the day after, and I'll listen, try to understand. Promise you won't tell the family, Ginger," she said. "Please."

"Isn't lying a sin, Mom?"

"Don't tell me you can't lie," she said. "Two months since it happened, and I'm finding out now." She folded her arms tight again.

"There was a good reason for that." My voice was tiny, a six-year-old caught feeding her green beans to the dog.

My mother faced me, no evidence of tears. "What reason?"

All right. There were plenty of things I could tell her, the fights about who would get the kids and about all those bottles of gin I wasn't supposed to be drinking and the way the lawyer's office always smelled like too much cheap air freshener and how the last time we had sex we were animals clawing each other apart and all the nights that went until the sun came up. All right. I could tell her that I wasn't a wife anymore, I was a divorced woman going to night school, keeping tabs on the job classifieds, typing and filing all day as a summer fill-in secretary because someone in Personnel had felt sorry for me. But I wasn't really a divorced woman either, because a divorced woman wouldn't stare at herself in the mirror for half an hour every morning, wouldn't call her ex-husband's phone number and hang up when he answered, wouldn't drive around and around the block the liquor store was on until closing time.

There was all that I could've told her, maybe mentioning how you can't put things like that in a letter or in a long-distance phone call or even now, really, face-to-face, because whatever I said would be wrong, would be a sin against the church and her way of living.

I said, "I guess I forgot to tell you," and what was supposed to be a smile twisted into a smirk that felt ugly on my face.

There was a long pause.

My mother said, "Your job is to hold your family together. No matter who wants to leave." She stepped away from me, put her hand on the swinging door to the kitchen, but looked back, waiting to see what I'd do. I shrugged. Then she pushed open the door, leaving me alone.

With a shaking hand, I picked up the blue vase off the table, pushed my thumb over the raised floral pattern along the base. I heard them in the kitchen, first a cupboard door, then the refrigerator opening and closing; she was getting them cupcakes, pouring milk into those glasses the kids liked from the gas station. I brought the flowers in the vase to my nose, pretending I was interested in smelling them, but these were plastic, faded pink roses so old that the petals were edged yellowy white. They'd been in this house, in this vase, on this same spot on this same table for years. If anyone ever looked at them, it was simply to dust them. That's how it was here.

Instead of setting the vase back on the table, I heaved it at the fireplace where it broke into too many pieces to be glued together.

If they heard in the kitchen, I couldn't tell when I walked in there.

It was late when I woke up the next morning, around ten, and my back ached from the too-soft bed. It was a double bed, though Jimmy had come up here with me only once, when Amy was a baby. I told my mother he couldn't take so much time off work for the driving and the visit, but it was more than that. "I don't like who you are when we're here," he told me that summer. "You're the kind of girl I tried to stay away from."

"What kind is that?" I thought he was teasing; we were upstairs in the too-soft bed, Amy in the crib, the room dark and still and hot even with the windows open, the two of us cuddled together despite the stickiness of the heat.

"The kind who's backed into a corner," he said.

"You don't really think that," I said.

He stroked my bare back with his hand, better than a backrub the way he did it.

I said, "What corner? What do you mean?"

"Shh, you'll wake the baby," he whispered.

So I was quiet, thinking we'd talk about it in the morning or later, sometime I'd bring it up with him, but I never did. He was right. I knew what he meant. In Detroit I couldn't relax. I could only fight or give up, the only two options a child has.

I didn't remember anything else about the summer he'd come up here, only that conversation.

My mother and the kids were in the kitchen, finishing pancakes for breakfast. Everyone's face and fingers looked sticky from the syrup, and flour was sprinkled across the counter, meaning Amy and Cal had sifted it.

"How many pancakes do you want?" my mother asked, standing up.

"None, thanks," I said. "Just coffee." I poured out a cup, sat down, pushed away the sugar and milk my mother nudged across the table.

"What kind of breakfast is that?" she asked.

Amy said, "That's all Mom makes for breakfast in our house, coffee and toast."

I shook my head.

Cal said, "Or cereal."

Amy said, "Dad hates toast."

I stirred my coffee fast, trying to cool it.

Finally my mother said, "I'm making you three pancakes, Ginger, and if you eat them, fine. Otherwise I can freeze them for another morning. But only coffee for breakfast is wrong."

She turned on the gas burner and in a moment, dribbled water onto the griddle. The water droplet exploded, so she poured batter for the pancakes I didn't want, wouldn't eat. When I finally looked at Amy, she was looking straight at me. It would be so simple if she'd just apologize—or if I would—but she was twelve, without a father, and I was thirty-four, without a husband, and we were both stretched too tight, always about ready to snap any direction. I said to Amy, "I thought you didn't like pancakes."

She said, "There's chocolate chips in these. You don't make them that way."

My mother said, "I'll heat up a little syrup," and she turned on another burner, stirred a pot on the stove, then flipped the pancakes with a spatula. "Don't you want milk for that coffee, Ginger? Black coffee is too strong for women."

"Fine," and I poured some milk into my coffee, watched it swirl and cloud.

"That's better," my mother said, reaching for a plate out of the cupboard, stacking the three pancakes, pouring a mess of syrup on top. "How about butter?" she asked.

I shook my head, but she cut off a hunk and plopped that on top. "There you go," she said, setting the plate in front of me, leaning to get silverware from the drawer. "Breakfast."

The pancakes were sweet and steamy, overloaded with syrup and melting butter, and it wasn't more than a few forkfuls before my face and fingers were as sticky as everyone else's.

Amy said, "Aren't the pancakes good?" and I nodded, and she smiled, and I smiled, and then Cal smiled at both of us. It was hard to be twelve, that's how I remembered it, as a yucky, awful age that's nowhere—not a child, not an adult. Add to that the only divorced parents in the neighborhood, and that's why Amy was acting the way she was lately. Maybe I was too easy on her, but being too easy was simpler than being too hard, and these days whatever was simplest was pretty much what I did.

There was a knock on the front door. My mother said, "That's Marge," and as she left to open the door, she said, "I've got to get her talking to her sister. Aunt Joane says it's been nearly three months."

I said, "You guys can go play outside, okay?" and Cal nodded, slammed through the side door.

Amy said, "I'm almost thirteen, I don't *play* anymore, Mom."

"You'll be bored in here. All we're going to do is talk."

She shrugged, poured out a cup of coffee and dumped in a couple spoonfuls of sugar.

"Since when do you drink coffee?" I asked.

"For your information, I've also smoked cigarettes," she said, shrugging, sipping her coffee, then spooning in more sugar, reaching for the milk.

My cousin Marge came in, followed by my mother. Marge and I hugged, exchanged comments about my long drive, the weather, our kids, as my mother poured coffee and sliced a coffee cake. Then there was nothing to say, and without meaning to, we both looked at my mother as if she'd have cue cards for us. Marge and I had never had much to talk about; she was nearly ten years younger than I was, so I mostly remembered her as the one who took too long to be potty trained, the one who sucked her thumb until her mother threatened to snap it off her hand—all the things I listened to our mothers and aunts discuss around the kitchen table. She was still a kid when I left home, and now she was married with kids of her own. I saw her with a bunch of other people maybe once during each visit to Detroit, so I didn't hardly know the first thing about her; I couldn't even remember if it was Tom or Tim Cizik she'd married until she referred to her son as Tommy Jr.

My mother started in: "It's so very sad to me, Marge, that you and your sister June aren't talking. It's not right." What the words didn't say, her voice did: You can't stop me from holding together this family.

Marge flushed and ducked her head.

My mother continued, "Your mother's done everything she can, so I offered to speak with you, to see how we can solve this problem."

Marge shook her head, but she still looked down at the table, her shoulders hunched like a question mark. Like Marge, I felt the vastness of the plan and its mission: the discussion between our mothers and the aunts, the decision of who would mediate, the story to lure Marge to my mother's house, her own mother volunteering to watch the kids while she was here, all of it moving together in this one direction, with this single purpose. Marge and June would be talking in, oh, say another ten minutes.

My mother licked her lips, said, "Your family is all you'll ever have that won't go away. Money, spent. Property, gone. Even religious faith can be lost. But family—never." I expected her to clasp her hands and hold them to her heart, but she didn't.

Marge said, "But June lied. She told me the money was for the doctor."

"I know," my mother said, her voice warm and creamy. "But the money isn't what's important now, is it? What's important is two sisters who haven't spoken to each other for three months. If June died today, you'd never forgive yourself. Right?"

Marge picked up a napkin and folded it in tiny sections. In the silence I heard Cal swinging back and forth on the gate outside, clang, clang, the way Amy used to.

The silence was too long. "That gate's going to break off its hinges," I said.

My mother shook her head. "That's what your father said back when you used to swing on it, and it hasn't broken yet, has it?"

Marge spoke slowly, as if her words had to be unfolded along with the napkin in her hands: "I think we're too far along, Aunt Helen. This is one of those problems that can't be solved."

"Nothing is so broken that it can't be fixed," my mother said.

"Is that true?" Amy asked suddenly, her hands curved around her full coffee cup.

"Absolutely," my mother said, reaching to touch Amy's arm. She looked at me, and then Amy followed her gaze, and with them both looking at me that way, I shifted in my chair, and reached for the coffeepot, watched the dark liquid steam into my cup, concentrating so hard on how it flowed that I poured too much and some went into the saucer.

"Mom, is it true?" Amy asked me. Her face was round and soft, a child, not a girl drinking coffee and smoking cigarettes, not a girl too old to swing on the gate. But then she looked back at my mother, and I realized I was wrong; she was asking the question because she already knew the answer, and she was challenging me to say it. "Is nothing so broken that it can't be fixed?" she asked.

Clang. Clang. Clang. My mother was right, I used to swing on that same gate in the summers, when there was no school, after my chores were done. There wasn't a lot of money for toys back then, and that gate turned itself into a horse, a merry-go-round, an airplane, anything I wanted it to be.

"Is it true?" Amy asked. "Is it?" Her voice was trying to pen me into the answer she expected.

Marge looked up from her napkin.

I looked straight at Amy. "Absolutely true."

Amy tried to hold back a smile but couldn't; she pushed away her coffee cup, sloshing a little onto the plastic-coated tablecloth. Marge swiped the spill with the napkin in her hands.

My mother said, "We're calling June right now. I'll help you two talk this over. You'll see."

Marge started to cry, dabbing her eyes with another napkin. "I didn't mean for this to happen," she said. "It's just that it was two hundred dollars, and she used it for a new carpet."

My mother patted Marge's shoulder.

"I would've liked a new carpet," Marge said.

"Ginger, will you go call June?" my mother said. "Don't say Marge is here, just ask her to run over, okay?"

I nodded, went into the front room where the phone was. I glanced at the fireplace, but all the pieces of the broken vase had been swept up, and the plastic flowers were in another vase, set in exactly the same spot on the same table.

I made the phone call, then went to sit in one of the lawn chairs on the front porch. The humidity was already pressing hard, and it wouldn't be long before the kids would be begging to get out the hose and sprinkler, waiting for the jingle of the Good Humor truck. Where we lived in Phoenix, everyone had pools. Houses were air-conditioned. You got popsicles from a box in your freezer. That way wasn't wrong, just different.

A moment later, Amy came out and sat on the bottom step in front of me, leaning back on her hands and staring up at the sun so long it made me squint to watch her. Then she looked away, said, "You told Grandma about the divorce last night, didn't you?"

"Yes."

"She got mad, right?"

I nodded, but she couldn't see me, so I said, "Yes."

"Is the reason Dad didn't ever come with us on these trips because it's not his family?" she asked.

"Because he couldn't get enough time off work," I said.

"You don't have to lie to me," she said. "I'm almost thirteen. I'm not a little kid."

"I know," I said. "But it's true. Four weeks at least he'd need because of all the driving, and he doesn't have that much vacation time."

"I don't mean that," she said. "About what you said in the kitchen. You know, things being broken. You shouldn't've lied."

In the pause, I realized that Cal had stopped clanging the gate. Now it was the rhythmic sound of a bouncing basketball. It would've been easiest then to protest that it wasn't a lie. But she was right, she was almost thirteen. That should mean something.

"You're right," I said. "I shouldn't've."

Amy said, "Anyway, I told her already. I wrote a letter and told her that you and Dad were divorced." She leaned forward, examining an anthill built up along a crack in the sidewalk.

"Amy!"

"I thought, maybe, she would, you know, do something."

"Like with Marge and June?" I asked.

She nodded.

Of course it was too late. Of course fixing a marriage wasn't anything like settling a squabble between two sisters. But I still asked, before I could stop myself: "What did she say? Did she write back?"

Amy sighed and looked up at the sun again before she spoke.

"She said it didn't matter how far away I was or where I lived, he would always be my father and she would always be my grand-mother, and I should remember that."

"Oh," I said, more a surprised sound than a word.

"I thought maybe she'd come down to Arizona or something," she said. "You know. Fix things."

I couldn't say what I was really thinking, so instead I tried to speak casually: "I guess not."

"Are you mad that I told her?" she asked.

"I'm not happy," I said. "It wasn't your place to get involved like that."

"Then what is my place?" she asked, her voice challenging. She scuffed the anthill with her toe, and scooted her butt up another step so she was in the shade of the awning, still facing away from me.

I opened my mouth to tell her, but there was nothing to say. Finally, I shrugged, said, "You're my daughter. That's your place forever."

There was a long pause. I watched the back of her neck, how the tiny hairs were flat against her skin, thought of Jimmy and me fighting over who'd hold her first in the hospital, who'd carry her through the door into our apartment.

Her voice shook as she said, "That's stupid." Then she swallowed and said, "That's something like your marriage counselor would say."

"That's all I know to tell you," I said.

"Well, it's stupid," and she stood up, wandered toward the back-yard. I closed my eyes. I didn't know the answer to that question.

My mother, too, had claimed that nothing is so broken that it can't be fixed. Were we both lying?

Any minute my cousin June would be here, towing along her noisy boys. The sprinkler would come out; someone would scream, "I'm telling!"; there'd be one or two who'd need a Band-Aid; we'd all eat fried bologna sandwiches and pickles for lunch, and someone would spill a glass of milk. My mother would convince June and Marge to make up, but June and I would find something to disagree about, we always did. The three of them would sit around the kitchen table talking about diseases and children and cooking and gardening and family while I'd think about what I'd be doing if I were back in Phoenix. They'd ask me how my husband was, and I'd say, "He's fine," while my mother held her breath and clenched her fist under the table. All these things would happen today.

But for now, right now, I could just sit in the steamy shade under the porch awning and listen to Cal's basketball pounding the pavement, Amy the one riding the gate back and forth, each clang rocking the house—that thought always there now, Is this the time the gate breaks off its hinges? but clang it goes, again and again and again.

Wigilia: The Vigil

H E L E N — 1 9 5 8

It felt wrong to celebrate Christmas in winter, in snow. Christ was born in the desert. There was no snow. Wise men weren't wearing snowshoes as they trudged great distances to the Holy Star. No icicles lined the eaves of the stable. Shepherds didn't stamp snow off their feet before kneeling at the manger. So to me something wasn't right about Christmas in December. But way back when I was growing up, we didn't question "why" to anything. Especially not anything in the Bible, not anything having to do with God— actually, not anything anyone told us.

All the questions I was afraid to ask ended up in my daughter, Ginger, who wasn't afraid of anything, certainly not questions. To my daughter, "why" was a curse with no answer beyond "because"—"Because that's the way this family has always done it"; "Because that's the way it is"; "Just because."

When my daughter told me she hated Detroit, I didn't have to ask why.

The summer after she finished high school, she packed two suitcases, bought a one-way ticket on a Greyhound bus, and left.

My sister Wanda said, "Two weeks." My sister Marie said, "Maybe a month at most." My sister Joane wiped tears off my cheeks. Everyone nodded and agreed that Ginger would be back.

"Why do you think so?" I asked. "Why?"

A quick silence spilled across the kitchen table, and they looked at each other. "Of course she'll be back," Wanda said.

"Of course she will," Marie said.

"Of course." My mother nodded. "Because this is her family."

Everyone nodded in unison with my mother, and that part of the conversation was over. We were just waiting for Ginger to come back home.

But then it was December—six months later—and Ginger was still in Arizona. She worked for a lawyer typing letters; she was living with a nice Catholic family with four children and a baby, helping out a little with the cleaning and wash; she even knew some Mexican ladies, and once she'd talked to an Indian. Everything she wrote felt far away. When the letters started to come to me typed out, it was like she was someone else, and I had to glance first at where she'd signed her name to be sure it was really her.

I passed her letters around the kitchen table so my sisters and my mother could read them. Wanda said, "Not a word about missing Detroit. Such a stubborn girl."

"Of course she's stubborn," my mother said. "Isn't she Polish?"

They laughed, someone poured out more coffee, handed around the plate of cinnamon cookies.

"Talking to Mexicans and Indians," Wanda said. "What next? Little green men from Mars?"

"That Ginger's something else," Joane said. "A way of doing things like no one else." She broke a cookie in half over a napkin, her way to tell me they were overdone.

"It's almost Christmas," I said. "Maybe I should mail the *opłatek* to Ginger." The *opłatek* was shared by Polish families at *Wigilia*, the Christmas Eve vigil supper, for good luck. It looked like a communion wafer and was blessed by the priest but wasn't sacred.

Joane broke her cookie halves in half; they snapped loudly in the silence. Wanda cleared her throat, turned the sound into a soft cough.

My mother said, "*Oplatek* goes to family members who are gone."

"That's right," Marie said. "And Ginger will be back."

"Of course she will," my mother said, nodding easy with the words.

The clock on the mantel chimed, and the talk shifted; instead of Ginger, now it was getting back to their houses, starting dinner, someone's new idea for fixing squash. Marie pulled her boots on over her shoes.

Then my mother said, "An unmarried girl doesn't spend Christmas away from her family."

"Not even Ginger," Marie said.

"Poor Helen," Wanda said. "Your only daughter. You should lock her in her room when she comes home. Keep her here with us."

"She'll be back before Christmas," my mother said, nodding again, ending it finally there.

I went to get the coats and scarves from the front closet, and just after I left the kitchen, Joane said, "I think Helen should send the *oplatek*."

I waited to hear the rest of what she'd say, but there was only silence, and I felt them looking around the table at each other, away from Joane. Of all my sisters, Joane had the loudest voice, the voice that pushed where no one else would go.

Joane said, "Ginger's not coming back. Don't we all know that?"

My mother said, "What I know is anyone so sure he knows something knows nothing."

"Helen's heart would break down the middle to hear you," Wanda said.

"What's going to break her heart down the middle is Christmas without Ginger," Joane said.

"No one's heart is breaking," my mother said. "Because Ginger will come home."

I went for the coats, and when I got back they were deciding that Wanda's daughter June's fiancé didn't give her an engagement ring because he was a good, frugal Polish boy, not because he was cheap.

After everyone left through the side door, I cleared away the coffee cups and the leftover cookies, shook the crumbs off the tablecloth. It was the tablecloth edged with yellow flowers that Ginger had given to me last Christmas. "For Mother," she'd written on the card with her elegant handwriting, "With Love From Your Daughter." Not "To Ma, XOXOX, Ginger," like every other Christmas. Even though I hadn't saved the card, I couldn't forget it.

It was my year to hold *Wigilia*, the traditional Christmas Eve supper for the family. Wanda offered to have it at her house, and so did Marie, but I told them no. Ginger might not get home until Christmas Eve, and I didn't want her walking into an empty house. Better everyone should be there to greet her; better she wouldn't have to go through the neighborhood looking for us. And getting ready for the supper was keeping me busy through December.

We were at Marie's house, helping some of the kids with their eggshell ornaments for the Christmas tree. The kids were maybe too old to be worried about decorating the tree, but there hadn't been a year yet when some of us weren't sitting around the kitchen table gently poking pins into eggs and blowing with puffed-up cheeks until the last bit of egg drizzled out into a bowl. Then the kids glued pieces of colored paper and straw to the eggshells and hung them on the tree on Christmas Eve.

Wanda set an empty shell onto a plate and leaned back hard against her chair. "My head's about to spin off my neck, I'm so dizzy," she said, and Marie jumped up for the coffeepot to refill her cup.

Every year Wanda got dizzy first. She was the most impatient of us, the one who broke too many eggs. Today she'd smashed at least four or five, making a big mess. Of course we couldn't waste eggs—we'd use them later scrambled or in cakes—so Theresa, Marie's oldest girl, was picking shells out of Wanda's bowl with her little finger.

The rest of the kids sprawled on newspapers on the floor, reaching for glue, fighting for their turn with the scissors, tossing straw at each other, ignoring our conversation as they jabbered about all the things they wanted for Christmas.

Theresa worked at the table quietly, as if she were afraid someone might notice and tell her to sit on the floor with the rest of the kids. She was almost seventeen, but that was hard to remember because she was so quiet. Not like my Ginger spouting an opinion on everything; Theresa was more like a cat, always right there, always listening. That's maybe why she and Ginger had been such good friends; Ginger needed to talk, and Theresa needed to listen.

Marie poured coffee for everyone. Purple spots floated in front of my eyes, and my cheeks felt permanently pushed out like big balloons. But we never rested until Wanda said she was dizzy.

Marie added milk to her coffee, said to the kids, "Someone has to make a rooster. Grandma won't be happy unless there's a rooster on the tree."

"What does a rooster have to do with Christmas?" Peter asked.

"It's good luck," Marie said.

Wanda added, "And if your grandma doesn't find a rooster on her tree, oh boy, it's bad luck for all of us." She laughed like it was a joke, but it wasn't. "There's been a rooster on Grandma's Christmas tree since before she was born, and there better be one long after she dies."

"Okay," Peter said, and he reached for an eggshell. "I'll make Grandma's rooster."

Marie said to us, "He's a good boy," and we nodded. He *was* a good boy, thirteen years old but still decorating eggs; the kind of boy who'd find a way to go to college and not miss a single Sunday dinner at home; find a way to be a doctor and still marry a girl from the neighborhood. All four of Marie's children were like that.

"Mama, may I help make the *Wigilia* supper this year?" Theresa asked. She'd fished out all the pieces of shell from Wanda's bowl. Her slim fingers were folded together, the way a girl's hands should look in church.

"You helped last year," Marie said. "Remember? You helped grind the poppy seed for the cake. You cracked the walnuts—"

"No, I mean really help," Theresa said. "I want to work all week in the kitchen with you. There's no school. I'm old enough. I won't be in the way. Please?" Her words tumbled faster and faster, as if she hadn't known it was possible to say so many in a row: the same way Ginger talked when she was losing an argument.

"Auntie Helen is in charge this year," Marie said. "You have to ask her."

"Auntie Helen, may I—?"

I couldn't wait for her to finish: "Of course you can, dear."

She smiled, and Wanda nodded at her, reached to pat her hand. "You'll see how much fun it is," she said to Theresa. "The kitchen is the best place. Those men don't know what they're missing. Right, Helen?"

What Ginger liked best was to sit by the fireplace and listen to the men tell stories about . . . whatever their stories were. I was never there to hear.

"Right, Helen?" Wanda asked.

I nodded, repeated, "They don't know what they're missing," and of course Wanda was right, there wasn't another way, and the kitchen was warm and filled with good-smelling food; the kitchen is where the traditions live on, my mother always said—either one of her many Polish proverbs or something she knew on her own, I never was sure which.

"Hello-hello!" My mother came into the kitchen, followed by Joane, who brought Marie's mail from the box outside. She slowly flipped through the envelopes. My mother said, "I see the rooster! Now Christmas can come, because my grandson is making my good luck rooster," and she leaned to kiss the top of Peter's head. "Good boy." Peter smiled.

Marie poured out two more cups of coffee, started brewing another pot. Theresa stood up, but Wanda said, "Stay, dear, there's room," and Peter went for extra chairs from the dining room to crowd around the table.

Joane said, "Letter from Ginger to Theresa," and she passed the envelope to me. The address on the front was typed, the lines neat and even, no mistyped letters or numbers, the return address the same way.

"The letter's for Theresa," I said, running my finger along the crisp edges of the envelope, around the corners. The stamp was on perfectly straight.

"We always pass around Ginger's letters," Joane said. "Theresa doesn't mind."

"Do you, dear?" Wanda asked.

"Of course she doesn't," Marie said, and she pulled a bobby pin from her hair and handed it to me so I could slit the envelope. "Go on, Helen. Read it out loud."

Theresa was looking hard at the stove, her cheeks tinged pink. She looked just like Marie. A couple of the kids on the floor set aside their eggshells and sat up to listen.

"Okay," and I slowly pulled the bobby pin along the inside of the envelope flap, pulled out the sheet of typewritten paper, unfolded it, and looked at the big scrawl of a signature. I said, "It's Theresa's letter."

"So let Theresa read it," Joane said, and I handed the letter across the table.

Theresa scraped her chair backward against the floor, and one of the kids cried, "Careful!"

"Sorry," Theresa said. She raised the letter, hiding her face.

Marie said, "Go on, dear. Everyone's waiting."

Theresa cleared her throat, starting reading too fast: "Dear Terry—um, that's what she calls me—um, Dear Terry, It's seventy-three degrees as I type this letter during my lunch break."

"Imagine that!" my mother said. "Seventy-three in December."

"Who would think?" Wanda said.

"Doesn't seem right," my mother said. "December should be all cold and snow."

"Let her finish," Joane said. "Go on, Theresa."

She continued: ". . . during my lunch break. Thanks for your last letter catching me up on all the aunties—don't their jaws get tired from all that gossip? Don't they ever run out of things to say?"

Someone else would've thought to look up to figure out what everyone was thinking—just one of Ginger's jokes? or something else?—but Theresa didn't stop, as if she couldn't hear the words she was saying: "The family I live with is like that, but late at night I sit outside on the porch and look at the stars, and there's only me and only silence. I love the flat desert all in front of me, the mountains in the distance; you can *see* how quiet it is here, and how much space one person can have. Not like Detroit, where every direction there's someone watching, someone to say 'no' and 'can't' and 'don't.' There's so much more in the world than they're showing us, Terry. Don't tell them, but I can't ever come back to Detroit. Not even for Christmas," and finally Marie yanked away the letter and crumpled it onto the table. Theresa stood up and opened her mouth as if she wanted to say something; then tears overwhelmed her. She grabbed the letter and ran from the room. The kids on the floor picked up their eggshells, started cutting paper circles, reached for the glue; they were suddenly silent as if not making noise would make them disappear.

Marie said, "More coffee?" and she held the pot so tight her knuckles bulged. In the silence we heard Theresa sobbing in the bedroom.

Wanda said, "She didn't mean any of that, Helen."

Marie set down the coffeepot. "Of course not."

They nodded; each reached for my hand. Their fingers were warm as they entwined with mine. I looked at my mother, waited for her to say something and nod that way she had.

She looked toward the window where outside the sky was that winter color everyone in Detroit called "factory-line gray." She said, "For this one year you mail the *oplatek*."

"Let's hope it's not too late," Joane said. "Arizona is far away."

When I got home, I slipped a wafer into an envelope, wrote out Ginger's address with a pen. I thought since I was spending postage anyway, I should put in a letter, but I sat at the kitchen table for twenty minutes with a piece of paper until the potatoes boiled over, and there was nothing to write.

I imagined Ginger opening this envelope with no letter. What would she think when she unwrapped the tissue paper, when she found the translucent white wafer with the nativity pressed lightly onto it? How she hadn't been to church for weeks. That her family was farther away than she realized.

I licked the envelope, pressed it shut. When she lived here, I didn't know what she was thinking either.

Theresa was setting the tables for the *Wigilia* supper, twenty-five places—always an even number of guests, because an odd number would mean someone would die within the year—and then add the extra place for the stranger who might arrive unexpectedly. My mother followed Theresa around the table, checking that everything was right, tucking more straw under the white tablecloth to remind us of the manger. "A guest in the home is God in the home," she said, nodding as she came to the extra place. She glanced at me, because we were both thinking of Ginger, who maybe still would come home tonight, maybe, maybe. "An old Polish saying," she said, and Theresa nodded, repeated it slowly as she lit the candles.

"First star's out!" Peter called as he and some of the kids ran in from the front porch, throwing off their coats and scarves, stamping snow from their boots. "Time to eat!"

My grandmother peeked through the curtain at where Peter pointed up at the cold sky. "Hmmm, let's see." She squinted, twisted her head this way and that, and smiled at Peter who was holding his breath. She said, "Good boy," then called toward the kitchen, "Time to eat! Everybody, time to eat. The vigil is over."

Everyone seemed to take up the cry—"Time to eat!"—and the men and kids started crowding in, jostling for places at the borrowed tables that had been pushed together every which way.

My sisters came through the kitchen door with the first courses: Wanda and Marie carried salad and bowls of pickled herring; Joane followed with a platter of *pierogi* still sizzling from the butter in the frying pan. Theresa poured coffee for the adults and milk for the kids, and I ran back to the kitchen for bread and butter and to give the kettle of fish soup one last stir.

When I returned to the table, all noise and commotion stopped as my husband John picked up his *oplatek*, held it out to me. "Good health and happiness in the coming year," he said. "May your deepest wishes come true."

I smiled and broke off a piece of his wafer, and then held out my own for him to break. Everyone around the table picked up their wafers, ready to exchange with each other. "Good health and happiness to you in the new year," I said. "May all—"

The ringing telephone burst in, startling me so much I could only stare across the table at my mother. The phone rang again.

"Not bad news on Christmas Eve," Joane said.

"Answer it, Helen," my mother said, and I squeezed around several chairs as the phone rang twice more.

"Hello?" I said.

"Long distance," the operator said.

"Long distance!" I said to everyone. "It's Ginger! Ginger, honey, it costs too much to call."

"We can talk for three minutes, Mother," she said. "Merry Christmas." Static fluttered between each word.

"Merry Christmas!" I said. "Where are you?"

"Mother, you know I'm in Arizona."

Of course she was.

"Where is she?" Joane asked.

"Is she on her way home?" Therersa asked. "Tell her we have an extra place at the table for her."

"She's in Arizona," I said.

"I wrote you that it's too much money to come back for Christmas," she said. "Otherwise I'd be there."

"Of course," I said.

"It's seventy degrees here," she said.

"Seventy degrees!" I told everyone.

"On Christmas Eve yet," Wanda said. "Imagine that."

"Do you have snow?" Ginger asked.

"Six inches two days ago," I said. "It's a white Christmas."

"Well, I've had enough snow to last me forever," she said. "I'm looking out the window, and there's a big blue sky and an enormous cactus reaching up into it."

"There's a big cactus outside her window," I said.

"Do you have to repeat every word I say?"

"The family's here," I said. "They want to know. They're interested."

"Have you . . . ?" Static crackled and hissed as she paused, breathed lightly in the phone.

"Have I what?" I asked. "We got your package. We didn't expect presents. Thank you."

"Did the first star come out yet?"

"Only a moment ago," I said.

"It's still day here," she said. "There's that big blue sky." More static, so I held my breath. "Are you, um, eating supper?"

"In a minute." I spoke quietly, fighting the static.

"Is everyone there?" She was quiet, too, almost a whisper.

"Twenty-four this year," I said. "June went to her fiancé's family's house and—well, and you. And of course William's at Fort Bragg, and Uncle Stanislaus is in the hospital, and Robby's on duty tonight so he couldn't—"

"Ma." Her voice cracked apart the word.

"Ginger," I said, and I looked down at the table, at the extra place setting that someone—Theresa?—had put near the phone. I started again, so careful, hoping so hard it was the right thing to say, the right way to say it: "Ginger, honey, the family's just about to share the *oplatek*."

"I'm holding it in my hand," she said. "I've had it with me all day. I brought it to work in my purse, wrapped up in tissue. It's right here."

"Break off a piece now, Ginger," I said, crunching the phone between my shoulder and ear so I'd have both hands free to tear the wafer I still held. "Good health and happiness to you in the new year. May all—"

"Your deepest wishes come true," she finished. "Oh, Mother, Ma, you know I don't really want to be here. Why am I so far away? Why?"

I closed my eyes. There was the blue sky above her, the deep silent desert, the first star yet to be seen. The operator clicked onto the line, so I spoke quickly: "Always so many questions, Ginger. I know you. You'll find answers for every one, I promise."

"Disconnecting," the operator said, and it was nothing but a toneless buzz.

"That was Ginger," I said as I made my way back around the table to my chair. "Calling to wish everyone Merry Christmas. She's fine."

My mother nodded.

"Of course she is," Wanda said.

Theresa said, "Auntie Helen, she'll be with us at next year's *Wigilia*, I know she will."

I blinked back tears, smiled. "Of course, dear."

Theresa's face was still cramped with worry, and she suddenly looked like the child she was.

I noticed the serving dish on the table in front of me. "Remember how pickled herring was always Ginger's favorite?"

"That's right," Marie said.

"I remember," Joane said.

Wanda said, "She'd eat a whole bowl if you didn't watch out."

"I remember that about Ginger," I said.

There was a silence that probably wasn't as long as it felt, then my mother reached for the pickled herring and spooned a bit onto the extra plate for the guest. "For Ginger who is far away," she said. "May she follow the stars through that desert of hers and find the way home." She nodded at her wisdom, at her answer.

The Wanting-To-Be-An-Artist Summer

AMY — 1975

It was the summer I thought I was going to be a painter. I wore a beret that I'd found at a garage sale. I said things like "You couldn't possibly understand" to everyone. My fingers were rough with turpentine from cleaning my brushes, and splatters of different colors dotted my face each day. "But you can't even draw," my little brother Cal said.

I showed him pictures in art books, paintings where there was no drawing, only swaths of paint, random color, all the emotion of a moment—of a life—strewn on canvas. "You couldn't possibly understand," I said, pushing hair out of my eyes.

"What kind of artist can't draw?" he asked.

"You're so linear," I said.

"Mo-om! Amy's calling me names!"

But my brother and I weren't among the few things my mother cared about that summer. As long as we weren't whacking off body parts she wouldn't get involved.

"Stop calling your brother names!" she shouted from inside the house.

133

She cared only because we were on our annual summer visit to Detroit, and my mother did things there that I never saw her do anywhere else, show-offy, I'm-a-good-mother kind of things that she'd always made fun of when I mentioned how my friends' mothers did them.

"You want to know what I called him?" I shouted back.

"No, just don't do it again."

"I called him linear," I said. "That's not a bad name."

"You heard me," she said.

"You're not even listening! All I said was he's linear."

"I'm warning you," she said.

I was being warned all the time that summer. I loved it. I felt dangerous. Like an artist.

> UNTITLED V. Oil on cardboard. Red, green, and yellow sprinkled like confetti. What it feels like for that one moment when you wake up after a dream and you can't think of where you are, who you are, and it could be anywhere, anyone—but then it's not, it's you.

That afternoon, Aunt Joane came to visit with my mother and grandmother. They sat around the kitchen table like always, drinking coffee even though it was ninety-five degrees and the humidity coated the room like wallpaper because my grandmother didn't believe in air-conditioning. The kitchen linoleum was about the coolest place in the house, so I sprawled there, filling pieces of notebook paper with my signature while conversation hovered like a haze.

"Why's she on the floor like that?" Aunt Joane asked. She was really my mother's aunt, not mine. Her voice was loud; she was born with an extra lung, my grandmother always teased.

"Amy's not used to this humidity," my mother said.

"Yes, Arizona's dry heat," Aunt Joane said.

"An oven's dry heat," I said.

"You're being a smart aleck," my mother said. "Just stop it." She sounded like a wrung-out rag; the colors I saw when she talked were dirty dishwater colors—beige gray, an icky pale yellow.

Aunt Joane said, "She needs a summer job."

My grandmother said, "She needs a boyfriend."

My mother shook her head, swirled her coffee. "Whatever she needs, she better find it soon, because this time I'm really at the end of my rope."

Like I couldn't hear. "What I need is an air-conditioner," I said. "Or a swimming pool."

"More coffee?" my grandmother asked, pouring into everyone's cups.

I did the wicked witch in *Wizard of Oz:* "I'm meeeeelll-tiiing."

"Pass over the milk," Aunt Joane said. "And I'll take another piece of pound cake, Helen. So much moister than your usual."

"It's that recipe out of the *Free Press*," my grandmother said. "Did you see it last Wednesday?"

"Can someone's blood really boil?" I asked. "I mean, bubbles and everything?"

"Amy, we're talking," my mother said. "Why don't you get out the hose and play with your brother?"

Like Picasso ever got squirted by a garden hose. "How old do you think I am?"

"Isn't there a swimming pool anywhere?" she asked my grandmother.

My grandmother laughed. "Who around here would have a pool?"

"A public pool."

Aunt Joane coughed, set down her fork. "No public pools." Heavy silence wedged all the way around the kitchen.

My grandmother nodded. More quiet pressed down.

Cal raced into the kitchen, calling, "I want to go swimming," in that whiny voice that made my mother sigh. Pretending not to see me, he stepped on my hand. I grabbed his leg and wouldn't let go. He kicked.

"Mo-om!"

"Isn't there a pool at the park?" my mother asked, all the calm strained out. "There must be."

"No pool." Aunt Joane folded her arms tight. So did my grand-mother. Together they looked like a wall.

I let go of Cal's leg so suddenly he fell backward.

"Mo-om!"

"Are you sure?" my mother asked. "At the far end of the park? Over by the merry-go-round? I think there is."

Layers of heat thickened on my skin like fur.

"That pool," my grandmother said.

Aunt Joane turned her head toward the window.

"I'm driving the kids over there," my mother said.

Going swimming was better than lying on the linoleum floor, and I could show off the hot-pink strapless bikini that my mother had forbidden me to buy.

Cal ran upstairs to get ready, and I was about to follow when Aunt Joane said, "You know you can't go to that pool, Ginger. The colored kids swim there." She still faced the window.

I paused at the kitchen door. "What are colored kids?"

"Get your bathing suit," my mother said.

"You mean black kids?" I asked.

Aunt Joane said, "Call them what you want, but they're different from us, Ginger. You should know not to let your kids mix with them."

My mother's mouth tightened into a knot, and she pushed her coffee cup. "That's not the way I am."

"All I know is my neighbor-lady's daughter's son played with a colored boy, and now he dropped out of high school and sings in a rock-and-roll band and smokes dope." Aunt Joane's big voice filled up and took over the kitchen.

"Amy's not going to be smoking dope after swimming at a pub-lic pool."

"What about when they rioted downtown?" Aunt Joane said. "You don't know these kids."

"For God's sake, Aunt Joane, neither do you. I'm taking Amy and Cal to the pool, and that's that." She shoved her chair back and stood up. "Amy! Cal! Let's go!" she screamed.

My grandmother started: "Listen to us, Ginger—"

"No, you listen to me!" my mother said. "There's nothing bad about black people, and my kids want to go swimming, so we're going swimming. At the public pool. With black people." She talked fast dark streaks.

My grandmother said, "What makes you so stubborn?"

As my mother came through the kitchen door she ran smack into me. "I told you to get your suit!" She grabbed my arm, started yanking me with her. "We're going swimming."

Aunt Joane said, "What Polish girl isn't stubborn?"

"Biddy," my mother muttered as we thumped up the stairs. "Maybe no one told her it's 1975."

The big attic bedroom where the three of us slept sweltered, like there was no air that hadn't already been breathed in and out a hundred million times. Cal was sitting on his bed waiting. I started digging through the dresser drawer for my bathing suit when my mother grabbed my wrist. I thought it was about the pink bikini, but she said, "Promise you won't be like them."

"What do you mean?"

"Like them. Like, all Polish people are stubborn. Like there's just one way to see the world," she said.

"I'm an artist, remember?" I said. "With my own clear vision."

"They don't know any better; they're not bad people."

She still had my wrist, like there was more to say, but after a moment, I held up my bathing suit with my other hand. "Should I go change?"

"I'm stubborn because I'm stubborn, not because I'm Polish," she said.

"Should I go change now?"

She let go of my wrist, pushed her hair off her face, blinked a couple times. She looked at me like she was surprised to see me standing there, like she hadn't been talking to me at all.

> UNTITLED XI. Oil on canvas. Midnight blue on crimson on black. Heavy layers of paint—an expensive experiment that takes weeks to dry. What my mother feels when she thinks no one sees her pouring from the bottle of gin she hides in the kitchen cabinet behind the canned fruit. Where she is when she drinks. Where I am.

My mother dropped us off at the pool, saying she'd be back in two hours. "Amy, watch your brother," she called out the window as the car rolled away. "Don't talk to strangers!"

"Isn't she coming with us?" Cal asked.

I watched as the car continued up the street another block, then jammed into a parking spot near a bar on the corner. "She's busy," I said, pushing him toward the pool entrance. "This is more fun. Now we can do whatever we want."

I waited for him outside the door of the men's locker room. He was probably dumb enough to pay attention to the signs saying showers required, that's what was taking him so long. The glittery cement under my bare feet was hot, so I stepped into a tiny corner of shade.

There were too many people in the pool; water and screams and bodies sloshed over every edge. Each time I decided one more kid couldn't possibly cram into the pool, someone cannonballed in, sending up another splash, another scream. It wasn't like the country club pool where our friends in Phoenix took us—or even the pool at the apartment complex where my mother's friend Ellen lived: not nearly as many people there, and palm trees surrounding the pool instead of wire fence, and people sitting on lounge chairs instead of faded bath towels. Even the lifeguards here were different; they slouched in their high-up chairs, twirling their whistles around one finger, their sunglasses mirroring the pool and the too-many kids. If someone were drowning, I really thought these lifeguards would think it over whether or not to jump in.

Cal came out, and sure enough his hair was slicked flat.

"Only dorks take showers," I said.

"Look at all those black kids," he said.

"Shut up," I said, whacking his arm. "They're no different than we are."

"All I said was look at how many there are."

"You sound like that biddy Aunt Joane." I started walking fast, looking for space to spread our towels.

"All I said was—"

"Shut! Up!" I dropped my towel and baby oil onto the cement near where the wire fence buckled outward, as if someone's body had banged hard against it. "Want me to tell Mom?"

"What did I do?" He set his towel on top of mine, and I kicked it away.

"You're just like them." I tugged the bottom of my bathing suit with my thumbs and twisted my way through the towels and bodies to the edge of the pool where I swished my foot in the cool water, squinted in the glare. All I had to do was jump; there'd be enough room, just jump.

"Nice bathing suit," a boy in the pool called to me, possibly a cute boy. I couldn't see who, so I smiled in a general way. "How does it stay up with no boobs?"

Everyone—from the little kids and mothers way over in the baby pool to the lifeguards who stopped twirling their whistles to the line at the diving board—everyone stopped screaming and splashing and dunking so they could point at me. Well, that's how it felt. I closed my eyes and dove in, crashing into someone underwater.

I came up sputtering, wiping my eyes, adjusting the top of my suit with one hand, the bottom with another—it was a stupid bathing suit, why had I bought something so ugly, so impractical, so pink? "Sorry," I mumbled to the girl I'd whammed.

"No problem," she said. "That was my nasty brother hollering at you. Want to dunk him?"

She filled out her strapless bikini just right; her smile was also just right, not too big and dopey, just friendly, a little dimple in one cheek. And she was black. I heard Cal screaming my name, watched him splash and tippy-toe through water that was too deep for him. He pulled at my arm, propping himself up so the waves weren't lapping over his chin. "Mom said don't talk to strangers."

I shoved him back toward the edge of the pool. If he couldn't make it, one of those lifeguards could drop his whistle and jump in. "My name's Amy," I said to the girl.

"I'm Lois Greene."

As we smiled at each other, an older boy lunged behind her, dragging her down into the water. When Lois emerged, she screamed, "Get him!" and she and I splashed off in pursuit of her nasty brother and his friends.

> UNTITLED XVII. *Oil on wood. Green circle within yellow circle within green within yellow within orange within yellow. My father left my mother last year because she's a drunk, because she promises each of her days will be different only they're all the same. Don't leave me, she begged. It's you leaving me, he said. I'm still here, is what I thought, always me still here.*

Lois moved her towel near mine; we'd nailed her brother in a remarkable ambush over by the deep end, and victory had exhausted us.

Lois was fourteen and she and her brother, Horace Jr., and her little sister, Tina, rode their bikes to the pool every day, all summer long. Her favorite food was macaroni and cheese, the bedroom she shared with Tina was painted yellow and blue, and they used to have a dog named Skippy but it ran away last spring and her mother was just as happy not to have to vacuum up all that hair. Her father pulled night shift at Ford and he'd been a high school star football player; people still recognized him at Kroger when they were buying groceries. When she grew up, Lois wanted to be a nurse or a ballet teacher or maybe one of those dancers on cruise ships.

The sun burned deep into my skin, into my damp bathing suit, and everything Lois said felt important, like I had to remember it to tell someone later, and I saw afternoons ahead at the pool and the letters we'd send during the year and her visiting me in Arizona and coming to my school and all my friends who weren't half as fun and full of interesting things to say as Lois, and maybe she'd be a ballet teacher in Paris where I planned to live and paint and wear my beret and eat French bread and French fries and French salad dressing. . . .

"You're sleeping!" Lois slapped at my leg with the back of her hand.

The sun slashed as I opened my eyes.

"Know any good jokes?" she asked. "I do."

I sat up, still blinking. My suit was almost all the way dry. "Where's my brother? I'm sort of supposed to watch him."

Lois sat up on her knees, visored her eyes with one hand, put the other on her hip. Two boys a couple of towels over nudged each other, pointed. So I sat up the same way, and I spotted Cal in the far corner, trapped underneath someone else's rowdy game of keep-away. "He's fine," I said, rubbing baby oil onto my arms and legs, turning my skin slick. "I don't know any jokes—you tell me." I squirted oil in my palms to do my shoulders, then nudged the bottle toward her. "Want some?"

"Can't you see I'm tan enough?" She pressed her arm against mine so our two skins touched, my arm shiny with oil, scrawny and the elbow knobby, tiny hairs lined up golden in the sun, hers dark. Stupid old Aunt Joane had probably never touched a black person; maybe even my mother hadn't.

"Everyone in Phoenix uses baby oil for conditioning," I said. "Otherwise we'd look like old cowboy boots." I held out my greasy palms. "I'll do your back," and I scooted behind her before she could say no. With slow circles I rubbed the oil like brush strokes. This is the picture that would terrify Aunt Joane and my grandmother, the picture my mother would hang in the living room instead of that stupid cow skull poster. She hadn't asked to hang any of my paintings yet. But I planned that one day my paintings would cover the walls of the house like a museum; wherever you looked, there I'd be.

"I'll do you," Lois said, and I moved in front of her. "Okay, everyone says I'm absolutely the best joke teller. Last Thanksgiving, Tina laughed so hard pumpkin pie came out her nose!" She snapped shut the cap to the baby oil, and I turned to sit cross-legged and our knees touched. "Okay. What's the difference between a dog and a Polack who've both been run over by cars?"

The dimple in her cheek got deeper, and I really liked the way she laughed—all round and wiggly—and what was a Polack anyway? It sounded like something I should know. "What?" I asked.

"No skid marks in front of the Polack!" There was her wonderful laugh, and the sound of it made me laugh. "Okay, this is my dad's favorite: Why do they put bowls of honey on the table at Polack weddings?"

"Why?"

"To keep the flies off the bride!"

I didn't exactly get it, but Lois watched me as she laughed, so I had to laugh, too.

She caught her breath. "What are the three greatest years of a Polack's life?"

"What?" I asked.

"Fifth grade!"

That one I got. We slapped each other a couple times; when it seemed like we were about quiet, one of us would say "fifth grade" to start us both up laughing again.

"I know tons more Polack jokes," she said.

"My stomach aches," I said. "Let me rest."

She grabbed my knees. "How many Polacks does it take to screw in a lightbulb? One to hold the lightbulb and three to turn the chair."

I couldn't stop laughing, my guts were about to splat onto the hot cement. "You're going to kill me," I said, smacking her shoulder. "Stop!"

"How can you tell which is the Polack at the cockfight? He's the one with the duck!"

That's when I remembered my great-grandmother saying things like "If they think we're just a bunch of dumb Polacks, they're wrong," the words blurry with her accent, but that one word, Polack, spit out hard like a bad taste.

"Don't you get it?" Lois asked. "Cockfight is with chickens, and the Polack's bringing a duck."

I smiled, laughed partway, not sure what I was supposed to think. It wasn't like Lois meant me when she said Polack.

We turned as the chain-link fence rattled behind us. It was my mother, her fingers curled through the wire diamonds like claws. She kicked at the banged-up fence with one sandaled foot.

"Amy!" she screamed, like she'd been screaming already for a while and was sick of it. "Where's your brother? Don't you know what time it is?" She shook the fence harder.

I looked across the pool at the clock above the locker room—twenty minutes until we were supposed to meet her outside.

"Where's your brother?" She pounded the fence. "Find him and get out here." Then she pointed at Lois. "Who's this? Your new friend?"

"Lois," I said. "She comes to the pool every day."

"I am absolutely delighted and thrilled to meet you, Lois." My mother was talking that slow, careful way I recognized, like she thought the words might break apart as soon as she said them. "You are a beautiful girl with a kind face, and Amy's so awfully lucky to meet someone wonderful like you."

Lois looked over at me like she knew she wasn't supposed to

say she was sorry, but that was all she could think of to say. My mother smiled and smiled, all fake and wide, like a jack-o-lantern you can't blow out.

"I guess I should go," I said to Lois, and she nodded. We stood at the same time, and she reached for her towel, wrapped it around her waist, tucking in the end so it stayed put. Than I did the same with my towel.

Lois said, "My mother says my dad's name should be Jim Beam."

"Is that a joke?" We started walking toward the locker room; I waved at Cal, pointed back to our mother. The towel slipped off my waist, and Lois retucked it for me.

"Jim Beam," she said. "You know, the booze."

I stopped walking, and the towel slipped again. She reached for it, but I draped it around my shoulders. "It's not at all like that," I said, walking fast, but she kept up. "It's different. Your dad is different. She's different." We reached the door to the ladies' locker room; from inside, I heard a mother spanking her child, choking sobs, the steady smack-smack.

"It just looked like—"

I cut her off: "You're wrong. She just—" but I didn't know the end of the sentence. The cement sparkled under my feet. Wasn't it different? She wasn't me.

Lois touched my arm with one dark finger. "I made this one up myself. Why did the Polack cross the road?"

"Why?"

"He saw the chicken on the other side and thought it was his mother calling him."

Just then my mother butted in from all the way across the pool: "Amy! Amy!"

We both laughed. It was too perfect.

UNTITLED XXII. Oil on canvas. Hard red and orange circles, yellow slashes ricocheting. Inside my mother's head on certain mornings when she says, Leave me alone, nothing's wrong, I'm fine, just will you please leave me alone, I'm fine, I'm fine. She doesn't consider that maybe there are things we want to say. We tiptoe across those mornings, we're so silent we aren't hardly there.

Aunt Joane came over again after supper; she and my grandmother were knitting baby booties for the church white elephant sale; they had a contest going between them over who would knit the most. My grandmother was doing pink, Aunt Joane blue, and blue was ahead by three. We were all out on the front porch, waiting for evening breezes, only there weren't any; the air stayed wet and washcloth-heavy. Cal was tossing a tennis ball high so he could dive to the grass and flop for the catch with his baseball glove. I had an art book spread open on my lap, but all I was doing was skipping around looking for wintery blizzards or ice blue lakes. Someone had switched the Tigers game on the radio in the kitchen, where the reception was best. All up and down the street there were families just like ours on their front porches, except they had a dad somewhere—either listening to the Tigers game or mowing the lawn or playing catch—and the mother was knitting baby booties or hemming a skirt, not like my mother: apart from the rest of us, hunched on the bottom step, slapping at mosquitoes that weren't there, fumbling ice cubes out of her glass of Kool-Aid to press against her forehead; she had a headache, she'd told us, she wasn't hungry; she didn't eat hardly anything at supper, just a spoonful of green Jell-O salad, and that was only after my grandmother told her she had to eat something.

Aunt Joane said, "Ginger, all these headaches. You should see a doctor maybe." My mother was so startled she dropped an ice cube onto the pavement. "I'm fine," she said, her voice closed off tight.

For a few minutes there was only the click of knitting needles, talking off the radio—not words, only sound.

Then Aunt Joane said, "Ma had a cure for headaches. Remember, Helen?"

My grandmother nodded. "Peel and slice a great big onion into a metal bowl. Pour near-boiling vinegar over it and breathe the smell for three minutes."

"Yuck," I said.

"It works!" my grandmother and Aunt Joane said at the same time. My grandmother continued: "Ma's mother and her mother and probably her mother were fixing the family's headaches that same way."

"It really works?" I asked.

"Cheaper than aspirin," Aunt Joane said. "Those doctors don't know so much as they think."

"Let's try it on Mom." I stood up, walked toward the door. "I'll slice the onion."

"For God's sake," my mother said. "I'm not sniffing a stupid onion. I took two aspirin, and I'm fine."

"You don't look fine," Aunt Joane said. "Ma's Polish cure won't hurt any—try it."

"Come on, Mom," I said.

Her voice sharpened. "It's idiotic to think an onion in vinegar gets rid of headaches. Aspirin cures headaches, not onions." She threw an ice cube way out into the grass.

Aunt Joane and my grandmother looked at each other, and I thought they were going to say more, but their knitting needles started up clicking again.

"First firefly!" Cal shouted, and he ran onto the porch to punch my shoulder, the rule I'd started years ago.

"Don't hit your sister," my mother said.

"He saw the first firefly," I said.

"So?"

"Whoever calls the first firefly gets to sock the other person," I said.

"I don't like you two hitting each other all the time."

"But it's tradition," I said.

"It's stupid," she said.

More silence, only knitting needles, Cal bouncing the tennis ball on the porch, a folding chair squeaking, the million-miles-away baseball game: the way all the nights here started and ended.

My mother suddenly spoke: "Amy made friends with a nice girl at the pool. Tell them about Lois."

I was standing near enough to the door that I could hear the baseball game clearly, that the bases were loaded and how were the Tigers going to pitch their way out of this jam? "Um, her father works at Ford," I said. "She takes ballet lessons."

"What else?" my mother asked.

"She's pretty."

"And she's black," my mother said. "You know, colored."

The knitting needles stopped. Someone whacked a home run, and the Tigers were behind by three. I went back to where I'd been sitting, picked up my book even though it was getting too dark to see the pictures. Cal missed his ball and it bounced down the steps into the grass, but he didn't chase after it.

"She's got one brother and one sister," I said. "She had a dog, but it ran away." It was like dropping something into a big empty bucket.

My mother set down her Kool-Aid, rolled her head from side to side so the bones popped gently, like something set loose. "Go on," she said.

"She's nice, you'd . . ." I was about to finish, "like her," but they wouldn't because their minds had been made up a long time ago—not like my mother, not like me. For God's sake, they were going around sniffing onions when there was aspirin in the medicine cabinet. "Wasn't Lois nice, Mom?" I asked.

"Very nice," my mother said, turning to give me her big full smile, the real one, not the boozy one. "An awfully sweet girl. I enjoyed talking to her."

Actually, I didn't remember much of a conversation between them, but my mother was smiling bigger and longer than she had since we'd gotten in the car to drive to Detroit.

"Will Lois be at the pool tomorrow?" she asked.

"Supposed to rain," Aunt Joane muttered.

I nodded. "She tells funny jokes."

"Tell a joke," Cal said.

"How about inviting her to come over here," my mother said. "Maybe for supper?"

My grandmother's knitting needles were silent in her lap, and she was looking into the front yard, maybe at the fireflies, maybe somewhere farther away. Seemed like thinking about Lois on this block, on this porch, on a night like this one, had yanked the headache out of my mother and jammed it straight into my grandmother's head. A true artist was supposed to have a clear vision at all times. I'd read that somewhere.

"Tell a joke," Cal said, a pest you want to slap away.

My mother said, "Lois could stay overnight." I'd forgotten how my mother looked when she smiled, like someone I never knew but always wanted to.

"Maybe," I said, a long, slow, uncertain word.

"Maybe," she repeated, firming it into for sure, yes—something we'd decided together.

"I want to hear a joke," Cal said.

My grandmother still stared straight ahead, at that place I couldn't see; I pictured violet, deep blue, rust, colors dripping away, fading. Aunt Joane's lips were so tight they'd disappeared. Who was I? I was in Paris and painting and bright colors splashing through the sun; I was as far away as forever.

"Yes, tell us all one of Lois's funny jokes," my mother said. Saying Lois curved her lips into a long smile. "Go on, Amy, honey."

My mother was listening to me now, so couldn't I say everything? Like, Are my paintings good? Like, I know you're still drinking after you promised you wouldn't.

"Tell us Lois's best joke," my mother said.

I only remembered one: "Why did the Polack cross the road?"

After a car passed by loud as a rocket I noticed no one had asked, Why. Maybe I hadn't really said it out loud: "Why did the Polack cross the road?"

"What's a Polack?" Cal asked.

"Shame on you, Ginger," Aunt Joane said, her voice bigger with each word. "Encouraging that." She stood up and walked into the house, the screen door slamming behind her. "See what happens at the public pool!" Another door slammed.

I was afraid to look at my grandmother, so I closed my eyes.

"I didn't do anything," my mother said. "I don't tell those stupid jokes."

"Maybe not," my grandmother said. "But neither do you tell your children who they are."

"What's a Polack?" Cal asked again.

"Just shut up!" I opened my eyes so I could smack his shoulder. He punched me right back, hard enough to make me think that I'd have to stop hitting him one of these days. But I got him again.

"Mo-om!"

There was a pause where she was supposed to say something. We waited.

"Stop it," she whispered. She sounded broken down the middle.

My grandmother stood, said, "Cal, your mother needs to talk to Amy alone."

He put his hand in hers. "Is Polack a bad word?" he asked.

"To Polish people it is," she said. "To people like us."

"Is Amy in trouble?" he asked.

"She didn't know better," and both doors closed behind them, the screen door and the big front door.

I didn't know what to say. "I thought you liked Lois so much"— which sounded dumb as soon as I said it; she didn't even know Lois. Neither did I.

It was almost too dark to see my mother nod the same old nod, the nod for when she didn't want to be bothered, the nod for when she was thinking about somewhere else. A breeze brushed my skin, fluttering the pages of my open book all the way back to the beginning.

"You told me not to be like them," I said.

"I know what I told you," she said. "You couldn't possibly understand, but no matter what we do, or where we go, we *are* them. We just are."

I nodded like I understood, that same kind of nod, which seemed to be all she wanted, and we sat outside together for a very long time, watching the fireflies search for each other, tiny nothing-lights alone against the dark.

UNTITLED XXX. Oil on canvas. Black and white. The last painting of the wanting-to-be-an-artist summer. Two black squares next to two white squares. I use a stencil and ruler to draw them out so they'll end up exactly the same. But they're not. I try again—still they look different. I measure the stencil, check the ruler. I don't understand. The one painting I ask her to hang on the wall, and she does.

Those Places I've Been

HELEN—1967

The front entryway to my house is like New York City: a bustling mess with winter boots tossed every which way, mud smears on the red tile floor, dropped umbrellas, slushy snow melting into stains that Ginger was supposed to scrub clean, someone's lost glove left over from last year, the kind of dirt and filth that digs deep, expecting to stay. This is the place you pass through before entering the real thing, the real life, the house.

Coming here from Poland, my mother saw the Statue of Liberty—even the men cried, she told us—and stopped on Ellis Island, but she didn't actually stay in New York City; instead she and my father boarded a train to Detroit, their destination printed on scraps of paper pinned to their collars. She wore that scrap of paper for a week after she arrived, still not sure she was really in Detroit. So no one in my family can tell me stories of New York City, but I imagine its confusion, noise, mess, slop, and what you feel when you come to a new place for the first time, the pinpricks of fear lining your belly, how everything behind you has melted into something slippery you can't hold. Of course I never once left Detroit, so I don't know, not really, not much at all.

Now, coming through the front entryway puts me into a different place because my husband is gone forever. My daughter moved all the way to Arizona nine years ago, and my husband passed away in early spring, and I'm a widow, standing in the front entryway, but the only thing I hear is silence, what used to be here, what isn't here anymore.

My mother and sisters had lots of good advice for me—keep busy, say the rosary, meet with the priest, light candles at church, put the life insurance money somewhere safe. What they said made sense, but it felt like the words were coming to me from far away. They liked to talk, wanted to fill the quiet. Most of the time that was fine.

My mother told me, "You shouldn't be alone, not at a time like this. Make Ginger come back home." It was that simple for her, because there was a certain way everything was done. Iron like this, wash your dishes like that, fix your cabbage this way not that way. Go to church and trust in God. Sometimes when I said the same things, I was surprised to hear my mother's words coming out of my mouth. Did that mean I didn't have my own?

Make Ginger come back home. It seemed suddenly, now, that nothing could be that simple.

What I wanted was not to make Ginger come home—because maybe I could find a way to do that—but for Ginger to want to come back. "It doesn't matter which." My mother sighed impatiently. "What matters is having her home. Getting your daughter back."

My mother had traveled around the world to come to a place she'd never seen and to build a new life out of nothing. When she saw the Statue of Liberty, she knew it was there for her. That's what she told me and my sisters, "The lady was standing there in the water waiting for me." We believed her.

*   *   *

My living room is like California, bright sun shoving through the lacy curtains in the morning, insisting that today will be another great day even though now I'm a widow.

That word.

In my living room, in the sun the morning after a too-long night when I didn't sleep any, that word can hardly be true, not even possible.

Alone. That's another word that doesn't exist in my living room, not here in California, where the pictures I see in beauty shop magazines show smiling tan people playing games on beaches, riding bikes on wooden walkways along the ocean, racing convertibles down wide sunny roads, wearing shorts and lounging on patio chairs, colorful drinks in their hands.

The living room is where the men and the children sit when the whole family gets together, when there's company. I don't know what they talk about; all I know is that it's different than what I talk about with the women in the kitchen. I imagine things that are easier, freer, sunnier . . . what they talk about in California where everything feels pretty and bright. It's the biggest room in the house, the living room, and still not very big, the way California isn't big enough for all the people who want suddenly to live there.

Once I asked my husband what the men talk about in the living room. He put down his newspaper, picked it up, put it down again. He looked at me as if my question couldn't be answered in the kind of words I'd understand. "We talk about things," he said. He picked up the paper and a moment later asked, "What do you talk about in the kitchen?"

"Things," I said too quickly.

California is on the edge of an ocean and that makes it feel farther away than it really is. One time I asked my mother, "How big is an ocean?" knowing she'd traveled across one to get to here. She said, "If we knew how far from one side, we wouldn't leave."

Is that what I'd asked? Her answers were like that, never quite saying what you wanted to know. But in school I learned distances and miles, and that wasn't the right answer either.

All that sun in my living room. I sit very still in it, thinking it should be somewhere else.

My mother was helping me plant my garden; I'd fallen behind, and the garden was important, all of us always, always had a garden—even if it was just a flowerpot on a fire escape, we had a garden, so to have this backyard without a garden was unthinkable. There's only one person instead of two, I wanted to say, so why grow all this food? but I already knew her answer: Someone in the family will need your extra tomatoes; someone will want the cucumbers, the squash, the beans.

The tomato plants were leftovers from the seeds my sisters started, the weakest, the stringiest, the stubbiest. Of course they kept the strong ones for their own gardens—only Marie set aside some good sturdy plants for me. It didn't matter; I was the best gardener, so by August I knew my tomatoes would be the biggest and juiciest, and Joane and Wanda would hide their jealousy behind smiles and whisper to themselves that I knew gardening secrets I wouldn't share. It was that way every year.

I was digging little holes and crumpling last fall's dry, brown leaves into the bottom of each hole, and my mother was behind me, ripping away the paper cup and setting the tomato plant deep, repacking the loose dirt, drizzling water from the watering can. Planting used to be my favorite part of gardening, but all I felt now was the sun scraping hot against my neck, the crick in my knees acting up; every hole meant more tomatoes I'd have to pick and can come fall. John was the one who loved tomatoes, standing in the garden eating them from his hand like apples. I didn't even want a garden. My husband was gone, so shouldn't things be different, shouldn't something change? Shouldn't I plant watermelons if I wanted to? Or nothing but pretty flowers for butterflies?

My mother must have been talking about something else because she looked startled when I spoke suddenly: "Maybe I'll move to Phoenix. Instead of Ginger coming back here, I'll leave and go there." That was the idea that came into my mind this morning when I was sitting in the sun in the living room, but now was the first time to say the words out loud. They sounded like nothing I'd ever said before, like having a dream and then seeing in daylight that it had really happened.

"You leave?" my mother said. "No."

"No?" I asked. "What do you mean, no?"

"No means no," she said. "No always means no."

I went back to digging holes and crumpling leaves, going faster and faster until I reached the end of the row. But she was keeping pace right behind me, already talking about something else, as if it had been decided that I wasn't moving to Arizona. In the morning it had been only a quick idea, in and out of my head, but now that I'd heard the words in my own voice, it was what I wanted to do. Move to Arizona. Leave Detroit. Do the most different thing there was.

Together we dragged out the stakes that John had neatly stacked in the garage last fall and pushed them deep in the dirt to the left of each tomato plant.

Did no always mean no? When my mother and father argued, they'd break into Polish, screaming awful things at each other, forgetting that my sisters and I understood every terrible word. The worst fights always ended with my mother shrieking, "You brought me here and then my mother died alone in Poland," and that's when the room seemed to tighten, and my father would shout, "No," refusing blame, but my sisters and I knew—the way you knew how to breathe—we knew he was wrong, she was right, that when a daughter left, the mother died. Again and again my father would shout no, over and over, like pounding a nail into the wall, and my mother would just watch him, not having to say anything. She knew we were listening.

The stakes were in, the tomatoes planted. "That's that," my mother said, nodding.

If I were a child, I'd run into that garden and stamp my feet all over it, grind my heels down hard on top of those tomatoes, yank the stakes and heave them as far as I could. Instead, we went inside to the kitchen, and I made coffee.

My dining room is New Orleans, down where the Mississippi River finds the Gulf, and all that water empties into the ocean; it's the place where the living room meets the kitchen, where the men join the women—the place we all end up eventually, drawn by the tinkle of forks against plates, the lace cloth cascading off the table like a waterfall, all the smells of a special dinner rolling through the house like waves.

The dining room is for holidays, birthdays, Sunday dinner— and the kitchen is for eating on regular dishes and the regular red-checked tablecloth. Food doesn't taste better in the dining room, but it feels more important, so the things we talk about feel more important, though they're not. All the really important things are saved and discussed in the kitchen, using low voices that won't carry past the doorway.

They have lots of parties in New Orleans because it's a place that loves celebrations. But there are hurricanes in New Orleans, and how can people have fun knowing their house might be swept apart by one of those big winds? That water could crowd through and carry everything away? That what you value most might suddenly be gone?

Just like that.

I've seen the pictures in the papers, on the news. Hurricane Betsy was the last big one, leaving behind muddy water flooding everything and people dying and a mess I thought could never be all the way gone; it seemed to me that people in New Orleans would never have another party after that.

Because we go to the dining room to celebrate, that's where I had the special dinner for Ginger's high school graduation, using the best dishes, the prettiest lace tablecloth, even four candles and honey wine Wanda's husband made for the adults. Ginger sat by herself at the head of the table, the place of honor, and we all stared at her: a high school graduate, part of the first generation of our family to finish high school. What could be next—college, married to a doctor, sons and daughters who won't know the kinds of bad dreams that come when you fall asleep hungry or sneaking out at night to steal the coal that's slid off the train. Their children millionaires, maybe.

"Now what?" Marie asked Ginger.

"She'll work and go to night school to be a teacher," I said.

"Get married," Wanda said.

"Start a job at Ford," my mother said.

"Now I can move away," Ginger said, and we all thought it was one of her jokes, something supposed to be funny that wasn't, and the men looked at the women and the women looked at the men and the kids stared down at their plates. No one knew what to say, so a couple men laughed, and Joane said, "Same old Ginger. Still joking about that."

Ginger's fists were clenched, looking tight and knotty against the white lace, and she stared at me too long, too hard. It wasn't a joke anymore. I hurried to the kitchen for butter for the bread because tears were about to overflow, and I stood holding the edge of the countertop with both hands, tears streaking my cheeks. When I looked up a moment later, Ginger was in the doorway watching me, and I waited for her to say she was sorry, but she said, "I can't help it." As if that explained anything.

I remember those pictures of the people in New Orleans after the hurricane, how they were clutching their things—wet books, frying pan, little dog, doll, pair of overalls. They couldn't hold tight enough. Everything they had could disappear in one tiny piece of a minute, and now they knew that.

*   *   *

I didn't own a suitcase because I'd never been anywhere over-night. Even my wedding night was spent in my mother-in-law's house where John and I lived for the first couple months to save money before sharing my sister's house. So why would I need a suitcase? I took my clothes over in the trunk my mother had brought from Poland and then returned it to her the next day.

I asked my sister Wanda to drive me downtown to Hudson's department store. She loved to drive on the freeways, not like the rest of us; she went fast, all the way up to the speed limit. I kept the window rolled down so the wind rushing in blew apart all the endless stories she was telling because she thought that was what I wanted. Everyone thought they knew what I wanted.

I'd told her we should walk around Hudson's looking at all the fancy clothes and furniture, maybe try on fur coats just for fun. She'd thought that was a good idea; "Get your mind off," she'd said. So when we went through the revolving glass doors into the store—Wanda only partway through the same story I'd lost track of back when we parked the car—and I suddenly interrupted to say, "Maybe we could look at suitcases," then she finally stopped talking.

"Suitcases?" she said, walking faster.

I nodded. We ended up in the perfume area, and I picked up the closest bottle and sprayed one wrist, rubbed it against the other. The perfume was too strong, and I coughed.

"For some kind of trip?" Wanda asked.

I nodded again, rubbed my wrists against my skirt, trying to get rid of that overwhelming smell, like wearing shoe polish.

She grabbed the upper part of my arm, shaking it. "Trip where?" Her fingers tightened, and I looked down at them clutching into my skin. "Just a visit?" I still didn't speak. "Right?" Wanda demanded.

The saleslady appeared behind the counter and asked, "Can I help you?" She smelled like the shoe polish perfume.

"Just looking," Wanda said, yanking me away from the perfume and over toward the handbags, where there weren't so many people.

"Can we just look at the suitcases?" I asked.

"Ma said Ginger was moving back here," Wanda said. "That's what she told us."

I pulled my arm free. "I've never been anywhere else," I said, crossing my arms. A group of ladies dressed up for shopping glanced at us as they passed, so maybe I'd spoken louder than I thought.

Finally Wanda said, "I've never been anywhere else. None of us have."

I nodded.

"This is where we live," she said, "right here," her voice rose sharply, "here. You know that." She picked up a black patent handbag, tilted the flat side this way and that so the overhead light bounced off it.

There was nothing I could say to her, nothing that could explain this to someone who didn't know. It felt like a long, long time before she spoke again: "Ginger is the one like this, not you."

She set down the handbag. We walked to the up escalator, rode silently to the floor where the suitcases were, and Wanda told the salesman I was looking for a nice, sturdy matching set, definitely on sale, maybe a floor model not too banged up that came with an additional discount.

We didn't talk much, not even on the drive home, not until we were carrying the suitcases into my house, and she asked, "What are you going to tell Ma?"

We set the suitcases in the middle of the living room. They filled the space like shadows. "I won't tell her anything," I said. "I'll send a postcard from Arizona."

We both laughed even though it wasn't funny, and as soon as she left, I moved the suitcases into the bedroom so no one would see them.

*   *   *

Our bedroom—my bedroom now—is dark: oversized dark wood bureaus and polished dark wood floor (carpeting only for the living room and dining room where company can see it) and one window looking at the wall of the neighbor's house and the other looking into the backyard, but it seems there's never a chance to look at the view out that window except late at night, not like windows in the kitchen where I'm seeing out all day long. The white bedspread is sad against this darkness, white curtains seem like ghosts; the mirror on my bureau reflects darkness, stillness, quiet, all thrown back on itself. Even the white walls are flat and empty, and I know if I pushed them aside there'd be only more darkness.

It's Hawaii, our bedroom, my bedroom, all those time zones halfway across the globe, the exotic place I know is always dark and quiet in the middle of my too-bright day. As night moves close, I switch on the lamp in the bedroom even though it's wasteful to burn a light for no reason. What am I trying to do? There's no easy way beyond darkness.

This darkness is for sleeping, for escape; it's where I go when the other places ache with light; this is where I curl up and close my eyes and darkness flows like lava, and I disappear into what, into nothing, into pure dark, into what there is before there's anything else.

This is where life begins, the bedroom, the way they say volcanoes made Hawaii, by rising up out of the oceans; the bedroom brings the sudden surprise you expect because that's what happens to married people, they have babies.

The first was so easy, and the others were supposed to come that way, quick and tumbling into our lives one after the other until our house was overflowing with babies and more babies.

When they didn't and still didn't, all we could do was lay side by side in the darkness in the bedroom, like someone had shoved half a world between us, and maybe we were thinking the same things, but neither of us knew how to say those words to the other.

*   *   *

The next morning I put the biggest suitcase on the bed and unlatched it, opening it wide so it filled my side of the bed. It was a nice light blue inside and out, and it smelled like the new cars John and I had seen at the auto show. A moveable cloth flap separated the two halves, and little elastic pockets lined the edges; the salesman told Wanda those were for "personals." Plastic straps reached from the top and bottom of each half so you could buckle your folded clothes down tight to keep them from wrinkling too bad.

This suitcase was prettier than my mother's old trunk, which was gouged with scratches and smelled like cobwebs inside. When she left Poland, she crammed the trunk with a goosedown quilt, pillows, two lace tablecloths, a bowl, a platter, candlesticks, some photographs, the Bible her mother had given her, bedsheets, and dried mushrooms and smoked sausages, then knotted it up with a thick rope. She and my father wore their clothes, as many as they could pile on. My sisters and I could almost tell the story ourselves, how the boat rocked from side to side until they were about ready to pray for it to go ahead and tip over; the husband and wife keeping everyone awake at night arguing in the language no one recognized but who wouldn't talk to each other during the day; how the food was nothing but lukewarm soup, boiled potatoes, and herring to help the seasickness; how everyone bragged about how much money they were going to make in America and how rich their relatives were; and everyone crowding to one side of the ship to look at the Statue of Liberty, to see New York City, America, and how even the men cried. My mother ended each story the same way: "To be alive in this country is a miracle. You should thank God every day."

But this was the only place we knew. How could someone else's stories make us understand?

I stood in Ginger's doorway and watched her the night before she moved away. She stacked piles of folded things on her bed, all the skirts here, the blouses there, socks, shoes (right on the clean spread, but I didn't say anything), a couple books, curlers, two hats, the good pair of gloves, dresses, a slip. The suitcase gaping open on the floor, waiting.

She was humming one of those songs off the radio, pretending she didn't see me. She had two suitcases she got from the pawnshop, and what was worse, to watch your daughter leaving or to think of her at a dirty pawnshop counter, haggling over the price of two battered suitcases where some stranger had kept his filthy things? She spent a long time arranging her clothes on the bed, making one pile higher, tidying the edges of another stack, pulling something else out of a drawer, taking something back, and still she didn't put anything inside the suitcase.

Finally she stopped fussing with the clothes on the bed and turned to look out the window at the backyard—the same view I saw from my bedroom window, just moved over a bit to get more of the garage, less of the garden. The sky was pinkish gray, day turning into dark, and there should have been something I could say, do. She slid her hands down onto her hips, and her elbows jutted backward like wings. I wanted to touch her, but I didn't move. She asked, "Do you think you can make me change my mind?"

Why did she say those words that way? She could've asked if she should leave, and I would've known to say no. Or if she'd asked if we'd miss her, I would've said yes. Or maybe those questions weren't so easy either, not when the open suitcase was there on the floor and she was maybe really going to go, the first one to leave, my only daughter, Ginger, who in so many ways wasn't like any of us but who was us. She wanted her own stories; was that so wrong?

And what did I want? I wanted her to stay, I wanted her here, I wanted to make her change her mind; I thought I could, I knew I could. She was my daughter.

But I stepped into her bedroom and picked up the top blouse

off the pile—the olive one with white polka dots, a hand-me-down from her cousin June; an ugly blouse I always thought, but one of Ginger's favorites—and gently set it inside the suitcase. "Only you can change your mind," I said. Where do words like that come from?

Ginger whirled and grabbed stacks of clothes in big armloads and piled them in the suitcase, jostling and shoving to make them fit. "Good!" she screamed. "Because I'm not changing my mind! I'm not! No matter what you say!"

So the moment was lost, and I cried as she dumped the rest of her things in her suitcases, and outside the window the sky slowly turned dark.

My mother would've said something different, my sisters, too. They would've said the thing to make Ginger change her mind. It was there, that thing to say. Did I not know it, or did I not say it?

So now it was my suitcase open on the bed, and what did I want? My husband back. My daughter. Something different. What?

The kitchen door slapped open, then closed—surely my mother; we all knew Wanda wasn't one to keep anything to herself—so I snapped shut the suitcase, shoved it back under the bed, and hurried into the kitchen. She would see that I hadn't washed last night's supper dishes; what I was thinking was, why waste all that soap lather on so few dishes?

My mother was running hot water into the plastic dish tub. There was a fresh poppy seed cake on the kitchen table. "What's this about a suitcase?" she demanded.

I pulled the wax paper off the cake and was about to crumple it and throw it away, but she said, "That's not so dirty," so I folded it and slipped it into the drawer with the old bread bags.

"Where are you going with this suitcase?" she asked. She turned off the faucet and piled the glasses into the dishwater, swishing them back and forth, rubbing them with a dishcloth, then added the silverware.

"I already told you," I said. "Maybe I'll move to Arizona now."

She turned the water back on too hard, quickly rinsed soap off the glasses and silverware, splashing onto the counter and herself, turned off the water. She opened her mouth, then shook her head, slipped the plates into the water. Finally she spoke slowly: "Yes, you told me." She lowered her voice, as if she thought someone else might hear us. "But did you tell Ginger? Does she want you to move down there?"

Anything I could think to say would break and spill open like an egg, so I just shook my head too hard. How did she know what scared me most?

She dropped the dishcloth in the soapy water, turned and wrapped her arms around me, held me close, murmured Polish words into my ear as she let me cry, exactly what a mother should know to do for her daughter.

Her arms were tight around me, her breath warm and damp and rhythmic. "No daughter should leave her mother," she said. "So Ginger will come home."

But you never went back, I wanted to say.

As if I'd spoken, she whispered, "I never saw my mother again. That's what I paid for my family to be in this country." She unwrapped her arms from around me to make the sign of the cross, and I automatically did, too.

We stood looking at each other. "Maybe that's not why she died," I said.

She didn't hear me because she turned around and stuck her hands back into the soapy dishwater. "Dirty dishes bring bugs in the house," she said, "like calling them by name." Or maybe she did hear me.

The attic is finished into one room big enough where a family could live; there's a bathroom John built in, a double bed, Ginger's old twin bed and a crib for babies; we could squeeze more beds up there, a sofa, a TV set. Whatever a family might want or need, we could find a way to put it up there because the attic is a big ranch in the west, all the space and time in the world; the place that's always there, waiting, waiting, the place that doesn't change when you're away, like mountains in the distance.

When they visit—only Ginger and her children, never the husband—things happen upstairs that we don't all the way understand: footsteps, squeaky beds, one of the kids fussing. John and I were like the owners of the ranch—things happen, cows go out, cows come home, fences break, fences get fixed. We never asked how or why because that's not what the owners do on a big ranch in the west where everything runs itself, where generations of the same family grow up on the ranch, and it's a sin worse than any other to sell your land.

But here's what happens when there's so much space, so much room: People become careless. Because it's a place you imagine will always be there, you don't think much about it. You certainly don't think about it disappearing. Isn't that why they made those big parks out west, because they knew people couldn't appreciate all that space unless pieces were taken away?

Upstairs, the big attic room waits for Ginger and her children. They'll be back; they come in the late summer and fill every inch of space with noise and books and games and dolls and shirts dropped right in the middle of the floor and unmade beds and glasses from the kitchen half full of melted ice and towels draped across chairs and all the mess and clutter of a family.

Ginger doesn't think, Is there room for us? She doesn't think, Does she want us to visit?

Out west, on a big ranch, things are simple. The family owns the ranch. The children keep the ranch going after the parents die. The sun comes up, the sun goes down. Everywhere you look there's plenty of space and mountains in the distance.

Every day I ironed and folded something else to add to the big suitcase until finally it was full. I could barely heave it on and off the bed. It sat along the doorway, latched and locked, waiting.

I could go by bus or train.

I could leave tomorrow or later in the summer or wait until the fall.

I could make a new dress to travel in or wear something I already had.

No one knew the suitcase was full. When my mother or my sisters came over, we sat in the kitchen and talked, and they always asked, "Have you heard from Ginger?" as they clutched my hand across the table.

"Ginger's fine," I told them, but that's not what they were asking, and they waited for me to say more, but the only thing more to say would be that I hadn't written to her about my plan yet.

If I left the kitchen for a moment and then returned, I could feel they'd been talking about me, wondering about this sudden change, this new brave Helen; their whispers hung like fog in the air, dissolving exactly when I walked back into the room.

I could ask Wanda to drive me to the station or I could catch the city bus or I could even take a taxi.

I could buy magazines to read on the trip, or I could bring along some knitting.

How could there be so many choices for one person?

If I slept at night, I dreamed of Arizona, of the stories Ginger had told me about big cactuses and funny little birds that ran fast but couldn't fly and empty blue skies stretched tall and thin and Indians and the heat rising out of the ground. In the day, it was my house, my garden, my mother and sisters and nieces and nephews all trying to keep me busy.

And the heavy suitcase sat in the doorway like a wall. At first I knocked into it on my way to the bathroom for a drink of water in the night, and I thought, Why is that there? before remembering. Then I got used to it and walked around it.

When I couldn't sleep, I sat in the kitchen and made up the conversation I'd have with Ginger when I explained my plan to move to Arizona. Sometimes it would be the conversation I wanted to have—she'd exclaim how happy she was, how there was a house just down the street for sale, or better yet, how about moving into the guest room in her house?—and other times it was the conversation I knew we'd have—too many ums and uhs before that one blunt word I didn't want to hear. It pounded through my head, no, no, no, the only word I could think of until it seemed like the only word there was.

I could call Ginger long distance or I could write a letter or I could just show up at her house.

I hadn't been keeping the weeds out of my garden like I should, so my mother and Wanda stopped by to help even though it was a saggy, gray, humid day, the kind of hot day that sticks to your bare skin. Wanda wanted to set newspapers out and weigh them down with rocks; my mother said no, that we had to pull out the weeds first because the roots were sucking the water away from the plants, so we did it my mother's way, tugging and digging each weed down to the root, tossing it onto a big heap over in the corner to be cleaned up later.

It used to be Ginger helping me weed this same way, digging down to the root. Where did all her questions come from? "Why is this a weed? Who said so? It has a flower on it, so why isn't it a flower? Why can't we let it grow and see how tall it gets?" On and on she went, always asking why, why, and I never knew any of the answers.

I dropped my trowel on the ground and sat back on my heels, wiping sweat off my forehead with my fist. A moment later the sweat was right back. Wanda glanced at me but kept weeding. The air was too heavy to breathe. I said, "Why?" then again, louder, "Why?" more demanding, and Wanda stopped weeding, half a dandelion dangling out of one hand, and my mother looked over at me from the corner of the garden.

"Did you say something?" she asked.

Wanda said, "She said 'why.' " It was already turning into a story to tell in a whisper when the kids weren't around, Helen's nervous breakdown. Or maybe it was going to be so bad that no one would even talk about it. It wasn't too late to kneel back down and yank out a weed, yank out another, just keep going the way it was.

But my mother asked, "Why what?"

I laughed. "Why anything?" I said, my voice sharpening. "Why can't we leave a couple weeds in the garden? Why do we wash all the dishes after every meal? Why do we always grow tomatoes and can them with the exact same recipe every year?"

"Poor Helen," Wanda murmured.

"Why can't I move to Arizona if I want to?" I whispered.

A big crow landed in the middle of the yard, and we all watched it pick at something in the grass. Then my mother clapped her hands together, and it flew away. "Is that what you really want?" she asked. "To live all the way down there in Arizona?"

I shook my head, nodded, felt tears pushing behind my eyes. "I bought suitcases," I said, blinking fast to keep from crying.

"I tried to tell her no," Wanda said. "I saved the receipt even so we can return them."

My mother said, "We all want to know why, Helen. Even when we don't ask, the question is there. Why does God make someone die? Who doesn't want to know that?" She quickly made the sign of the cross, and so did Wanda, and like a shadow, so did I. We were silent for a moment, and all I could think was why-why-why. Was this what it was like to be Ginger, restless and unhappy, always wanting more, needing so desperately an answer that can't be, running, running, running, jumbled between Detroit and Arizona? I shivered and wrapped my arms around my body, but I still felt cold. Goose pimples tightened the skin of my arms, and my fingertips were like icicles ready to snap off.

Tiny purple spots danced in front of me, so I closed my eyes but that made more spots, purple and green and blue, and it was the whole world spinning around and around, going too fast, whirling out of control, and I put out one hand to try to hold it still, but I couldn't quite reach, so I stretched both arms as far as I could, but there was my mother's voice—"Helen! Helen!"—and everything stopped spinning; the world floated in front of me like a glass bubble, and I opened my eyes. I was on my back in the dirt next to and on top of the carrots, and my mother and Wanda were leaning over me; Wanda was pouring warm buggy rainwater from the watering can over my wrist, and my mother's hand was gentle across my forehead.

"You scared us," Wanda said.

"To feel better you need an ice cube in your mouth," my mother said.

"No more gardening today," Wanda said. "I'll finish weeding; you go into the kitchen with Ma. Sit down, drink some water."

"An ice cube," my mother said. "That's what works."

"Okay, an ice cube," Wanda said. "An ice cube, then maybe some water." She stood up, and I watched her legs hurry toward the house, heard the kitchen door bang. The heat was like a soggy blanket pressing the air out of me.

After a moment, I asked, "What happened?"

"One minute you're moving to Arizona, and the next you're flat on the ground," my mother said.

The dirt was soft underneath me, almost comfortable. Seeing her from this view, my mother looked old suddenly, and tiny, like someone else's mother you can't really fear. How had this little woman left everything behind to get on a boat to come to America? Who was the person who could do that enormous thing?

Wanda hurried back outside, a towel draped over one arm and two glasses in her hands. She put the damp towel on my forehead as my mother fished an ice cube out of one of the glasses and put it in my mouth. It clunked against my teeth, too big to hold on to.

Wanda said, "I saw that suitcase when I got the towel from the linen closet. I tried picking it up."

Tiny streams of water ran off my forehead and onto the dirt. Wanda never wrung out the towels enough; when we helped our mother do the wash for other people back when we were girls, we always had to tell her to wring out the towels more before pinning them on the line.

Wanda said, "You put clothes in it, didn't you?"

My mother said, "Helen, you packed a suitcase? This is real?"

There was a long moment where I should've been thinking of what to say; I couldn't talk with the ice in my mouth, and I slowly removed the ice cube and tossed it toward the tomatoes. It pinged against one of the metal stakes.

Until I heard myself say them, I didn't recognize where these words came from: "Do you think you can make me change my mind?"

There was not even a tiny pause before my mother said, "Only you can change your mind," and she reached deep into the glass and pulled out another ice cube with her fingers and set it gently in my mouth. It burned cold against my tongue—but how could it feel both hot and cold?—and how did she know this was exactly what I needed to feel better? How had she known what to say?

It wasn't Arizona I wanted, but why not, when I thought I was so sure?

"Come inside," Wanda said, as if everything were ordinary.

"Yes, into your house," my mother said.

Together they helped me stand and held me steady for a moment before we started walking.

"You can rest," Wanda said.

"Or we can sit in the kitchen," my mother said. "Turn on the fan maybe."

"It's such a nice house," I said, and they didn't understand, but they nodded anyway, one after the other, exactly as I knew they would.

There's always coffee in the kitchen and something good to eat. There's the toaster over there, the bread box over there, the drawer for plastic bread bags to reuse, the butter dish always in the corner.

My kitchen smells like bacon in the morning, fried bologna at lunch, and sauerkraut or *kielbasa* at supper. I wash the red-checked tablecloth on Tuesdays and mop on Mondays and Thursdays. Those are the days my mother mops, the days my sisters mop.

The kitchen is the kitchen. It's where we laugh and cry, share secrets and think about the secrets we don't dare tell. It's where we ask questions and where, maybe, we find answers. Am I a mother or a daughter, a wife or a woman, someone who wants to leave or needs to stay?

And sometimes, sometimes, what's best of all is to sit alone in the kitchen late at night and not have to say a word at all.

Things Women Know

R O S E — 1 9 2 5 – 3 5

Pins

"For good luck, you must wear three new things to Mass on Easter Sunday." There is no money now for new clothes or new anything. What I have are two handkerchiefs, a tiny square of lace, and an arm's length of ribbon the watery blue of Helen's eyes. Since that is all, my children and I must go to Easter Mass without three new things, and we will have a year of bad luck; isn't there a way to find three new things my children can wear? Can't I hold off bad luck?

My husband says the old ways don't follow us to this new country, but only last week he cured his toothache by pressing a slice of warm onion against his ear for an hour.

The night before Easter, I move through a dark dream filled with bad luck—hunger, sickness, death, factory strikes. I must bring good luck. All I have is an unopened box of straight pins on the bureau, and in this dream, I slide three pins deep into the seams of the children's dresses, the hem of my husband's pants, the edge of my sleeve. By morning I've forgotten; by morning it's breakfast, and I'm getting the children dressed and pouring coffee for my husband and putting up my hair.

But at Mass, when I lean my arms on the pew ahead of me to ask for God's blessing, a pin jabs my wrist, and again, and I move so I am pricked more. No one else understands my smile.

The old ways don't follow us here. We brought them, carrying them with us as any piece of china or silver candlestick or photograph, wrapping them carefully as we did all our treasures.

Helen

"To cure any wart, you must rub it with a chicken foot." My Helen won't ask the man at the butcher shop for a chicken foot to cure the wart on her hand. Twice I've sent her; twice she's come home with nothing. "He'll think we're eating it," she says. Her voice rises: She thinks there could be nothing worse than eating a chicken foot, when, in fact, I could explain that what's worse is eating nothing. She tells me, "He says 'dumb Polacks' when he thinks the door's closed behind us." Doesn't she know they all do? But she's a pretty girl who likes her pretty thoughts.

I know this man at the butcher shop, and a smile goes as far as a quarter with him. A chicken foot for no charge is a matter of asking in the right way.

Men don't have this option, and perhaps that is why women feed the family. What men know best is force; what they know is the sweating, hulking heat of days or nights at the factory, how small parts get banged into an automobile; men know hard edges and angles. Women understand that force is not the best way to put food on your table.

It was the sixth week of the strike. Baby David had only just died, the doctors and the funeral man taking all the coins and crumpled bills in the jar in the closet. We dared not buy death on credit and risk more bad luck. I watched the food in my pantry go bite by bite until what was left was nothing. The money the children brought me from their odd jobs wasn't enough, not when there was rent and coal and something for the church.

My husband wouldn't look at me across the table as we went from three meals a day to two, and it was because he was ashamed, I know, but every turn of his head, each flicker in his eyes told me to do something, to feed our children, to find a way.

So I went to the butcher. It wasn't him I looked at—his tiny eyes, his hands all knuckle and veins—but at the hams I wanted to boil and serve with horseradish and tiny peas; and the ducks that should be roast brown, crispy-skinned, and overflowing with sauerkraut stuffing; and the pork loin to bake slow and crusty with applesauce and sugar. My stomach filled with strange twists to think how I wanted that food on my plate.

He greeted me, listened as I told Wanda to take her sisters down the block to wait outside the church, that I'd be along in a moment to go to confession. He watched my children leave the shop, heard the door soft behind them, felt the silence gather. He'd known before I'd come through the door; he'd known it would happen sometime, it didn't have to be the baby dying, the strike. It could have been taxes, the flu, a factory accident, the house burning down. Anything. All women live that close to walking into the butcher shop the way I did that afternoon.

He pulled out his ledger from under the counter and spent what felt like too much time turning over the pages. "I don't buy on credit," I said.

He closed the book, brushed the cover back and forth with one finger.

"It's the strike," I said.

His finger tapped the ledger book, once, twice, three times. "Such hard times for us all." But his face was round and pink and looked every day at a full dinner table. "With the strike, I can't give credit."

"I don't buy on credit."

"As long as you understand."

When his hand touched mine, I closed my eyes to see pork chops and sizzling strips of bacon. I thought about meat, how I'd cook it for my family—stew, braise, bake, fry. I felt its soft roundness, slicing through the grain with a sharp knife, the slap of it dropping onto my kitchen counter.

I remembered that time my mother brought home a chicken, and how no one asked where it had come from, where she'd gotten it, because it was food, because we wanted so bad to eat it—we were hungry then, too, and my mother knew we were.

Lace

"**This is how to find your true love: Sleep with a mirror right underneath your pillow for three nights, the third a Friday, and you will dream of the man you will marry on that third night.**" There are many years yet before my girls will marry, but just the same, one hour each week they embroider pillowcases, learn to crochet doilies that will later turn into tablecloths, knit baby booties for babies that will come. We sit in the front room, the crib shoved to the corner and the blankets folded off the couch where Joane sleeps, and none of them complains about the bent-over work that is so hard on the neck; none asks why; no one reminds me there are no boys stealing kisses, no boys wanting to marry them and take them away from this house. Their fingers simply guide the needles in and out as I direct, leaving trails of red roses on the pillowcase edges as we talk about neighbors and family, sharing stories that make us laugh so hard we jab our fingers, drop thimbles and watch them roll across the floor. When the hour is over, there should be something to say, but I don't know what it is.

I wonder, do these girls see that the sheets they sleep on every night, their pillowcases, are edged with the same red roses? When they sit around the table for Sunday dinner, do they finger the lacy tablecloth and whisper to one another, Oh!

My mother told me I couldn't marry anyone until I had at least eight pillowcases, four sets of bedsheets, twelve napkins, three tablecloths, ten feet of bobbin lace, two feather quilts—each more perfect than the others. So I knew what that meant, sitting on the chair with my mother's eyes close on each stitch of my needle, a wedge of sun slanting through the window that grew narrower the more stitches I made, as if my needle and thread were closing it shut. Of the daughters, I was my mother's favorite. My older sisters chattered like chickens in the yard, spinning out long stories with no beginning, no end; but I watched my mother, following her face with my own: when she smiled, I smiled; when one of my sisters' stories was too harsh, my face showed the same frown as my mother's; I nodded her short, firm nod when we approved of what was being said.

My sisters especially liked stories about boys with blue eyes that moved like the sky and hands big as loaves of bread and a voice steady enough to still rabbits. My mother frowned through these stories, so I did, too, even though I liked them and the way my sisters' faces turned soft as they talked.

One afternoon, there were too many stories about these boys who didn't live in the village, who didn't exist, and my mother interrupted, keeping her words underneath the click of her knitting needles: "Marry the man who puts food in your mouth." Her whisper scraped like dead leaves blowing through the dust, harsh and dry, then gone. "That's what love is." None of us knew what to say, so we said nothing, and the look on my mother's face was one I couldn't imitate, sort of happy and sad and confused, like the times she brought a new baby to show us and my father grunted and said, "One more place at the table, eh?"

I heard that whisper of my mother's each time my father came in from the fields, washed his dusty hands and face in silence, prayed long thanks as the food on the table grew cold. My mother

sat very still during his prayers, almost as if she'd stopped breathing, but once he finished, she came to life again, started serving
up potatoes and reaching for sauerkraut and helping the little boys
with their forks and knives. He didn't look at her; he didn't look
anywhere, just at the food on his plate, with nothing to say unless
he wanted more tea.

People told me how beautiful my mother had been as a girl,
how when she walked, men's words dropped away as they turned
their heads to watch her, how they kept on watching where she'd
been as if by staring hard enough, she might come back. I saw
many things in my mother, but never that. Still, that's what people
told me. She could've married anyone, they said, there were so
many who loved her.

When my father was taken from us, struck by lightning, my
mother wouldn't cry—not when they first told her, not when the
priest spoke over my father's casket, not when she walked away
from the grave. Not until Sunday dinner when my oldest brother
Stefan gave thanks. His voice stayed loud and clear, rising above
her thumping sobs, and after we murmured "Amen," there was a
long moment, so we looked at her, not sure what to do next, what
we could say. She must've felt us staring at her, because she took
her hands from her eyes and said, "Eat, that's what it's there for,"
and that was the last time I saw her cry.

After my sisters found their husbands, it was my turn. I married
a good, strong man who didn't drink more than most; he married
me because I was a good, strong woman with "eyes like the sun
shining through them." Everyone called it a good match, and after
the wedding, my brothers brought over my trunk packed with my
sheets and tablecloths, and as I spread the sheets on the bed while
my new husband finished the chores in the barn, I heard my
mother's whisper. Maybe there was a different way to love a man,
but I didn't know what it was.

There are nights when I dream of my true love—a tall, bold
man with the biggest farm in Poland. His barn is filled with hay

and horses and their sweaty sweetness. My true love looks at me with eyes that move like the blue sky and holds me with hands as big as loaves of bread; when he walks, men and women turn to watch him pass, but his voice is soft enough to still rabbits and to reach its way deep into my heart. I wake from these dreams, my husband's snores rising gentle against the early-morning light, and this is better. This is good, and it's time to start breakfast, coffee first for me, alone in the kitchen before they come, then the food for them: bacon and eggs and oatmeal. The smell wakes the children and my husband. The smell moving through the house brings them to me. At breakfast our prayers are silent, but always there, and I know what it is I don't ever see in the dream about my true love—a house, beds, pillows, the table set nice for Sunday dinner.

Weeks follow weeks and I watch the children as we sit and sew. Pillowcases are as remote to them as Poland and the memory of my mother feels to me. But soon enough the men will come—a store owner, a foreman, a baker, a doctor maybe (why not, since it's a dream to myself?)—and one by one my children will leave me, and what will they take with them? Eight pillowcases, four sets of bedsheets, twelve napkins, three tablecloths, ten feet of bobbin lace, two feather quilts—all perfect.

February

"Potatoes will bake in half the time when you boil them first for five minutes." Such a good thing to know in July, when the kitchen is hot enough you think Hell's got you by the throat, and sweat coats your body like something stiff you long to peel off. Someone brought bushels of cherries as a favor from a farm outside Detroit, but you don't see fruit the way others do; you see kettles of boiling water billowing into clouds of steam and globs of shimmering fruit melting down into preserves—jar after jar after jar, all labeled and dated, lined up in rows on a shelf in your pantry in the basement, the jars squeezed tight together and pushed to the back to save room for what's coming—green beans, tomatoes, sauerkraut, pickles, corn. You're the one who planted the garden with seeds you dried and saved from last year; you watered it through the dry days, tied vines to stakes, picked bugs off thickening stalks and leaves, sprinkled crushed eggshells and coffee grounds into the dirt, and dug out each weed to the root. To reward your work, the garden has given you more vegetables than last year, than the year before—each year is a bigger harvest, or perhaps it only seems that way in the kitchen in the summer.

And then someone with another favor: apples from an orchard, or twelve giant pumpkins, or baskets of grapes for jelly. You fill every jar you've carefully washed and saved (each shattered jar is a scream and a swat at the child who broke it), and every summer you have to buy a couple dozen more jars, and you think, So I'm set for next year, but when it's next year, still not enough jars, the big box of lids never enough either.

The girls help as girls can, mostly stirring and peeling and cutting and pitting and shucking, but there's always one moment, no matter all you do to avoid it, and in that moment there you are, alone in the kitchen, and all you see are the splatters and stains you'll have all winter to scrub out, and the clock saying it's time for supper, and only you know there is no supper because you've forgotten about it, and every dishrag in the house is soaked through so you'll be doing one last load of laundry tonight, standing in the dark to pin the towels on the line where they'll dry overnight to get soaked again the next day, and this is the moment: you standing there, in your kitchen, all alone, and what you think is, Why isn't there something more than this? But it's gone as soon as you think it because now it's time to get supper, and cold food isn't a real supper, so you grab some potatoes and turn on the oven and fill a pot with water and start supper, because you know that once you do that, there isn't room for anything else except thinking ahead to February, how you'll open a jar of beans, the dull pop of the seal breaking, the way the beans look in the bowl with the pink roses painted along the rim as you place it in the center of the table and call out, Supper! and how your family passes the bowl around the table, dishing a couple spoonfuls onto their plates as if there's nothing to it, as if this is how it's always supposed to be, green beans in February and pork chops and sauerkraut and baked potatoes with butter melting deep into them, and yes, I suppose that is how it's always supposed to be.

America

"A mole on the neck means you are very patient." There is a tiny mole in a place I can't see on the back of my neck, but I know it's there because my mother spoke of it often: "Lucky you to be born patient instead of having to learn it like the rest of us." Sometimes I reach behind my neck and touch this mole that makes me patient, maybe when the children are crying like hard sheets of noise; or my husband hasn't come home yet and it's payday; or when he tells me not to send the children to collect the coal that's fallen off the train, that it's better to go cold than scavenge in the dark like thieves; or when my neighbor-lady tells me the bedsheets hanging on my line aren't as bright-white clean as hers—that's when I reach behind my neck and touch the mole that has promised me patience.

Marie asks, "Why does a mole make you patient?" The mole on her chin means she will have many wonderful friends in her life-time—already all the girls in the neighborhood tell their secrets only to her.

"It just does," I answer.

"If I touch it will I be patient, too, Ma?" Helen asks, reaching for my neck, her fingers cool and sticky on my skin.

"Am I patient now?" she asks. "Am I?"

"I don't know, are you?"

She nods, but only a moment later she's in the kitchen, turning up the flame under the bacon, burning it crisp, the way no one in the family likes it.

"It's just a mole," my husband says when he finds me angling a hand mirror at the bureau mirror so I can see the back of my neck. "In this country a mole is nothing but a mole." Then he kisses it, and maybe he's remembering the long boat ride, all the clothes we owned in layers on our bodies, how the waves pounded the thoughts out of our heads; walking up the stairs on Ellis Island, praying the doctor wouldn't yank one of us aside, praying there'd be no one with a hand out for money, praying so hard we couldn't remember to breathe; where and how we lived when we got here and how his brother hadn't all the way told the truth about America in the letters home; studying English together, the words a jumble that didn't fit in our mouths—the many things we had to do, and how and where I was able to find patience where there was none.

Yes, it's just a mole, a blemish that happens to be on my neck and not my cheek (contentment), not my temple (happiness in love), not my nose (business success). "Better to have it than not," I tell my husband. His face is perfect and smooth; he can't understand, but he smiles as if he does.

Now my daughters chatter in English, words roving too far past me, leaving for me only the smiles on their faces, the laughs that go longer in English than Polish. I was the one who came to this country, who wanted American children, but there's no way to tell them that. Instead, it's me telling my daughters how we do things in the old country; they do what I ask, but their eyes already say, This is America.

All the women like me—the women at daily Mass, the women who set the *Wigilia* table on Christmas Eve, who take the basket of food to be blessed by the priest Saturday afternoon before Easter, who greet each other with *dzien dobry ci*, not that chirpy-bird "hi"—we tell each other how much better it is here in America. We talk about the new country while sitting on our front steps as the heat melts off summer nights, over shared laundry lines, when we're adding up the cost of what we want at the market, then adjusting down to what we need, at the union picnic every September. We know how good this is, here, now, and how one day it will be even better for our children, and their children, and this is why we came, we remind each other—when the baby's sick, when there's a strike, when a brother loses his arm on the factory line, when the tax notice comes but the money went for food—we tell ourselves that everything we do is for our children. We came to this country with nothing, we tell ourselves. Our two hands, one says. Strong backs, says another. Only what God gave us, someone says, and the voices of the women bend and curve like something in the distance, and I find my fingers touching the back of my neck.

I Want You to Have This Now

They visited this afternoon, sitting in the two chairs against the wall. They looked at each other, out the window, at the TV—anywhere but at me.

"Is there something we should bring you from the house?" my daughter asked. "Anything you need?"

My granddaughter said, "Anything you want?"

Leftover seed packets: tomato, squash, pole beans, radish, carrot. Three bowling trophies from the Friday Night Ladies' League. Rosary from Poland in my Sunday purse. Envelope of sand sent from Lake Michigan. Braided dried palm fronds. That picture of eight-year-old Amy riding a horse, looking like she's king of the world, waving straight at the camera.

"Why does Grandma have plastic wrapped all over everything anyway?" I asked. My mother and I were in Detroit, at my grandmother's house. I touched a lamp shade covered in crinkly cellophane.

My mother shook her head, looked at the glass of red Kool-Aid sweating in her hand.

I pulled aside the corner of a white sheet and looked at the sofa underneath. It was yellow-gold, soft like the color of a cat, and I don't think I'd ever seen the fabric before; it wasn't until a few years ago when I turned twelve that I was allowed to sit on the sofa in spite of the sheet covering it, in spite of the towels spread along the back of the sofa on top of the sheet.

"Everyone in the neighborhood did this," my mother said. "Whenever you got a new piece of furniture. Everyone in the family, too. You wanted to keep it looking nice as long as you could."

Sandy, the real estate agent my mother was interviewing, looked up from her clipboard and said, "Nowadays we just Scotchguard everything and replace it in three years."

"We got this sofa when I was ten years old," my mother said. "We all went to the big Hudson's department store downtown to pick it out. Furniture was all the way up on the twelfth floor, and I remember holding my mother's hand as I rode up the escalators. I couldn't believe the stairs were moving underneath me. The old sofa we gave to Aunt Marie. Her daughter-in-law has it—re-covered now in a floral print, but I bet that's the same one. Did you notice it when we were over there the other day, Amy?"

I nodded, but one sofa was the same as the next to me.

My mother said, "I wasn't allowed to touch this sofa," and she pulled back a corner of the sheet and brushed her fingers along the fabric, catching against it with a ragged fingernail.

Sandy said, "Of course we'll clear away all this plastic when we show the house, right? Maybe hang some brighter drapes? Freshen up the paint? This house will move in a couple weeks, I'm almost certain. People are always looking for original-owner houses. And this one's in excellent condition." She nodded again and again, each bob up and down like a hammer hitting a nail head-on.

I watched my mother press the glass of Kool-Aid to her forehead, roll it from side to side. It was hot in Detroit—and no air-conditioning except a small window unit in the back bedroom where my grandmother used to sleep. I took long, cool showers

every night and tried to fall asleep before my hair dried. Sometimes my mother did that, but most nights she stayed up late;
often I woke and heard her walking through the dark house, and
even with no lights on, I never heard her bump into anything.
But if she was back to drinking, I couldn't tell because she never
looked tired the next morning and never wore her dark glasses in
the house.

"So, what do you think?" Sandy asked. Her voice was bright
like the flame off a match.

The clock on the mantel chimed the hour, taking a long time
to get to four o'clock. We all stared at it.

My mother said, "I'll call you," and closed her eyes, didn't open
them until Sandy was out the door and down the front walk.
Through the open window we heard her high heels tap the sidewalk, her car door open and slam shut, her car driving away.

"Did you like her?" I asked.

My mother shook her head.

Sandy was the eleventh real estate agent that had been by since
we'd come up from Arizona to move my grandmother to a nursing home.

"What's wrong with her?"

"If a woman's going to dye her hair, at least she should make
sure her roots don't show," she said.

"Mom, do you know what you sound like?"

"Yes," my mother said. "A child."

What about me, I wanted to say. I'm the one who should be
spending the summer at an internship or doing volunteer work—
something that looks good on a college application. Not this. "You
have to choose someone," I said.

She closed her eyes again and didn't say anything.

"You're looking good," my daughter said. "You look like a million bucks."
But she got mad when I called her Theresa. "I'm Ginger," she said. It's

hard to remember. "Can we bring you anything?" she asked before leaving. "Need anything?"

Cracked picture frame John never got around to fixing. Postcard of the Grand Canyon. Jade plant more than twenty-five years old. Wooden bowl for bread dough. Cigar box where we put the money to give each week to the life insurance man. Ginger's pink and white baby blanket, torn in one corner. Hat I bought from Crowley's with my first paycheck—looks like an upside-down bowl of cherries, my sister told me. Champagne cork. A pair of white gloves that button to the elbow wrapped in tissue—never worn.

It was too hot to cook, so my mother and I went out to dinner every night. My mother let me drive, and I had a hard time following her mumbled, half-remembered directions to restaurants that weren't where she thought they'd be. She liked eating at fast, simple places that were clean and well-lit: coney dogs, BBQ ribs, pizza, gyros, hamburgers. Places without liquor licenses. Our favorite was the coney dog place, the one with the white tile walls and the big street-front windows steamed white from the icy blasts of air-conditioning and damp hot dog air. We sat at long tables like children at a school cafeteria, gave our order to a Lebanese man wearing a paper cap: coney dogs, extra onions, fries, Vernors ginger ale. There were no salads at this place, no vegetables, no milk. The only dessert was a Detroit Cooler—a huge scoop of vanilla ice cream floating in a glass of Vernors. Someone was always mopping the floor at this place or scrubbing down the counters with a handful of steel wool the size of a cabbage.

That night after ordering, I said, "Sandy's in the million-dollar club," and I put her brochure on the table.

My mother sipped ginger ale through a straw. "What about her hair?" she asked.

"Her hair doesn't matter." I looked away. Behind the counter someone dumped frozen French fries into the fryer, and the hot grease hissed.

"I don't know what's wrong with me," my mother said.

I waited, thought how I'd never been to this kind of place with my mother in Phoenix. Thought how my mother never ate food like this in Phoenix or even knew how to find it there.

My mother said, "That stupid house. The toilet ran over all the time. That creepy basement with the clotheslines twisted around for drying laundry in the winter, spiders falling off the ceiling. Furniture you couldn't sit on, dishes you couldn't use. All that junk she wouldn't throw away."

"It's where you grew up," I said.

"My whole life, all I wanted was to get away from that house," my mother said.

We got our coney dogs and fries at the same time the kid mopping the floor reached our section, so we ate with our feet propped up on the chair rungs as the kid mopped underneath us. The water smelled faintly of pine; the fries were just out of the fry basket, perfectly salted and crisp. Chili sauce dripped off the coney dogs as we ate, and there was no skimping on the onions. Even the ice in the ginger ale was just right—chips, not cubes.

No one should talk, no one should move. Even the floor should stay as it is, streaky from where the mop's been.

My mother wiped her mouth with a napkin. "I'll call Sandy tomorrow," she said. She pushed aside her fries, dropped her crumpled napkin on top of what remained of her coney dog.

They brought me flowers, an expensive arrangement with nine roses, more money than I would think to spend on flowers that are dead. But the vase is cut glass, something to keep on a dresser.

By the end of this visit, it's them talking to each other. The sun shines through the glass vase.

My daughter turns at the door. "Need anything?"

Home run baseball John caught at Tiger Stadium and the ticket stub. Old diary of Ginger's: "May 10—Why is my mother so old-fashioned? Everyone else wears lipstick now." Bottle of La Noire perfume for special occasions. Ballpoint pen that writes upside down. Matching set of light blue suitcases, never taken out of Detroit. Tiny sheet-metal box Joe made for me on the battleship during the war. That nice set of pink towels I bought on sale at Jacobson's last spring—I was going to send them to Amy when she goes to college next year.

The next day my mother called everyone, all her aunts and uncles, her cousins, her cousins' children, and said if anyone wanted anything from the house they should come over on Sunday and take it.

Sandy stopped by with a contract for my mother to sign. "Give me a ring when you've finished cleaning up," she said. "Then I'll send the camera people over pronto so we can get this house on my weekend TV show."

"We'll be ready on Tuesday," my mother said.

"This Tuesday?" Sandy looked around the room. "I really think— I mean, I recommend to all my clients that they shampoo the carpets and touch up the walls with a little paint, wash the windows, clear away any clutter, fix up the yard with some bedding plants. You know."

"We'll be ready on Tuesday," my mother repeated. "You won't recognize this place."

"Well," and Sandy flipped through her clipboard. "You two certainly have your work cut out for you," and she smiled the exact smile that was on her business card photo.

"Don't worry about us," my mother said. "We're motivated sellers."

"That's the best kind there is," and Sandy smiled again, handing us each a pen with her phone number printed on it before leaving.

"We can't get all that done by Tuesday," I said.

My mother looked out the window, and I looked, too, but there was nothing to see. Finally she said, "Be sure to mark whatever you want from this house so no one takes it."

"There's nothing I want," I said.

"You should take something to remember your grandmother by," she said. "What about the clock?" and she pointed to it on the mantel. "I remember how you stood and watched, waiting for it to go off. You were amazed every time I told you when it was about to chime," and she walked to the clock, picked it up.

"I figured out how to tell when it's about to chime when I was six," I said.

My mother said, "It was a wedding present from her mother. Take the clock, Amy."

I shook my head. "I don't want it."

"Your grandmother would want you to have it." She held it out until I reached for it. The wood was varnished to a buttery smoothness, and it was heavier than I expected. I'd never held it before; it was always on the mantel each summer when we visited, chiming every fifteen minutes, and I'd touched it only once, one afternoon when everyone else was on the front porch. My mother said, "When you look to see what time it is, you'll think of your grandmother. She loved this clock."

"Then maybe you should keep it," and I held it out to her. The second hand swept away a minute, and another, and then the clock chimed the quarter hour, vibrating in my hand like something alive. "Don't you want it?" I asked.

"Nobody has clocks like this in their houses anymore," she said. "All that chiming. You get so tired of it, always knowing that's fifteen more minutes gone by, fifteen minutes you don't have. I hated that clock when I lived in this house." My mother looked around the room, lifted her hair off the back of her neck, let it drop. "Don't let me do this to you, Amy. Don't let me leave you with roomfuls of useless junk like this. A chair covered with towels. A clock that could chime you to death. What's the point?"

The phone rang; my mother answered. "How are you?" she said. "By all means come on over. There's tons of nice furniture, and Mom will feel better knowing family's enjoying it instead of strangers. Whatever's left I'm donating to St. Vincent de Paul. I'm sure that's what she'd want. Three-thirty sounds good. See you then," and she hung up. "Flock of vultures," she muttered, but when she saw me looking at her, she smiled. "This is what Grandma would want," she said. "It's what the family does when someone dies, lets everyone take what they want or need from the house. That way nothing's wasted. I remember Grandma taking plenty of things from other people's houses. That end table, for example, belonged to her uncle Stanislaus."

"Grandma's not dead," I said.

"You don't have to tell me that."

I set the clock on Uncle Stanislaus's end table with the scattered plastic doilies and little ceramic chickens. "All I meant was—"

"I know exactly what you meant," she said. "But everyone's coming over for the furniture and that's that. That's the way it's done. We can't just leave everything here like nothing's changed."

"We could wait until the house is sold," I said. "If it will make you feel better."

"I feel fine," she said. "All I'm worried about is that we don't have enough time. Why'd I tell that woman we'd be ready Tuesday?"

"We can call her," I said.

My mother shook her head. "We've been in Detroit way too long. We'll just work our butts off, that's all. The drive back to Phoenix will seem easy after this, huh?"

"Let me do it," I said.

"Do what?"

"I'll stay here to clean up and take care of everything. You can fly back home. Then I can drive to Phoenix by myself. It will be fun."

"This isn't supposed to be fun," she said.

The mail dropped through the slot in the door. Every day it was less and less as my grandmother was taken off mailing lists and subscription cancellations were finalized. My mother went to the entryway and brought back the mail, which she tossed on the sofa near me: supermarket advertising circulars, a coupon for pizza, a shoe catalog, and a card from a photography studio confirming an appointment next week.

"I'll call and cancel that," I said.

My mother said, "I don't know why you think I can't handle this. I'm an adult woman." She yanked the towels off the easy chair where my grandmother used to sit and knit in the evenings. The exposed chair looked naked, and my mother dropped the towels so they fell in a little pile on the chair. She said, "Let's start with the basement; what do you think?"

I nodded, and I would've put the towels back, but she waited for me to go downstairs first.

They were supposed to visit today; instead it was a phone call. "We'll be by next week," my daughter said. "Maybe sooner. Promise."

This is how it begins.

In the basement pantry: Two cases of Faygo Redpop, what Amy asked for, and Rock 'n' Rye for her brother. Beans—string, wax, kidney, green. A shopping bag full of other shopping bags—Crowley's, Jacobson's, Kroger, Hudson's, Penney's. A box of used birthday candles. Kool-Aid: grape, cherry, strawberry, seven packs for a dollar. Three jars of applesauce. A ten-pound sack of potatoes, three-quarters gone. Christmas candy—half price in January. Onions. Spam (John was the only one who'd eat it). Hershey's chocolate syrup. Birdseed. A jar of caviar from a gourmet store Ginger found downtown in the Renaissance Center. Graham crackers. Flour. Six packets of yeast. A bottle of vodka in the back I wasn't supposed to know about.

I woke up because I'd been dreaming about my grandmother, and I thought I'd heard her downstairs, singing that Polish lullaby she sang when I couldn't sleep.

I looked at my watch; it was just about three in the morning, and I flipped my pillow over hoping for a cool spot. My body ached from hauling boxes all day, moving old bedsheets and towels and *Family Circles* and half-used balls of yarn and blankets and baby clothes and board games no one had played with for years and packets of Burpee seeds dated 1974 and tulip bulbs and cases of empty Faygo soda bottles waiting to go back to the store for the deposit and all the rest of the stuff down in the basement. "Can you believe all this crap?" my mother kept saying. "Who would save all this stuff? Baby clothes? For pity's sake, I'm the baby, that's how old this stuff is!"

I flipped my pillow again. Neither of us would sleep in my grandmother's air-conditioned bedroom downstairs; even the night after we moved her out, we both went to our beds in the attic, mine in the dormer, hers a double bed across the room (although my father had visited only once when he and my mother were married). My brother's bed in the corner remained empty—he was with our father on a river-rafting trip in Colorado where they were supposed to bond.

A breeze whispered at my face through the open window. I sat up, looked at my watch again: 3:05. The clock downstairs hadn't chimed for three o'clock—unless I'd missed it. But you just didn't miss it.

My mother's bed was empty, and I heard a cupboard shut downstairs. She did this even at home, just got up and started walking through the house. When I was little, I'd wake up and see her face looking over me as she stood at the end of my bed.

"Mom?" I called, walking down the stairs. "Are you all right?"

One lamp was on in the living room, and the cellophane-wrapped shade glowed like the heart of a candle; shadows twitched along the sheeted furniture as headlights from outside spun in. It looked like no one had lived in this room for a very long time.

My mother called from the kitchen: "Thirsty?" Her voice was cheerful, hostessy. She was drinking. I started back up the stairs, but a floorboard creaked, and she called, "Amy, don't leave!"

I said, "You know what I think about your drinking."

She came to the stairs, reached her hand out to me. "I had one little drink," she said. "I swear that's all. It's Kool-Aid for me from here on out." She showed me the glass of grape Kool-Aid she held in her hand. "Taste if you don't believe me." When I reached for it, she snatched it back. "You don't trust your own mother?"

"I'm going back to bed," I said.

"I'm kidding," she said. "Here," and she walked up to where I was and put the glass in my hand.

I gave it back. "Whatever you say."

She laughed too long, too loud, but I let her pick up my hand and lead me downstairs. She yanked the sheet off the sofa like a magician, said, "Voila," and giggled as she sat down, scooting deep into the couch. I sat next to her, perched on the edge.

"Where's the clock?" I asked. It wasn't on the mantel or on the end table where I'd left it.

"That stupid thing," she said. "Aunt Joane wants it, so I packed it up for her. Someone should have it."

"I just don't want it," I said. "I don't want anything from this house."

"What would your grandmother say if she knew you refused to take anything to remember her by?" She rubbed her fingers along the couch.

"Why do I need a thing to help me remember?"

"Next time we go over, tell her you took something. That will make her happy."

"I'm not going to lie," I said.

"Then I'll tell her," she said.

"No."

"All anyone wants when they're about to die is to think they're going to be remembered," she said.

"What will you tell her *you* took?"

"There's other stuff you could take." She waved her arm, pointing at things in the room. "Those porcelain figurines. The picture of that waterfall. Ceramic chickens. The mirror and brush set in the bedroom. That African violet."

"What will you take?"

"We're talking about you, not me." She took several quick sips of her Kool-Aid.

"I'm going back to bed," I said.

"You wouldn't be so snotty to me if you knew what I'm going to tell you." Her voice slopped over its edges. "Please don't leave me alone right now." My mother held on to my arm. Her fingers looked awkward, like dry sticks.

When she drank, she overflowed with confessions and revelations, apologies and explanations. None of it lasted through the next morning's headache. But I said, "Tell me what?" It was why I'd come, wasn't it, to take care of her?

She said, "Just a sec," went into the kitchen and came back with a full glass, no ice. "Putting her in the nursing home was the hardest thing I've ever done," she said. "Harder than leaving home." She sat down next to me.

"It was the right thing to do," I said.

"What do you know about it?"

"She couldn't take care of herself," I said. "You had no other choice."

"Susan moved back from Lansing to take care of Uncle Joe."

I said, "No one expects you to do that."

She started to cry, long tears that stretched the length of her face. Without the clock, it was impossible to know what time it was; without the chimes moving us forward, I felt trapped in this moment. My mother said, "She told me it meant I didn't love her. You went into the bathroom and she said it. I couldn't breathe, and she said it again. And then you came back."

I remembered that moment, my mother standing with her hand on the wall, my grandmother turned to look out the window, someone saying, "Well, look how late it is," glancing at my watch, a nurse wheeling in a cart of food trays.

I said, "Grandma didn't mean it."

Then I said, "She knows you love her."

My mother wiped her nose with the back of her hand. "I hated living here. I left as soon as I could. For all the family around and all the talking they did, no one ever talked about whether I was pretty or good or nice or anything. Just Ginger, don't wear that dress with your blonde hair; Ginger, is that lipstick you've got on; Ginger, we didn't see you at Mass on Sunday. I hated the sound of my own name because always right after it was something I was doing wrong. It never stopped: Ginger, you're pregnant, don't sit in the sun. Ginger, why do you live so far from your home and family? Ginger, what did you do to make your husband leave you?" A clump of sweaty hair stuck to her forehead, edged into her eyes; she didn't blink or push it away.

"Maybe that's how she showed that she loves you," I said.

"Why do you think you always have the answer!" she cried. "I didn't like her, and she didn't like me. That's the answer. That's what it is. How can you live knowing you don't like your own mother?"

I looked away. "You're drunk, Mom. You won't even remember this in the morning."

"Is that what you think?" In the shadows, the curves of her face looked carved out of wood.

I said, "Yes," set my face just as hard as hers.

"I'll remember," and she tilted what was left of her grape Kool-Aid so it poured onto the sofa cushion. "I'll see this big ugly stain tomorrow, and I'll remember everything."

I jumped up and ran to the kitchen for a sponge, but when I got back, my mother had slid over so she was sitting on top of the stain.

"I want to remember," she said. "This, I want to remember."

I stood with the wet sponge in my hand, water dripping onto the plastic walkway on the carpet, and watched my mother cry.

When I looked a the picture they gave me, I couldn't tell them apart. "Who is this?" I asked the nurses. "Who is that?" They smiled, made up answers.

Doilies my sisters and I made for our hope chests, filling idle moments with lace—they sold theirs, I saved mine, if not for me, then for my daughter, her daughter, a daughter somewhere along the way who would unwrap the tissue and find my doilies. A set of dishes for eight we collected from buying gas at the station on the corner—plates, coffee cups and saucers, bowls, dessert plates; too pretty to use, so I saved them, still in the original boxes, still taped shut. Invitation from Joe's wedding. A pen they gave me free at my bank. Fur-lined gloves Ginger gave me five Christmases ago—supposed to keep my hands extra-warm, she said; they were so soft inside; I used to pull them out of the box and stroke the insides, even in the summer. But in the winter I thought of rabbits hopping through a field, and I couldn't wear them.

The clock on the mantel. I could add up how much time passed me by counting every chime I ever heard.

I explained to everyone that my mother had a headache, was upset, was sick, was napping—any story that felt believable. I expected questions, challenges—sick how? napping since when? upset why? But my mother's aunts and uncles and cousins and cousins' children all nodded, looked grave; the women murmured "Poor dear," and touched my arm with their soft hands, making me think for just one moment they meant me, that I was the "poor dear." It wouldn't be so bad, would it, growing up with this kind of family?

But then they turned their attention to what they'd come for: to take the things they wanted from the house.

They took the chairs and the dining room table and the little table in the kitchen and the never-before-used towels and sheets and the canned food from the pantry downstairs and the TV set and the bed my brother slept in upstairs and the sewing machine and the toaster and the silverware. Someone promised to come by later with a truck for the china cupboard and someone else took the dishes. They ripped the cellophane off the lamp shades and took the lamps; they took the stationery out of the desk drawers and they took the desk and the chair. Someone with a baby girl took the mixer and all the cookie cutters. "Can I have this?" I heard a thousand times, "are you sure you don't mind?" "Yes, you can have it; no, I don't mind," I said, whatever it was. Take it, take it. Take it all away. What did they mean, anyway, all these things?

My mother stayed in my grandmother's room, door shut. Standing in the hall, I heard nothing, just the rumble of the air-conditioner.

"Take it—It's yours—She'd want you to have it—Enjoy it": there were a hundred ways to say "get it out." A neighbor came by, and I let her load up all the houseplants in a red wagon and wheel them three doors down. "I've got the perfect place for them," she said. "Very sunny, protected from breezes." She waited for me to approve, and I nodded. She didn't move, so I added, "She'd want you to have them."

It was still hot, and I was running around getting drinks for everyone, using paper cups after someone wrapped the glasses in newspaper to take. My responses were automatic, a chain link of words: "Take it—It's yours—She'd want you to have it—Enjoy it," but when someone's daughter asked, "Has anyone said they want the sofa?" I said, "Yes. It'll be picked up later."

She said, "I just asked because it would look nice in my new family room. My curtains are gold and blue and tan plaid."

I was in the kitchen mixing a pitcher of orange Kool-Aid, stirring briskly to dissolve the sugar, admiring the depth of the whirlpool my stirring had created.

She kept talking: "It's really a nice sofa, in excellent condition. I mean except for that stain in the middle. But I guess that cushion could just be flipped over, right? Who's taking it?"

"I don't remember." I stirred faster.

She said, "Maybe I could call just to make sure they really, really want it. I mean, it will match those curtains so perfectly. Maybe if they knew about my curtains, they wouldn't want it."

I stopped stirring, watched the whirlpool in the pitcher slow and finally disappear. I said, "I'm really sorry."

"I should've come by earlier," she said. "I wanted to, but I had a roast in the oven."

I poured out a paper cup of Kool-Aid and handed it to her. "I know she would've wanted you to have the sofa," I said before walking into the other room with my pitcher of Kool-Aid and stack of paper cups.

The last people left at ten that night, taking with them a box of magazines, a magazine rack, a roasting pan, the kitchen stool, a shopping bag full of yarn, and two throw pillows.

I thought the suddenly bare rooms would turn the house into a different place, but it was still my grandmother's house, even without her things. There was a smell, a look, a feel. My grandmother would always be here, no matter who lived in the house or what kind of furniture there was or where her ceramic chickens or her clock ended up. So why did everyone need those things?

I tapped gently on the door of my grandmother's bedroom, said, "Mom? Want to go get a coney dog? Everyone's gone."

My mother didn't answer, so I opened the door a crack and peeked inside. She was sprawled on her stomach across the bed, her feet hanging over the edge, a tiny bedside lamp cast enough light so I could watch her body move up and down as she breathed, silent and peaceful as a child.

I tiptoed in and turned off the lamp; the slight snapping woke her up. "What?" she said.

"Shh." Moonlight came through the window, put a bluish tinge on the furniture promised to family members, on my mother. The air conditioner hummed steadily, yet the room felt silent.

I stepped back to the door, but she said, "Wait," and she rolled over, patted the bed.

I sat down.

"You've been so good about all this," she said. "I don't know what I'd do without you."

"I'm sure you'd manage," I said.

"No, I'm really glad you're here," she said. "I couldn't have done any of this without you. Look at me. I fell apart. I simply fell apart." She said it like I could look around and see the pieces.

"Well, most of the stuff's gone. So the rest should be just a matter of cleaning up. I called Sandy and told her to give us a few more days."

"Wonderful," my mother said. "What a good job you've done. I'm very proud of you. So who all came by today?"

I told her the people I recognized, the names I remembered.

Then she asked me who took what, and I told her what I remembered of that, and she made comments like "Figures," and "Mom would die if she knew he got that," and "That's exactly who she'd pick to give that to."

When I couldn't think of anything else, I said, "And no one took the sofa."

"That ugly thing," she said. "How're we going to get rid of that? Those St. Vincent de Paul people said there's a three-week wait to get large items picked up."

The air conditioner shifted itself into a lower speed.

"What about—" and then I didn't say anything else.

"What about what?" She stood up, yanked open a window, pushed up the screen, and stuck her head through.

It seemed to be a long time before either of us spoke again. She pulled her head back in the room, said, "How about dinner? I'm starving, aren't you?"

It was so simple to nod.

We went for coney dogs. It was the same Lebanese man who waited on us the last time we were there. "Yes, good evening, ladies," he said. "I remember you. Two coneys, extra onions, French fries, Vernors. Right?"

We smiled at him, nodded, and ate the food he brought us. We didn't talk much, but people around us were talking and mopping and scrubbing, and the steam was thick on the windows.

As she was paying the bill, my mother slipped a book of

matches into her purse. She didn't see that I saw her. Then on my way out, I took one for myself.

I was living in Thailand, teaching English to children, when Aunt Joane died. I asked for the clock back. I told them to send it insured, that whatever the shipping cost was, I'd pay it. It didn't end up being as much as I expected, and they'd wrapped it for me very carefully.

Farang

AMY — 1 9 8 7

In Thailand, I thought everything was faraway. Letters took weeks, months to arrive. It could be some never even got to me.

I was halfway around the world. I imagined a globe with something long and thin and very sharp skewering Phoenix and through the heart of the earth straight on to Bangkok, trying, trying to jab me. But it couldn't reach. I thought nothing could reach.

I liked standing in Buddhist temples and amid temple ruins to feel silence, to feel thousands of years of impossible questions without answers. There, the world I knew dissolved like something you mean to keep but can't—snow, the sand under a wave, all the minutes in a day.

In Thailand, I didn't fit in with my blonde hair, my height, my light eyes that were round therefore unattractive, my English words. I was the teacher, I was the Westerner—the *farang*—I was always the person from somewhere else, the person from far away.

I used to think that there wouldn't be one moment when I decided to leave home, to really leave; I used to think the decision would be many moments jumbling like a kaleidoscope, but I was wrong; there *was* one moment: I was trying to steer my mother into her bedroom, but she wouldn't let go of her gin bottle; she was waving it like a club, nearly whacking my head a couple times, and finally I managed to grab hold of both her wrists, all the while murmuring I don't know what in that soothing voice I used on the cat in the vet's office, but she yanked herself free and said tightly, "Amy, if I were you—" and I interrupted: "Well, you're not me, you're not!" and there was a moment of her looking at me, me staring back; then she said—same tight voice: "How do you know?" I let go of her; she dropped the bottle, and it shattered on the kitchen floor—a mess of green glass and that same-as-always wretched gin-stink I couldn't escape—and my mother collapsed down into it all, so there was blood and green glass and that stench and both of us crying and the cold tile kitchen floor. In the emergency room, I filled out all the paperwork, carefully printing her name again and again. That was the moment.

I liked taking trips to see the country. Any breaks we teachers would get, I'd go somewhere, anywhere, just to see something new: the beaches of Ko Samet, the annual elephant round-up in Surin, the old capital of Ayutthaya with its ruined temples and castles. When there wasn't enough time for a real trip, I'd go somewhere new in Bangkok: the Temple of Dawn, the *klongs*— river streets—of Thon Buri, a market. I had a long list of all the places I wanted to see that I used as a marker in my guidebook, and I was always scribbling one more thing onto it until my writing filled both sides of that scrap of paper.

So with a vacation coming up, I read my list over and over, each place a different vision in my mind, until it was impossible to pick and my mind became as cluttered as the paper. I was trying to explain to the sweet lady who taught me Thai what flipping a coin meant, when she asked very politely in English, "Why keep a list? Just see what you see-*kha*."

I looked down at my workbook so she wouldn't see me smile

at her insistence on perpetually making English more polite than it was by adding *kha* to the end of her sentences. I said, "What if I miss something important?"

"What if?" she said.

"That's why I have a list," I said.

She said, "But this list only tells you what others have seen-*kha*."

"I don't understand," I said in Thai. It was one of the earliest phrases I'd learned, *mai kawjai*, repeating it over and over that first lesson, the words fluttery like birds. That was the day my teacher told me I'd be a good student of Thai because I was so eager to learn.

My teacher said, "Look for things not in your book. When you shut the book cover, when you travel away from what is written on your list—only then you will know why you came here."

All I wanted was a vacation, to go somewhere I hadn't been, somewhere farther than Bangkok, but I just nodded, said in Thai, "Thank you, teacher," and smiled. A smile was about as good as cash in Thailand and could ease any situation. "But I know why I came here," I continued in English. "To see sights. To learn about Thailand. To get experiences I can talk about back home." She looked down at her fingers on the table. I added, "To see the world."

"There are many reasons for leaving," she said, almost a whisper. I leaned closer. "Some we understand, some we don't-*kha*."

It sounded wise. Or maybe when you were far from home about anything could sound wise.

I decided to go to the north, to Nan Province, to see the mountains, the hill tribes, remote villages. It was a place regular tourists didn't often go. I wrote it on my list so I could cross it off later, even though that felt like cheating. When I told my teacher where I was going, she nodded. I wanted her to be impressed, but all she said was, "A beautiful place, many notable temple ruins. Wat Phra Thep is the most beautiful, with paintings of Singha lions, swans, Nagas. And the most famous painting of Kala." She watched me write down the name of the temple, then she added, "My family is in Nan Province," and I kept my pencil ready because I thought she'd give me a name, a village, but it was as if she hadn't realized she'd spoken those words out loud, and she said, "Be careful, Amy-*kha*," what your mother is supposed to say when you go far away.

I made a list of all the things I wanted to see on my trip: Wat Phra Thep and the paintings of Kala, a trek to a hill tribe village, the city of Nan—all things mentioned in my guidebook. So at the bottom of my list, I wrote "opium poppy fields" with a question mark. This was not in my book because tourists were not supposed to think about the opium and heroin trade in Thailand just as they were not supposed to think about the AIDS epidemic raging through the little girl prostitutes or where the beggars in the streets went at night. But once I'd sat next to an American man at a hotel bar in Bangkok who liked to hear himself tell stories about how he'd backpacked all throughout Southeast Asia before getting his job with IBM. One story was seeing the poppy fields in bloom in the mountains in the north. "Incredibly beautiful," he'd said, "the wind catching all those red flowers and rippling them like waves. Then I turned around to see ten guys pointing machine guns at me, happy to escort me back down the mountain. Not the typical friendly Thais, if you know what I mean. I tell you, you really learn something about the kind of person you are when you've got a gun at your back." He offered to buy me another drink and was surprised that I was drinking plain Sprite. He was even more surprised when I didn't invite him back with me at the end of the night. "So why're you hanging out in bars?" he asked. "What're you looking for, sister?" But he wasn't the kind who waited for an answer.

I didn't show this second list to my teacher or to anyone.

When I told the headmaster I was taking a trip over our break, he didn't ask where I was going. Instead he told me that when I returned I would have to let the school know if I planned to teach for a second year, that he was trying to get teaching staff organized, that I'd pushed my decision as far as I could. He spoke politely and smiled the whole time as if it didn't really matter, the typical easy-going Thai way that still surprised me. But I didn't know what to say. I'd come here thinking one year, but there were still so many things I hadn't seen.

"You are a good teacher," he said. "Students and parents like you."

I smiled, thanked him.

"But of course your family is far away, and you're here alone," he said, his smooth forehead creasing with lines of worry. "So to decide cannot be easy."

I smiled again, nodded, my face suddenly stiff like a mask. I said, "No, it's not easy." What was easy was letting time move from school day into night and back, never thinking about how many days were ahead because everything was far away in Thailand. My letters and notes from the States usually came in a clump, several days worth of mail arriving all at once, and I read the letters like that, all at once, and the letters from my friends were interesting, gossipy, funny, thoughtful, and the letters from my mother seemed the same way, but I lingered longer over them, rereading them, hoping to find that thing that wasn't there—the "I miss you," the "hurry home," the "I need you," the "please come back"—that simple thing I couldn't ever quite find.

The headmaster smiled at me. I smiled back. In Thailand I could simply smile at problems that didn't have solutions and that was considered solution enough.

I liked the province, liked what I was seeing. People were very friendly, chatting with me on the buses I rode, in the villages showing off to me their one or two words of English. My teacher had told me where her family lived, so I stayed one night with them in their village where I showed photos I'd taken in Bangkok and postcards I'd brought from the States. My teacher's mother unfolded a page ripped off an old calendar with a date circled— after many hand signs and some stuttered Thai, I figured out it was the day my teacher left home for Bangkok. In the city of Nan, I bought an armful of chunky silver bracelets from a sweet woman who invited me to have dinner with her; every time I told people I was an English teacher in Bangkok, they brought over their children who were taking English lessons so they could practice with me. Then I trekked into the hills for a week with a guide and took ten rolls of film of one of the most remote hill tribes. Just being away from the noise and confusion of Bangkok was a pleasure, and I filled pages of my journal with all the things I wanted to remember, the stories I would tell people back in Bangkok, back in the States.

Then I rode another bus north, getting close to the border of Laos, eating crackers so I wouldn't get sick on the mountainous ride, watching rice fields pass and burned patches that used to be forests about to become farms. There was a village to see, the temple with the murals my teacher had mentioned, and maybe even the border itself. I hadn't spoken English for at least a week, and my dreams at night were taken over by the things I'd seen during the day, the strange dialects I'd heard but couldn't understand. No letters, no decisions, no one to take care of. This was exactly why I'd come to Thailand, to find this faraway place. But there was no one to explain this to when I arrived at the village, just smiles from the friendly owner of the guest house when I chatted in Thai about the food, the weather, the school I taught at in Bangkok; smiles from his wife and three children.

The next morning my mouth ached from so much smiling. The guest house owner had told me his brother had two motorcycles that he rented out, so my plan was to rent one and tour the countryside better, find the temple ruins my teacher had mentioned. Maybe I'd end up looking across the border at Laos.

Even after much haggling and smiling, the brother insisted on keeping my passport as insurance I'd return with his bike and battered helmet. Back by sundown, we agreed, which seemed like a long time away, and after two seconds of instruction about shifting gears, I put on my sunglasses and was ready to go.

Even though the Thai bus system was decent, it felt great to be driving, to be in control. On certain nights back in Phoenix things would cram in close, and the only way out was to drive my car too fast along the straight roads cutting across the city, watching numbers tick by on the street signs: starting at 55th Street near my mother's house, the street numbers lowering one by one as I drove west until I reached Central Avenue, where the streets turned into avenues and the numbers started rising. Sometimes it wasn't until 83rd Avenue or so before I'd feel ready to turn around, to reverse the process and go back home. Other people might drive to the empty dark roads of the desert, but I liked seeing the street signs pass, knowing exactly how far I'd gotten. Here, of course, there were no street signs; there were barely even roads, and all I had were verbal directions to the temple from the guest house owner that I may or may not have translated properly with my Thai–English dictionary.

The road was rutted and bumpy, very narrow and twisty, doubling back on itself as it climbed steeply into the mountains. I'd been told that the road would fork three times and that the temple was to the right of the third fork. At least I thought it was the right; when I'd held up my right arm and pointed to verify, the guest house owner had smiled and nodded, then held up his left arm, as if he were my mirror reflection. So when I lifted my left arm and asked in Thai, "Turn left?" he held up his right arm and smiled. So I just nodded, hoping there'd be someone on the way I could ask. But the road was empty.

On and on I went, jiggling with the road, the dry heat pressing tight against me, the drone of the motorcycle like a friend who won't shut up, and the road wasn't branching anymore—in fact, if anything, it was getting less like a road and more like a footpath, barely wider than my motorcycle.

So different than those drives in Phoenix, where I'd be rolling down the driveway with my eyes closed so tight I'd see yellow streaks—not crying, not crying—my mother hanging out the front door, drunk and screaming her usual promises. That was so far away it was like it had never happened. I almost had to think to remember it.

The road widened abruptly, big enough for a car, so maybe I wasn't really as lost as I'd thought. Gravel crunched under my tires and spit up at my ankles. Deep grooves were worn into the road, and fresh patches of gravel filled the ruts, trying to even out the road, and I don't know what happened, but somehow I hit one of those ruts exactly the wrong way and I tried to steer out of it, wrenching the handlebars to yank my bike straight, and I skidded and twisted and fell, the motorcycle sprawling on top of me, suddenly silenced.

I was disoriented, with my face pressed into gravel, my sunglasses shoved sideways up my forehead, and inside my helmet my head felt as if it had been smashed apart, then every last piece stepped on and kicked. My knee was tight under the bike; when I tugged at it pain jagged and echoed in my head. Sun glinted off the dulled chrome and into my eyes, so I closed them for a moment. But when I opened them again, nothing had changed except that I noticed a piece of the motorcycle, a thingamajig that looked important, a short distance away in the road. There was a nagging tickle along my temple, and after pushing aside my broken sunglasses and pulling off my helmet to scratch my head, lots of blood smeared my fingers. I was lucky the sunglasses had only gouged into my skin and not gotten my eye. But I didn't feel especially lucky.

There was nothing here, there was only silence and the trees and the mountain and more mountains far off in the distance. Laos somewhere. Ruins of Wat Phra Thep.

All that silence was suddenly slashed apart by voices that seemed to come at once from behind me and in front of me, male voices chattering in a Thai dialect I couldn't understand, quick clipped words like marching feet, and within moments four men were grouped around me staring at where I lay. They weren't dressed like the typical farmers I'd been seeing in their blue work shirts, and they definitely weren't members of one of the hill tribes; they wore cut-off khaki shorts and sloppy, faded, not-quite-right-English-slogan T-shirts with the sleeves ripped out, and one man wore no shirt at all, and I stared longest at him because it was so unusual to see a Thai man's bare chest—let alone Thai men wearing messy cut-off shorts and ripped shirts. It wasn't right, not for the countryside. They had gotten here so quickly, but they obviously weren't farmers. I didn't understand.

I greeted them in Thai: "Hello," and they all laughed hiding their laughs behind their hands. I was used to this reaction from Thais when I spoke their language. My teacher assured me it wasn't the way I spoke as much as it was the surprise of Thai words coming out of a *farang*'s mouth.

The man with no shirt spoke quickly and quietly to the others, and within moments, one had lifted my motorcycle, another picked up the mysterious piece of machinery off the road, and the third knelt beside me and peered at my bleeding temple, tilting my head this way and that. His fingertips were sticky.

"I am a teacher in Bangkok," I said. I'd practiced that sentence a thousand times with my Thai teacher, along with "I don't understand."

The man looking at my temple glanced at the shirtless man who still stood in the road. I waited for him to speak, but there was nothing, just the other two men jiggling parts of the motorcycle, tapping here and there with their knuckles, one pointing out something, just the third man's sticky fingers on my head. It was too much silence. There was time for me to think how there was no village out here, and there was no reason for these men to be dressed in such an untidy way when most Thais were generally very neat. Time for me to notice how well they communicated without speaking, better than brothers, like they spent a lot of time together.

I spoke again, louder, "I'm a teacher in Bangkok. American," and the man standing in the road, the bare-chested one, nodded, and I felt like I was supposed to know exactly what that nod meant, but I didn't, and my head hurt even more, which I wouldn't've thought possible.

He said something that went too fast, and then he spoke in regular Thai, going very slow so I would understand, "Come with us," and they started rolling my motorcycle down the road, and I couldn't get my passport back without that motorcycle, so I struggled to stand up, and purple sparks crackled in front of my eyes, and the man with the sticky, sweaty fingertips supported me, and it felt so natural the way he reached for my camera case and my backpack that I handed them over, and I pressed one palm against my temple because blood was oozing out, and I didn't want it to mat my hair. I tried to hurry to keep up with the motorcycle because all I could think was where would I be without my passport? My leg twinged with every step, but at least it wasn't broken.

The man with no shirt said to me, "L.A.?" and I thought it was a Thai word I didn't know so I told him that I didn't understand, and he added, "California?"

It seemed easier to nod and smile than try to explain Phoenix. The men with the motorcycle were way ahead of us now, around a bend ahead in the road, and when we turned the same bend, we'd reached a camp, like a small army base, and why hadn't I thought of that? They were soldiers. We passed khaki canvas huts and a helicopter over to one side and a couple men, wearing cut-off shorts and ragged T-shirts, leaning against tree trunks, cleaning guns—they watched me pass, then looked at one another, and though no one spoke, I had the definite feeling that each knew what the others were thinking. When I smiled, no one smiled back. A couple chickens scooted past, and even they seemed to be watching me.

I was led to a tent that was set apart from the others and before going in, I asked, "Where is my motorcycle?" and the man with no shirt said something and smiled, so maybe he said it was getting fixed and maybe he said we're going to kill you so it doesn't really matter much, does it, blondie? But I said, "Thank you," and we went inside. The tent was arranged like a school nurse's office, with a line of three cots, a small metal cabinet, a glass jar filled with cotton balls, bottled water in the corner, a battery-powered fan. All that was missing were the "Just Say No" posters on the walls; instead there was a shrine with a framed picture of the king and a statue of Buddha draped with dried flower garlands on top of a crate against the far wall, right next to a big two-way radio.

They sat me on the far cot, next to the metal cabinet, and the man with no shirt said a few words, and the other man nodded and left, taking my camera case and backpack with him.

The shirtless man tilted his head to the right, looked at me, not meeting my eyes. Now that I was closer to him, I noticed a jagged scar cutting down from the corner of his mouth, across his chin, and just under his jaw, like a child's naughty scribble.

"I am Taklaw," he said, and he peered closer at my temple, and I shifted my eyes so I wasn't looking directly at him. Then he opened the metal cabinet and pulled out two gauze pads, one so I could wipe the blood off my hand, and one that he pressed against my temple. "Very big," he said, speaking slowly. "Deep. You must stay here."

It wasn't clear if that was an invitation or a command, so I pretended it was an invitation. "No, thank you," and I smiled as if he'd asked if I wanted more tea. "I must go home." He didn't say anything, and I wasn't sure I got my words right, so I added: "I am a teacher in Bangkok."

"Teacher of English?" he asked.

I nodded. "Are you in the army?" My teacher's brother was; maybe this was his base.

Taklaw laughed, but not the way you laugh at something funny. "Okay, sure," and he laughed that same way again. "Why are you here?" he asked, sitting on the cot opposite me.

I had to think for a moment of the Thai words I knew. I said, "I like to travel, to see the world," and he stared at me, and I wondered if I had just told him he was a pig or something, but the longer he looked at me, the more I felt like he knew the parts I wasn't saying, that he understood why someone might want to see the world. He was about my age, and back in Phoenix he'd be in graduate school or already hating his first job out of college or looking for a new apartment or trying to decide whether to marry his girlfriend. Here, there was more than that.

Much more. Maybe it was how that jagged scar moved when he smiled, maybe it was the bare chest, maybe it was the way he listened and understood exactly what was said and wasn't said, or maybe it was that laugh a moment ago, but he was not a soldier and this was not an army base. It's not like opium drug runners would have a big welcome sign. I smiled, God, did I smile.

Taklaw said, "The world is not as big as we think." He removed the gauze pad and showed it to me; it was soaked with dark red blood. With one hand he made little looping circles, two fingers and thumb pinched together—he wanted to give me stitches. Exactly what I did not want, some drug lord stitching me up with an unsterilized needle, leaving behind a gaping scar like his on my temple.

"No!" I said in English, shaking my head. "No stitches!"

He showed me the bloody gauze again, and I shook my head more vigorously which made me dizzy and a little woozy. I pointed at the metal cabinet, at the gauze pads, and he pulled out another and pressed it against my head, then put my hand on top of it for me to hold it, tilted my head back. His fingers were smooth, cool. Maybe he was a doctor. But I didn't ask because I didn't want to hear that he wasn't, and I was pretty darn sure he wasn't.

He pulled out of the cabinet a plastic bag filled with brightly colored pills and started sorting through them, picking out red ones and white ones which he piled next to himself on the cot.

"How long have you been a teacher in Bangkok?" he asked as he worked.

"Almost one year," I said. "Ten months."

"Not so long," he said, but he didn't know it *was* a long time, it was forever. I'd had way more than ten months of experience and thoughts and questions and confusion in those ten months. I'd forgotten what it was like to go through a Taco Bell drivethrough, I hadn't been able to vote against my slimeball senator (and I'd almost forgotten why he was a slimeball). Time was different here—it didn't stack up like a brick wall you can't get over, it melted away as pleasantly as ice in a cold drink. "Maybe it is long for your family," he said. "Alone at your home."

I smiled and nodded.

He returned the plastic bag of pills to the metal cabinet and slid the door shut. There was no lock on the cabinet. "I want to be a teacher," he said, then shrugged. "But my father. . . ." and there could be so much behind that, so many different stories. But it was the shrug, the tiny sigh, the glance toward the entrance that made me certain I knew the part of the story he didn't say: His father was in charge here now, but eventually this family business would be his. That simple, that complicated, same as my story. There were things I wanted to say, and I opened my mouth, but I didn't have the right Thai words.

"My father said Bangkok was too far." He looked at the two piles of pills, nudged them farther apart. We both knew Bangkok wasn't the only place with schools.

I said, "Bangkok is a nice city."

He said, "I was there once." I watched his fingers arrange each pile of pills into two neat rows. I was trying to figure out how to ask him what he saw there, and when I couldn't get that right in my mind, I started adjusting to ask how he liked Bangkok. He spoke suddenly: "But then my father found me," and all the words I knew weren't enough. He swept the rows of pills back together with one hand, then began dividing them by color again.

I quickly said, "It's very pretty here."

He shook his head. "We are not here because it is pretty. Do you understand?" There was a pause as he concentrated on sorting the pills. "What is your name?"

"Amy," I said.

He repeated my name, turning it into a question. "You *farang* come here thinking you will be far from home," he said, gently pushing aside my hand that held the gauze pad on my head. As he looked at the cut, his breath tickled my skin. I wanted to explain how it was in the United States, that there were as many reasons for leaving as there were for staying, that no one was sure they were doing the right thing until they were doing it. He said, "The west is different. To leave home is okay."

I said, "To stay at home is okay, too."

He said, "Here I am my father's shadow. In Bangkok I was nobody."

It was almost the same thing, sometimes, wanting to be nobody and wanting to be somebody. I nodded, said, "Maybe some day you will be a teacher."

"It is too late," he said. "This is what I know." As if to punctuate his point, an older man came to the doorway and murmured something in that dialect I didn't understand, looking at me the whole time. Taklaw listened, stood, and asked the man a question. He answered and laughed, not a nice laugh. Taklaw asked me, "Where is your passport?" His voice sharpened as he repeated the question. The man in the doorway smiled, not a nice smile, either. "Answer now," Taklaw said.

Suddenly it was like I was talking to a different person; Taklaw's voice was wound tighter and he seemed taller. The scar pulled across his chin like a rope. "In the village," I said, because the whole motorcycle thing and back before sundown was way too difficult to explain. Was the man in the doorway Taklaw's father? My breath didn't feel like my own.

"Who are you?" Taklaw asked.

"I am a teacher in Bangkok," I said.

"Why are you here?" and he pointed to the ground, meaning right here, and this was all getting very scary, and there was no way to know what was the right thing to say.

"Wat Phra Thep is near?" I asked.

The two men spoke at length, going back and forth, and it became clear that Taklaw was in charge so the man couldn't be his father. I tried not to make any noise or even move, even breathe. Finally they stopped talking, and there was a moment of silence that was more frightening than the talking. Taklaw said, "Wat Phra Thep is not near here."

"I want a photo of Kala." I was trying to sound knowledgeable, as if I really knew something about this temple, but the only thing I remembered was the painting of the mythical creature Kala trapped in the process of devouring himself. I couldn't remember why he was devouring himself, what that represented, and as the silence built up again, I wasn't even sure if Wat Phra Thep was the temple with Kala, or if Kala existed, or who I was and why I'd come to Thailand, let alone Nan Province. My mouth was dry, and I cleared my throat, which instantly sounded exactly like the noise a guilty person would make, so I coughed instead, which sounded even more suspicious.

"*Farangs* cannot understand Kala," Taklaw said, and the man in the doorway nodded slowly. Then he said something and the only word I recognized was "time," but I nodded as if I'd understood.

In my mind I saw the page in my guidebook with the drawing of Kala: the chubby hands stuffed inside the jawless, toothy grin as he shoveled chunks of his own flesh into his mouth, blank eyes that somehow looked both evil and knowing, that decorative headdress and the pointed ears. I remember thinking Kala looked like the naughtiest kid in nursery school . . . or an old man you crossed the street to avoid. But I couldn't remember the significance. I thought I knew so much about Thailand.

The radio crackled with static, and the two men spun as if tapped on the shoulder, but there was nothing more than that.

My arm was tired, and when I removed the gauze pad it felt as if the bleeding had stopped or at least slowed, and I lightly touched the cut with one finger. So refusing stitches was one thing I'd done right.

Taklaw frowned and tapped my hand away, then reached into the metal cabinet and pulled out an aerosol can which he sprayed on the cut, shielding my eyes with one hand. The liquid felt cold and sharp like ice, but I tried not to grimace. Then Taklaw got out another gauze pad, taping it onto my temple with white tape that he ripped from the roll using his teeth. The whole procedure took no more than twenty seconds, as if first aid were something he did regularly, and probably I would've been okay with him giving me stitches, but it was the scar on his chin like a second grin, like a dead-end road on a map, that scared me.

I watched the other man, and it seemed to me that a decision had been made because he wasn't looking so intently at me anymore. Instead, I watched him watch a large striped beetle crawling up the canvas wall above the doorway. As the man reached a finger to flick the bug down to the dirt floor, I closed my eyes so I wouldn't have to see him crunch it under his bare foot.

When I opened my eyes, Taklaw's outstretched hand was in front of me. In the middle of his palm was one of the red pills. "One red now, one red later," he said. "Two reds tomorrow. Then one white twice a day for five days."

I picked up the pill with my thumb and one finger. There was no writing on it. It was bright red, like a stop sign.

He poured out half a glass of water from the water bottle. I tried to look in his eyes as I took the cup with my other hand, but he glanced away, spoke softly to the other man who nodded.

I set the pill on my tongue and waited a moment as a bitter taste burrowed down. They watched as I lifted the glass of water to my lips, swallowed. Either it would be a story to tell everyone, or I'd die. It was that simple.

They watched me, and I closed my eyes, lay down on the cot. But I still felt them watching, even after I'd fallen asleep

There was one moment when I half-woke, thinking I was in my bedroom at home, and my mother was standing in my doorway, watching me, and there was a half-filled suitcase on the floor between us, but she didn't say anything.

Another moment, later, I woke up enough to think I saw Taklaw sitting on the cot opposite me, flipping through the color picture pages of my guidebook, but I may have dreamed that also.

Afternoon shadows covered the canvas walls when I woke, and my stomach twisted with hunger. As I sat up, my head throbbed, and that's when I remembered exactly where I was, what had happened. I saw my backpack and my camera in the corner, near the door, which could be a good sign. My body was coated with sweat, and my knee—with its big bruise the shape of a banana—ached.

The pills were on top of the cabinet, two neat piles of red and white.

I thought about how I would tell this story to everyone back home, the letters I'd write about being in a drug runners' camp and getting my prescription of "red pills and white pills," and how sweet Taklaw was to me even though he had that tough-guy scar on his chin, and how I'd answer when people asked, "Weren't you scared?" I almost heard myself saying, "Except for the guns and helicopter, it was like stumbling into a Boy Scout camp." It would be the kind of story people would remember and say, "Oh, Amy, tell the one about the drug camp." And I'd tell it, and people would look at me and mouth, "Wow," and they'd secretly wonder what they would've done in the same situation, and I'd smile because I knew; I knew exactly.

Taklaw came in, still without a shirt, he carried a tray with tea and bowls of food. He set the tray on the metal cabinet, handed me one bowl of chicken *laap* and another of sticky rice, poured the tea, then sat down. He smiled, touched his head.

I smiled back, nodded, said in English, "Okay," and gave the thumbs-up signal. Then I started rolling the sticky rice into little balls with my fingers to dip in the *laap*. I hoped he was impressed that I knew the proper way to eat sticky rice. The *laap* was delicious, the balance of mint, chiles, and lime juice just right; obviously drug runners cared about eating well—another detail for my story.

"Your motorcycle is okay now," and he made vroom-vroom noises like a little boy playing.

I laughed. "Thank you."

"When you go to Bangkok, it is better not to tell anyone where you were today," he said. "Better for me . . . better for you." He spoke very casually, same slow careful way he'd been talking to me all along, and he rubbed the scar on his chin, tracing its path up and down, up and down. Then he picked up his cup of tea but did not drink.

Outside the wind rustled the trees, and the shadows on the canvas walls curved and knocked together. I nodded. "Okay." I reached for my tea, hoping he didn't notice how my hand shook the tiniest bit, but some of the tea sloshed over the edge of the cup onto the dirt. We both looked at it.

"Maybe you will come to Bangkok," I said.

He shook his head. "I am always my father's son," and he stared down into his tea, as if something so close could show him something important.

I wanted to explain it all to him, to urge him just to go, to leave, to tell him that you had to start somehow, that if you put miles between you and them that was the beginning, but my Thai was limited, so all I could do was smile and nod and let the words clutter my brain like dry leaves pressed up against a fence by the wind. Finally I said, "Your father must be a good man."

He looked up. "My father is dead," and I didn't understand right away so he repeated himself, and then I understood the words, but only the words. If his father was dead, why not go to Bangkok? Why stay trapped here? But they were rude questions.

He sipped his tea, sipped again. "He is still my father. Nothing changes."

Outside the wind picked up again and brushed against the canvas walls, buckling them in toward me just a bit. A shadow of a flying bird crossed the far wall, behind where Taklaw sat. Everything seemed far away and close at the same time, like the mountains you always saw but never reached.

We sipped our tea. I could've been back home, worrying over what to say to my date.

There was too much silence. I pointed to the scar on his chin. "How did that happen?"

He touched it quickly with his forefinger as if surprised that I'd been able to see it. "This?" he said. "This is nothing," but he kept stroking it, so I knew there was something, some drug lord war, or run-in with soldiers, or some impossibly exotic story that I couldn't even begin to imagine. Then he said, "This happened when my father found me in Bangkok." He pointed at my head. "Yours is not so bad."

I touched the gauze pad taped to my head, my souvenir. I didn't want to think about his scar, about his father traveling all the way to Bangkok to find him, to bring him back. So I thought about myself: Did no stitches make a cut more or less likely to leave behind a scar?

He set his empty teacup on the tray then stood and walked over to where my backpack and camera case were, put them on the cot next to me and sat down. "I looked at your book," he said. "There are many things to see. The world is so big . . . for you."

That's what brought me here, thinking the world was big, thinking it was big enough. I thought everything could be different over here, and some things were different, sure, like the food and the smells and the things to see, but really nothing was different, nothing.

"You have a camera," he said.

I set down my teacup, started to apologize, to promise I wouldn't take any photos—I didn't want him keeping my camera; it was an expensive one that I'd bought just before leaving Phoenix—but he said, "Please take a photo of me. Take my picture to Bangkok." He looked away from me as he asked, and that's how I knew it was important to him.

I took my camera out of the case, removed the lens cap. Taklaw stood straight at attention as I focused on him. He was as serious as he'd been when he and the other men were deciding what to do with me, but at the last second he smiled, and I snapped the picture. Then another, just in case.

He thanked me. Then I thanked him.

Was he right; was the world big? There were ten million people in Bangkok alone, and Bangkok was how many thousand miles from Phoenix, and when I walked through the markets of Bangkok, no one knew who I was or why I'd come here. All they thought was, *farang*, someone who doesn't belong.

Taklaw touched my temple with his thumb, then touched his chin. "We are like brothers now, yes?" he said.

A couple of Taklaw's men rode with me back to the village. They pointed to the road I should've taken to find the temple ruins. Just outside the village they turned and disappeared into the forest without saying good-bye.

The next day, though, I didn't go to the temple and I didn't go looking for opium fields and I didn't try to go to the Laos border.

My head still hurt, so all afternoon I ate mangoes and sticky rice as I lounged in the hammock on the guest house porch, adjusting the colorful triangular cushions until I was perfectly comfortable. I read my guidebook, studying the pictures of the places I'd been and the places I'd go to and the places I'd never see. I read about Wat Phra Thep, about Kala, forever devouring himself, signifying the endless passage of time. And I browsed through my Thai dictionary, learning new words and discovering that Taklaw means "very brave" in English.

When I got back to Bangkok, there was a letter from my mother in which she talked about this, this, and this, but not about that, not about would I come home, not about missing me or needing me, and was it a lack of courage or just plain stubbornness that led me to find the headmaster and tell him that yes, I would stay to be a teacher in Thailand for another year and possibly even another year after that.

Best Friends

GINGER — 1987

After Amy left for Thailand, I started writing letters to her every night after the late news ended. I sat outside where I listened to the slow night noises I'd forgotten: wind rolling along the desert, coyote howls stretching the distance, an owl. I let ice cubes and tonic dilute my gin, and I listened and wrote letters to my daughter.

I didn't send all these letters, just a few. The rest I kept for myself in a manila folder tucked between my mattress and box spring. There was no one else in my house, no one to hide these letters from. Yet they seemed to want to be hidden.

I never wrote to my son down in Tucson. There was no reason why not, unless it was that things always came easily with him, his birth, his toilet training, his adolescence. Not one thing challenged me. He was a gift.

Dear Amy: This is something I never told you. When you were sixteen, I called the police and reported my car stolen. You and I were fight-

ing—I don't remember what about, that awful boyfriend and the way the house smelled like pot the minute he walked through the door, or was it my drinking again?—probably that—and you screamed that you hated me (like I'd heard you say several times before), but I screamed back that I hated you, too. Your jaw went suddenly slack, still, your eyes widened. You were surprised to learn that a mother might hate a child, even for an instant. We stood in front of the hall mirror, and as I watched your face, I looked beyond it to see my own. I remember thinking, So that's what a mother who hates her daughter looks like.

The tears dried as you stared at me, and I kept watching my face in the mirror, waiting for it to change, but it didn't. You walked away, too quiet—no stomping, no screaming, no breathing—and you grabbed my car keys off the bookcase where they always were, and you were out the door, no slamming, just a soft click shut. I don't remember hearing the car's engine start, but when I looked out the window, you were gone.

Then I called the police. "My car's been stolen," I said, and I gave the license number, the make and model. I was so calm that the woman filing the report asked me twice if I was all right.

That night you still hadn't come home, and I realized I'd reported the tag number of the old station wagon I drove when you and your brother were children, before your dad moved out.

When I called to explain, the police found no record of my report. I was on the phone, and you came through the front door. "Hi, Mom," you said, hugging me quickly before walking to your room. "Are you all right?" the policeman on the phone asked. "Never mind," I said.

Something else I never told you. I hated you only that single instant. When I saw what hating you looked like, I knew I could never do it again. I saw what hate is, Amy, and then I knew that though you said you did, you didn't truly hate me, not even one instant, not ever.

I wasn't surprised when Amy told me she was moving to Thailand. What surprised me was that she had already accepted a job, that the school where she'd be teaching was paying for her airplane ticket, that reservations had been made, dates set, that everything was arranged and planned, lined up one-two-three like a flight of stairs.

She told me all these details over dinner at Rosa's Place, her favorite Mexican dive: sticky tables and great tamales, mismatched silverware and handmade tortillas. No liquor license.

"How did all this happen?" I asked her.

"Filling out paperwork," she said. "Just a matter of time."

The waitress brought a second basket of tortilla chips that we hadn't asked for, smiled at us, picked up a napkin off the floor, lingered as if there was something more to say or do, finally was summoned by another table.

"You knew I wouldn't stay here forever," Amy said.

I nodded.

"I've been here all my life," she said.

The way she spoke she found no possibility of contradiction in those two statements.

"Growing up, college, job," she said. "All of it here in Phoenix."

I dabbed one of the chips in the last bit of salsa.

"It's time to go," she said.

The waitress overheard her and scribbled out a final total on the check, ripped it off her pad and placed it upside-down by my elbow. She waited next to the table, smiling, humming with the jukebox, and there was no choice except to pay the bill right then.

As we waited for the waitress to bring back my change, Amy said, "Mom, I'm twenty-four years old. I should've left a long time ago."

But you didn't, I thought. Your father left, your brother left. I said, "I hear it's real hot in Thailand."

"Guess I'll find out," she said.

"Of course it's hot here in Phoenix," I said.

"There's weather everywhere," she said.

The waitress apologized profusely that my change was in quarters, so I smiled and said I needed them to do my laundry. As Amy and I walked through the parking lot, she said, "Why'd you lie about the quarters?"

"To be nice," I said.

Amy stopped at her car, dug through her purse for keys, didn't look at me when she said, "You've always been nicest to the people you don't know."

Only a daughter would know to say such a thing, when exactly to say it.

Dear Amy: It wasn't easy for me. Isn't that how we all begin an apology, by apologizing to ourselves first? I had no idea how to be a wife, how to be a mother. All I knew—maybe all anyone knows?— is that I didn't want what I'd seen. There was noise always around me, people talking, too many relatives wanting to know what I was doing now, was doing next, what I did yesterday. Aunt Joane stopped by to visit, and the first thing she said to me was "So, Ginger, I hear you became a woman last week." You couldn't sneeze without pneumonia setting in. When I got a B on an exam, everyone knew I was flunking out of school and that I'd never be the teacher they expected me to become.

It shouldn't be this easy to leave behind your family. There should be some part of you that doesn't want to go.

Do you know how I saved enough money to take the Greyhound bus out of Detroit? How badly I wanted to leave? I stole tips off tables in restaurants. Tips my dates left, tips other people left. I had a job at the five and dime, but that money was for helping out the family. So how could I dare use that same money to escape?

I hated Detroit, hated being Polish, hated the way my grandmother spoke so slowly in English, so carefully, each word made of glass.

The food we ate was slow and heavy, dense, took too many bites to chew. Winter and snow and slush stretched across too many months. We all looked alike; my cousins and I were confused with one another at school and church. That made me feel I'd never get out, knowing that months after I was gone, someone was calling my cousin Theresa "Ginger."

But was there one part of me that refused to go, one part wanting to stay behind?

I never thought anyone else would know this about me, but I was crying as the Greyhound bus pulled away from the curb. I was bawling so hard that women looked away instead of handing me tissues from their purses; they were that afraid of my sorrow. I hated that I cried that way, what it meant.

Amy, go back and reread this letter, and X out the paragraph before this one because this is really what I thought no one would ever know about me: My mother cried; my grandmother, my aunts, my cousins all cried. Even my father slipped off his glasses and wiped at his eyes with a handkerchief. But when the bus pulled away from the curb, I was still waving my white gloves out the window, calling my promises to write lots of letters, and it wasn't until halfway down the block that I realized I hadn't cried. I remember thinking, Now I'm going to cry; I'm going to cry because I should have, and I didn't. The entire bus trip I didn't. Are you surprised?

Are you? You didn't cry at the airport on your way to Thailand. You kissed, hugged, fussed with luggage, waved, bought magazines, ate a sandwich, but you didn't cry. I watched you.

As you watched me. I didn't cry until after your plane was no longer a number on the flight monitor, after I found the airport bar and had a martini (maybe it was two, more likely three, probably four). Not until then.

You learned about leaving from me. What else?

Sometimes when the phone rang, I knew it was Amy before I answered. "You didn't know," she'd say when I told her that.

I would keep quiet.

"You're making that up," she'd say.

I still wouldn't say anything.

Finally she'd ask, "So how did you know?" And I'd ask why she was calling or tell her I only had a minute or say I was happy she'd called or whatever because of course I didn't know how I knew.

The conversation went like that every time. I liked to think it meant something but couldn't figure out what.

A week before she left, she called asking for addresses of my family back in Detroit. She had some, but she wanted everybody's. "What for?" I asked. The phone cord didn't reach to where I'd left my drink on the counter, so I just stared at it, at the water droplets collecting on the outside of the glass, rolling down the smooth sides.

"So I can send letters from Thailand," she said. "So everyone knows how I am."

"All you have to do is send one letter," I said. "They'll all read it. Or at the least hear about it."

"Still," she said. "I want to write to them." There was a pause, and I didn't want this to be a fight because what were we fighting about? I should be happy she wanted to send my family letters. "I want to write to *all* of them," Amy said.

I went for my address book and grabbed my drink, too. If cold were a taste, that's what that drink at that moment would be. Or if clear were a taste. Let her write a thousand letters to my family; what did it matter?

I picked up the phone again, crunching it between my head and shoulder, but before I could start reading off addresses, she said, "It's not wrong to keep in touch with them."

"I never said it was."

"They're my family, too, you know," she said.

"Of course they are." I tilted the phone away from my mouth and sipped my drink so quietly she couldn't possibly hear.

She sighed, a sharp breath that I swear I almost felt. "Just give me the addresses please." How many times had I heard her voice sound that way, that hard?

After I read off all the addresses she needed, I was sure she'd hang up, but she asked, "How come you didn't know it was me when the phone rang?"

"Of course I knew." I shifted the drink to my other hand because my fingers were too cold.

There was a pause, and I felt her trying to decide whether or not to believe my lie.

"But you didn't say anything," she said.

"I thought by now I didn't have to." I pressed my cold fingers to my cheek. When I took them away, I still felt their imprint on my face.

"No, Mom," she said. "You always have to, always." There was another pause. "You should know that." What she meant was: A good mother would know that.

"Next time I'll say something," I said. "Promise." But she'd hung up.

Dear Amy: Like you, I sent letters back home. I wanted my family to know what I was doing. I wanted them to know I was just fine, that everything here was great. So I typed a letter every Friday on my lunch break at the law office where I worked. My words looked so important, long black lines on crinkly pieces of typing paper. Very few mistakes; I was an excellent typist. No misspellings—even if it meant looking up words in the dictionary.

I knew that every letter I sent my mother would be read out loud around the kitchen table, so I wrote imagining her voice reading my words. I could picture exactly the way her mouth would twist when she came to something she didn't quite understand, when she'd nod, when she'd pause and look at her sisters and mother. I knew what she'd say after finishing each letter, I knew what they'd all say and who would speak first and who would disagree just to disagree.

I knew what they'd be eating as they read the letter—poppy seed cake or pound cake with coffee—and how each one of them took their coffee and who would say, "Not another cup for me, thanks," and when.

In fact, I still know all those things. How far away do you have to be before you forget? That's what I used to wonder.

I have to tell you this. I thought I was writing those letters to make them realize they never understood me, to force them to see that now they never would because I was doing fine, doing better in this whole new life without them. Maybe they thought that; I don't know. What I do know is that I never knew I knew them until I wrote those letters.

Amy asked, "Do you need a drink to get through the day?" She was reading out of a magazine. I knew exactly what she was getting at. She was fourteen, certain she was sly.

I said, "No."

"Does your drinking affect your job?"

"No."

"Is it why Dad left?"

The magazine was on her lap, and she was looking straight at me. I set down the memos I was reading, pushed them aside.

"No, that's not why Dad left," I said. I opened my briefcase, pretended I was looking for something at the bottom.

"Does your drinking make you lie?" she asked.

The briefcase fell shut. I couldn't tell if she was reading from a magazine article or not, if in fact she'd ever been reading from the magazine. It was still in her lap, still open.

"Are you saying that your mother lies?" I asked.

"Just answer the question please."

"No," I said.

"Is that your answer? Or is that 'no, I won't answer the question'?" She sat up straighter, pushed her hair behind her ears.

"Just no," I said. "What are you reading anyway?"

"None of your business," she said.

"What makes you think these questions are your business?" I asked.

"Dad left because you're a drunk, didn't he?"

I was tired of working a full day and taking two classes at night, tired of trying to hold everything together. There should have been a joke that would get the smirk off her face and the sweat off mine, a joke that could put us together into a hug, a giggle, but hell if I knew any joke that good. I said, "He left because we decided it would be the best thing for both of us."

"Is it the best thing for me?" she asked.

"It's better for all of us," I said.

"I don't believe you."

When did she get too big to send to her room? I said, "Ask your father if you don't believe me."

She said, "I already did."

"So you believe him, not me?" I could sound casual, too, tossing off words like they were nothing.

The bulb in the overhead light suddenly fizzled and popped. Odd shadows off the lamp on my side criss-crossed the wall. Amy flipped her magazine closed. "You don't know what he said, do you?"

I knew exactly what he said. I'd heard it over and over and over. "What did he say?" I asked.

"That you're a stinking, disgusting drunk, and you're always embarrassing everyone by drinking too much wherever you go." The words came out one by one, stacking up until she was sure she had enough.

I stood up. I thought I would walk from the room. I thought I

would pick up my papers and my briefcase and go into my bedroom, turn on the radio to soft music, read my memos and then
look over my chapter for tomorrow night's class. I thought that's
what would happen next.

Instead I left my papers on the table. I walked to where Amy
slouched sideways in the overstuffed chair, and I leaned toward
her the way you lean when you're about to hug someone.

I slapped her. My hand against her cheek was a quick, hard
thwack.

There was silence. I had never hit my daughter.

"I'm sorry," I said.

"No, you're not," and she was the one who took her magazine
to her bedroom and turned on thumpingly loud music that played
on "repeat" all night, even after she was asleep.

I was the one who sat in the room with the burned-out light
bulb, watching the level in the gin bottle sink lower and lower
until I reached the bottom and then I could cry.

*Dear Amy: I don't even know if you drink, how much you drink, what
you like to drink. Is it gin and its coolness whisking down your throat,
or the slow burn of scotch, or the jolting yip-yap of tequila, or smooth,
invisible vodka? Beer? Wine? I should know this, of all people I should
know this.*

*But you never told me. Or did I never ask? I think maybe there are
lots of questions I didn't ask. Why did you stop painting pictures? Why
don't you let me meet your boyfriends anymore? Why did you leave?
Or—better—why didn't you leave sooner? Why did you stay with me
so long?*

*I make up answers. I pretend I know why. But then I measure out
another g&t and then I do know why.*

*There is a question you never asked me, either: Why do I drink?
You must have wondered; you must have thought about it; you must've*

talked with your brother, your father, your shrink. Do you know, no one ever asked me, not ever? For a long time I thought there didn't have to be a reason. Like, why is yellow a color? It just is. I just do.

But that doesn't answer the question you wanted to ask.

The first time I drank a martini was at a bar with my boss, the lawyer, in my first job. It was what he ordered, so I said, "The same," and he was surprised and impressed. "Aren't you quite the little firecracker?" he said. That was the way he talked, funny phrasings that no one else dared use. The first sip shot down to my toes and straight back up. I coughed, but he pretended not to notice, kept telling me about his wife's ugly poodle, "like a drowned rat and a half," he said. I laughed. I would've laughed anyway because he was my boss, but the martini helped. "You have a lovely laugh," he said, "which it occurs to me you don't present very often." So I laughed again and took another sip, and soon we were both laughing and eventually he leaned close and kissed me with his ginny lips, and I was farther away from Detroit than I'd ever been, than I'd ever imagined it was possible to be. So that was the first and second and third martini.

But what does that mean? Liking to laugh doesn't make you a drunk. Neither does leaving home.

Your father and I had some wild times. You wouldn't remember much, because by the time you were old enough to remember, he'd quit, or quit enough. I hated that once he made up his mind about something, that's the way it was, that he could decide to cut back on drinking and do it like it was easy, like it was a walk around the block. Once that happened, there was nothing we could understand about each other anymore. What we'd understood in the beginning was a party that started at five on Friday and didn't really end until seven Monday morning. We knew the way a headache could grind apart every last thought in your brain. We understood taking all the lights on yellow and barreling crooked into the parking lot to get inside before the liquor store locked up for the holiday. We knew a special boozy kind of love *that ended with us exhausted and sweaty, the sheets a tangle, ice melting in the glasses, and us collapsed into each other's arms, missing the big moon right outside our window.*

But loving someone who drinks doesn't make you a drunk either.

I only vaguely started to think about what I was doing to your father when it was too late. Certainly what I was doing to myself was of no interest whatsoever. But—and you probably won't believe this—I always thought about you and your brother, about what I was doing to you. I wanted you to love me. I wanted to be a good mother, the best mother—fun and young and fresh and free and all the things my mother, trapped in Detroit, wasn't. And I was some of those things. I know I was. You must love me. I'm your mother. You do love me?

Why I drink. Could it be so simple: Now I can't imagine my life without it. Who would I be? Where would I fit? What would I want if I didn't want that next drink?

When I got back from taking Amy to the airport, I went straight into her old bedroom and sat at her desk. It didn't matter that she hadn't lived here for several years. The room was still hers. There was a framed picture of the two of us on her desk: we were sitting in front of the Christmas tree, wearing our pajamas. She must've been about sixteen. I held a half-full glass of orange juice in my hand. We were both smiling, and we looked so normal, like we could've been a magazine ad, a TV family, the people everyone else wanted to be. Around her neck was the string of pearls I'd bought her for Christmas with her father's money.

I stared at that picture for the longest time.

Then I remembered the rest. It wasn't just orange juice in that glass. Amy and I got into a huge screaming fight, and I knocked down the Christmas tree. Ornaments rolled across the floor, and

I stomped on a few before kicking the tree again and again. There was more I didn't want to think about, didn't remember exactly. But she would remember exactly: cleaning up the mess and each awful thing I'd said, me ripping the pearls off her neck. Of course she'd remember, with the picture or without, here or in Thailand.

I was sorry, so sorry. But even as I thought it, her voice came clearly into my head—"Mom, you're *always* sorry. So what?" But this time I really was, this time was different. But she was already gone.

I turned the picture over and slid the backing from the frame, removed the photo. There was an envelope in the desk drawer, and I put the photo inside, and printed her name on the front of the envelope with a pen.

The next morning I drove to the post office and mailed it to her even though my head ached and the sun was way too bright.

Dear Amy: What do you miss? Do you miss chips and salsa? Is there a TV show you'd like to watch? Have you forgotten the smell of apple pie in the oven on a chilly November day? Is there one type of bird you're used to seeing that isn't there? This is how I think of you now, someone going without. I forget about the new things you're finding in Thailand.

The women I work with talk about their daughters. "My Anne-Marie and I wear the same size shoe," one says. Another says, "Susannah's treating me to lunch today, isn't that sweet?" "Shelby and her boyfriend and Paul and I went camping together in the White Mountains this weekend—what a blast!" someone else says. When they look at me, I smile. "Amy and I are best friends," I tell them. They believe me as easily as I believed them.

It's never the men talking this way about their sons or daughters, or the women talking about their sons. Only the women and the daughters, the mothers and their girls.

I remember the afternoon I found out I was pregnant with you. I never told you this: Your father and I weren't married yet. Maybe you guessed? I borrowed a friend's wedding ring and went to a doctor on the other side of Phoenix. The wedding ring was too big, and I kept spinning the diamond around and around my finger. "Positive," the doctor told me. The room was cold; there was a window air conditioner clacking and dripping water into a pan. The doctor's hands smelled like the soap in the ladies' room. He didn't say anything, didn't say "congratulations" or "I'm sorry." Just once he brushed the hair off my face, and I heard the tick of his watch as his hand passed by. It was as if he'd entirely forgotten about the crowd of pregnant women sweating in his waiting room.

The first thing I thought of was not your father or my mother or even me, but you. Tiny you all alone in my uterus, waiting for me to speak. I knew the options. I knew the choices.

My friend who loaned me the ring had said this doctor knew people. He would have helped me. He liked me. There was always a way to find money.

I didn't think: This will be my best friend. I didn't think: She and I will wear the same size shoe. I thought: This is part of me.

The doctor smiled, put his hand on my shoulder, said, "Congratulations."

So I became a mother and a wife. Like my mother before me, and her mother and back into the past, and like a long mirror looking into itself, there you were. I knew you'd be beautiful. I knew you'd be smart. I knew you'd be able to tell a joke well. I knew people would like you. I knew one day you'd leave.

Amy, don't think about what you miss. Think about what you have now that you didn't have before. Don't live always fighting against what you don't want; instead fight for what you do want. Of all the times I asked you to believe me, this is the time I mean it the most.

I wanted to tell you this not at the airport, not the day at the Mexican restaurant when you told me you were moving to the other side of the world, but that first day in the doctor's office.

I wrote a letter to Amy every night. I imagined her doing the same, writing a letter to me, except that her night was my day. Or was it my today was her tomorrow? Whichever it was, it never matched exactly right.

Braiding Bread

There were too many things I wanted to remember about Thailand: tourist places that were more than pictures in guidebooks; and tiny details you wouldn't notice unless you'd lived in the country for almost three years as I had; and ideas and reasons-why I couldn't understand because I wasn't Thai. I typed long letters to friends and my family back in the States describing what I saw; I wrote every afternoon in a journal; I shot rolls of photos with an expensive camera; and I bought souvenirs of every place I visited. I looked at these things again and again, the copies of my letters, the Thai knickknacks, everything I accumulated.

But the Sunday when I returned to school after my vacation trip north to Chiang Mai and the Golden Triangle, I sorted through the mail they'd stacked in my dorm room during my month-long absence. One envelope seemed whiter than the others; nothing was written on the outside, and it was sealed *and* Scotch-taped, so I slit it open immediately, and I sat on my lumpy bed and read the letter written by the headmaster in his too-perfect, too-formal English—they were sorry they'd been unable to reach me, they'd contacted the Embassy, they'd spoken to several government bureaus in the north, they'd called hotels, they'd called and faxed everyone they could think of to call and fax, trying to find me to tell me that my mother had died, that my brother had called the school many times, my father, a lawyer.

I didn't read that letter a second time.

"Everything's been taken care of," my brother said.

"But shouldn't I come back?" I heard clicks and scratches, as if he were sliding his hand over the bottom of the phone receiver to answer somebody else's question. It was five in the morning in Phoenix, so he must be sleeping with someone. It seemed like maybe I should know who she was, that a sister might usually know that sort of thing.

"What I mean is, there's nothing really to do now," Cal said. "Everything's been taken care of."

"You said that." I was sprawled flat on my bed, staring at how the water stain on the ceiling tiles had grown while I was away, how it looked like a seagull now.

"I don't know what else to say."

"What about Grandma?" I meant, Who called her in Detroit? Who knew words to explain what couldn't be explained to someone who didn't know her own name anymore? The people in the nursing home? My brother? Some lawyer?

And what about everyone else in Detroit, the great-aunts, cousins and cousins' children, all the people I'd been sending letters to. Who told them? There was a whole chain of people; was I the absolute last to know?

"Grandma's so bad now," he said. "No one's sure if she understood."

The pauses between our sentences felt like places you couldn't go back to.

Finally, I said, "I can't believe this happened." It was something to say, but it was also true. I'd thought people used those kinds of sentences only to fill space.

"Jesus, Amy, where the hell were you?" he shouted suddenly. "Why wasn't there a phone number? What were you thinking?"

There were reasons: There weren't phones at the guest houses I stayed at or in the hill tribe villages I trekked to; the planning and structure of teaching drained out of me whenever school ended; I traveled to see the world, and I'd learned you don't always know where it was until you got there. But mostly, you don't expect something like this to happen.

A voice murmured in the background; Cal mumbled, but I couldn't hear. "I'm sorry," he said to me, and I felt the weight of all the things he wasn't telling me, all the things he'd never tell me—no matter if we were sitting across a table in the same room or separated by an ocean into night and morning.

"Will you pick me up at the airport?" I asked.

I felt him nodding into the phone instead of talking, doing what I'd done as a child when we were long distance on special occasions with our grandmother in Detroit. "She can't see you," my mother always said, glancing up from the clock she was watching to make sure we didn't pass our five-minutes-each time limit. But it seemed to me that some people had to see nods, while others could feel them, because my grandmother always seemed to know what I was telling her, and then Cal said, "I'll be there."

The man next to me on the plane asked the flight attendant for three little bottles of gin. He poured them over ice and gave the glass three quick shakes every few seconds as he read a thick business report. He looked like the kind of father who called his daughters Princess and his sons Tiger and his wife Angel, the kind of person whose company pays for business class instead of getting a frequent flyer upgrade from their father as I'd done.

I had the window seat. I was trying to sleep, but my eyes opened every time he rattled his ice.

Suddenly he said, "Last night I dreamed this plane crashed.

That's why I'm drinking all this gin." He had the smile of someone who knows how to sell.

"I don't care how much gin you drink," I said.

"It seemed like you were noticing," he said.

"My mother drank that same kind of gin," I said.

"In my dream, the back of the plane caught fire, and as the flames moved closer, people jumped out of the door where some kind of cruise ship was waiting. I was too afraid to jump. I kept grabbing people as they went by, saying, 'I'm not ready.' They shook me off and kept going. When I woke up sweat was on my forehead." He jiggled his ice.

"Don't make up a story just because you want a drink," I said.

He stopped smiling. "I'm not making anything up." He turned through too many pages of his report.

The plane ride was so smooth that it didn't feel like we were going anywhere.

A moment later I said, "My mother just died in a drunk driving accident."

He set his report on the tray table and said, "Those scum ought to be shot. They're a menace to society."

He would've kept going—he would've called me Princess and lent me his handkerchief and found me a cush job in the multinational corporation he was CEO of and introduced me to his Harvard MBA son and presented our firstborn with a pony and a mutual fund—but I cut him off: "She was the one who was drunk."

The plane seemed filled with silence, as if everyone had heard me, as if rows and rows of people had decided my mother was a menace to society.

"That's her gin," I said, reaching over to pick up one of the little green bottles from the man's tray table. I tightened my fingers into a fist around it. "I'm going back home for the first time in almost three years."

"For the funeral." His voice collapsed into a "poor dear" murmur.

A nod would bring me back to Princess and the son, Whoever

Jr. who was in line to inherit the multinational corporation, but I said, "Actually, I missed the funeral. I was on vacation and they couldn't find me," and the look on the man's face was, Why won't you make this easy for me?

I closed my eyes for a moment, then opened them so I could set the green bottle on his tray, next to the other two. "I was on vacation," I said. "I didn't know."

He swallowed the rest of his drink, rolled the glass between the palms of his hand. He said, "In my business you have to be ready for anything," but I didn't ask what his business was though he wanted me to; I didn't talk to him anymore. I pretended to sleep, and then I really was sleeping, and I dreamed the plane was burning and people were running all around while I sat reading a really interesting magazine. They ignored me when I asked them to please be quiet.

There was no plane crash. In fact, the pilot landed us smooth as silk at LAX, not even a jiggle.

It felt like someone else's country, being back in the United States. The L.A. airport was like too many of your favorite toys on Christmas, so you didn't know where to go first—should it be the pizza stand or the drinking fountain with as much cold, free water as you needed or gumballs or fifteen different kinds of potato chips or Lakers T-shirts that weren't crummy knockoffs with the name spelled wrong or was it enough to stand still and listen to American music coming over invisible speakers? It was too much; it was so much that when my father pushed through the crowd to hug me and he told me to speak Thai, I couldn't think of one word.

My father looked more tired than I felt, as if too much had been squeezed out of him. He and my mother had been divorced for fifteen years, and he lived in L.A. now, but I used to imagine there was one part of him that still loved my mother. There was no evidence beyond occasional checking-in phone calls, lent money that wasn't always repaid, birthday cards; I only wanted to think that there was a certain kind of love that could outlast everything, even the end of a marriage. But now I knew what it was like to grow tired of loving someone as difficult as my mother—especially once you saw what your life was without her.

"We tried to find you," he said, reaching to carry my backpack. I let him, even though it was heavier than he expected, and his shoulder slumped.

"Cal told me."

"This isn't the way it should happen," which seemed like a sentence he'd been saving, as if it had special meaning. As if there was one way anything should happen.

We were on the escalator heading down to the parking garage, and I watched the swoosh and glide as the steps disappeared into themselves, not listening to my father who was saying things I didn't want to hear, words like burial and lawyer and police report and house for sale. I was thinking about summers when my mother, brother, and I visited my grandmother, and how I liked to ride up and down the escalators in Hudson's in downtown Detroit, holding my grandmother's hand while my mother shopped for school clothes for me and Cal. All the way up to fourteen (the "employees only" floor) and then back down to B, the bargain shop, where my grandmother said my mother could've saved money by buying seconds and sale items. Then back up. I asked my grandmother where the stairs went, but she didn't know. "They go where they're supposed to go," she said.

"Are you sure you don't want to stay longer than tonight?" my father asked as we stubbed our toes against the grate and stepped off the escalator.

"I need to get to Phoenix," I said, and that didn't sound like what I meant. "Back home."

He opened his mouth as if he were going to start spouting out more of those words I didn't want to hear, so I spoke quickly:

"Where do the escalator stairs go?" and he laughed, not thinking it could be a real question, and I laughed with him.

I woke up suddenly at four-thirty. The guest room in my father's condo was too quiet, the way a group gets before someone says something that makes everyone angry.

There was still one part of me that couldn't believe she was gone; Show me the body, it said. I hated that thing inside me that needed proof, that always asked why and how and when.

But did I hate it worse than the part that whispered terrible secrets like, All that drinking she did, she deserved to die; or, You'll never have to pick her up from some lowlife bar the night before two finals or listen to her cry and tell you she's sorry and then not remember any of it the next day or have to see her hiding behind those stupid sunglasses?

Or was the worst part the one that said, Stop—because you don't understand how much you'll miss her?

That's what happened now at night—or morning or afternoon or a thousand times a day.

My father was only trying to make me feel better—"It shouldn't happen this way"—but it *did* happen that way, so now what?

It was only fifteen minutes or so of being awake, but it felt like three days I'd never get back.

Cal hustled me off to some lawyer's office straight from the Phoenix airport the next morning, and things were explained to me in immense detail and I signed documents and I did a lot of nodding and smiling and sipping too-strong coffee a secretary brought me. I murmured "I understand" many times—sometimes when I did understand and sometimes when I didn't. We were seated around a table strewn with documents, and I faced a big picture window that looked out onto the tops of the palm trees lining Central Avenue, behind them a blue sky, off in the corner the rough edges of Camelback Mountain. The words for these forgotten places came back to me as I twisted in my chair one way and the other as the lawyer explained, and I pretended to listen. The Sugar Bowl in Scottsdale where we went for ice-cream sundaes on our birthdays. Eating tamales at El Molino in the junky courtyard where the wild cats begged for handouts under the picnic tables. Sneaking out of school with my boyfriend and his friends to drive to Mesa and catch the Cubs at spring training at HoHoKam Park, everyone thinking I was cool for knowing how to keep score. Sunrise horseback rides in the Superstition Mountains, certain we'd discover the Lost Dutchman's Mine and return with our pockets full of gold. Carmelita's Bakery in South Phoenix and the handmade tortillas so perfect you bought one to eat right then with butter along with your two dozen to take home. Hiking with my mother to the top of Squaw Peak to watch the sun come up over the valley, how we looked at each other and felt like we were the only people alive even as we stood by three chattering tourists. All things I couldn't take with me to Thailand. It wasn't only leaving behind long screaming fights with slamming doors and waking up to see my mother wearing her dark glasses and knowing what the day would be from that and racing to finish my homework before I heard the crack of the ice tray.

The lawyer (Mr. White, Mr. Green, Mr. Brown; his name was a color, but I couldn't keep straight which one) leaned over and patted my hand and asked if I had any questions. He asked it like I shouldn't have any because he was a busy, billable man. He even started to stand up, and so did my brother.

I said, "What did you say about the house again?"

"Now that you're back, we can put it up for sale," he said. "It's a slow market right now, though we think that—"

"I want to stay there while I'm here."

"But you said—" Cal started.

"I changed my mind." At the airport it had seemed like a good idea to stay at Cal's apartment. Now, I wanted to be home, to see what "being home" really meant, to see my mother's house, my mother's things.

The lawyer raised his fingers into a little tent and looked down through them.

Cal said, "Is this such a hot idea, Amy?"

"It's my house."

"Yours and your brother's," the lawyer said. "Of course, your father stepped in to take care of some of the necessary payments and such."

"No one's really cleaned it out," Cal said. "It's like she's still there."

"That's fine."

The lawyer tilted his arm to glance at his watch.

Cal said, "We'll stop by after lunch. Then you decide." It was the way an adult handled someone else's embarrassing child.

"Very good," the lawyer said, already on to his next client, his lunch meeting, the rest of the day. We were something that happened ages ago.

On the way to the elevator, Cal said, "Well, that's over," as if he were looking at a long list of things to do, things to say, people to see. His life was listed out: this degree followed by this job then this promotion and this career move and on and on like a board game that's not all that fun; he kept an appointment book, filed people's business cards, and always left a phone number where he could be reached.

We went for Mexican at a place I'd never been to, the kind of place I didn't usually go to, with piñatas hanging off the ceiling, colorful blankets stapled along the walls, waitresses who say, I'll be your server today, the kind of place where cab drivers steer tourists. But Cal claimed it was good, had won an award for best machaca burritos. And best margaritas, I noticed on the menu. Maybe my mother had been here.

After we ordered, Cal pulled out his wallet and took out some newspaper clippings about the car accident and the obituary. I pretended to read them but the words blurred, like a language I wasn't used to seeing.

"I can copy them for you," he said. "Or take these."

"What for?"

"Don't you think someone should keep them?" he asked.

I set the torn-out pieces of paper on the table, right into a ring of water from his iced tea. A dark stain grew in the middle of the obituary, right under her name in bold print. "I thought she wanted to be cremated."

"We went through all the papers and nothing said that." His fingers drummed the table, and I thought of the lawyer, of the two of them sorting through a drawer of stuff, not knowing the truly important papers would be hidden somewhere—under a mattress? behind sofa cushions?—making their own sense of what my mother left, the two of them arranging things the way they saw them. "Makes you realize you've got to get all this down in writing, even at our age," Cal said. "I'm setting up one of those let-me-die-if-I'm-a-vegetable deals. You should, too."

"Remember how she said thinking about her body underground made her sick to her stomach?" I said. "On those drives to Detroit when we were kids, remember we used to talk about what was the worst way to die, and she always right away said buried alive?"

"You're the one who said buried alive," Cal said. "She said eaten by rats."

"Nobody said anything about rats," I said. "She said buried alive, I said a hundred razor blades slicing across my neck all at once, and you said getting gored by a bull at the rodeo. Still worried about that?"

"Okay, so I was six years old." Cal dumped another packet of sugar into his iced tea, spun his spoon around.

"You never used to drink iced tea," I said.

"I always drank iced tea." His voice was hard.

"It's just that—"

"She wasn't alive when we buried her, Amy."

The waitress brought our burritos; she was laughing at something someone else had said, and her honking laugh was like geese crowding a small room. As soon as she walked away, both Cal and I mimicked it perfectly, and then we laughed.

"Rats, bulls, razor blades," he said. "It's never what you think."

"Or when," I said.

"You couldn't've saved her," he said, parroting words some professional had told him.

"That's not what I meant."

"Then what?"

I said, "You just never know when things will happen."

"Well, duh, Amy," he said, "it's called, That's Life," and I realized he was still angry, would maybe always be angry at me.

Across the room the waitress laughed, but it didn't seem funny now. There was a too-long silence. Had I really been to Thailand?

I asked Cal about school, and as we ate, I let him talk about being back in Phoenix after living four years in Tucson, and the MBA program at ASU, and how his statistics class was a bear, and how his marketing professor asked him to help with some research over the summer for a paper to be given at a conference, and all the rest. It was a conversation you wouldn't mind overhearing, but like always, it didn't say what we meant. That's what had been so perfect about letters and postcards in Thailand, they never pretended to be what they weren't.

We came in through the kitchen door, the sound of the lock unsnapping just as I remembered—too loud, too sudden, as if there could be no secret comings and goings in this house. But of course there were; you had to know how to ease the key just right, to bury it in your fist. The kitchen looked exactly as it had the last time I was here—champagne brunch the day before I left for Thailand (she made a big deal of drinking orange juice)—but the smell was different. It was like how you could walk into someone else's house with your eyes closed and you just know it's not your house but you couldn't say how you know.

I tugged the string to the blind in the kitchen. Its clatter filled the room, and light angled in at my feet. I stepped out of it. The plants lining the sill were brown. I touched a leaf; it crumbled into pieces. No one could think to water a couple plants? "How come nobody's been through all this stuff?" I asked.

Cal shrugged. "I don't know."

"You were waiting for me?"

"Not that."

I opened the kitchen cupboard. There was an open box of Triscuits, the wax bag not all the way crumpled shut; the crackers were stale. My father always complained that my mother constantly left boxes open, crackers, cereal, cookies. I rolled the wax bag down tight, tucked in the box flap, returned the box to the cupboard, and closed the door. "So, am I supposed to do it all?"

I looked away, at the dead plants, at the stupid, dead plants. I'd been the one watering them when she was alive; no telling how long they'd been here, just sitting all brown and crackly in their hard, dry dirt. I wanted to fling my arm along the sill and knock them onto the floor. But doing that would just leave me with a bigger mess.

I set my hands on the counter; for a moment they didn't even look like my hands, and I stared at them until the moment passed, then I repeated my question: "Am I supposed to do it all?"

"I'll get your stuff from the car," Cal said abruptly, walking to the door, and as soon as he was gone, the house felt still, like something holding its breath, and when the air conditioner hummed on, I was so startled I gasped and felt my heart pound harder. I reached to turn on the radio by the sink; it was tuned to an oldies station, and I imagined my mother alone at night, singing with the Supremes as she did the dishes, no one to make fun of her bad voice, no one to tease that she was getting the words wrong. It was the only time she sang, in the kitchen. I opened the cupboard door under the sink and knelt to look inside. Tucked behind the Windex and the Mr. Clean and the extra rolls of paper towels was a half-empty bottle of gin. Can something still be a surprise if it's what you're looking for?

Cal came through the door, and I stood up. He dropped my suitcase and backpack on the floor.

"What?" he said.

"Nothing." I turned off the radio; it was a commercial for the bank where I'd had my first savings account.

He said, "I hate being here." He folded his arms across his chest. They were big now, and looked like they'd be hard if I touched them, as if he spent time lifting weights. It struck me that maybe he was good-looking; he'd told me that someone had asked him to stop by to audition for the "Boys of ASU" calendar, but he blew it off. He said, "It's like . . ."

"Like what?"

"I just hate it."

"I guess we're supposed to put it up for sale," I said.

"Real estate market's down the toilet," he said.

"It's probably stupid for Dad to pay for electricity and stuff if no one's using it," I said.

"It's like, here's her house," he said. "She's gone, but her house is still here. A house lasts longer than a person."

"Thais build houses for the spirits to live in," I said. "Little shrines outside the real house, and supposedly the spirits prefer living there." I sounded like a teacher, as if I were pointing to a chalkboard as I spoke. It seemed like someone else's life back when I was taking photographs of spirit houses, writing everything down in that stupid journal. For what? To keep in a drawer?

"It's still under the sink, isn't it?" he asked abruptly.

"And probably in her underwear drawer, and in a shoebox in the back of the closet, and shoved behind the *National Geographics* in the bookcase," I said. "We used to find bottles all over the place."

"You poured them down the sink."

"She never said anything."

"I won't drink," he said. "I was the only guy who pledged my fraternity sober." When I didn't say anything, he said, "What about you?"

Silence stacked up between us. "Because she drank too much doesn't mean I can't drink at all," I said, and I couldn't shake the teacher voice. "I'm living my own life, not some rerun of hers. Things are different in Thailand. I'm different."

He looked at me like, Wherever you go, you'll still be the daughter of an alcoholic. "What do you need from the grocery store?" he asked. "I have to stop for a couple things, and I could pick up stuff for you."

"I missed baking," I said, nudging the flour and sugar bins to see how full they were. They were some long-ago Mother's Day present; "Flour, sugar," she read off the fronts, "how cute," but I was the one who remembered to pour the bags of flour and sugar into them after trips to the store. I looked inside; there were half-empty, ripped bags of each. I said to Cal, "Milk, eggs, butter, flour, sugar, chocolate chips. The sugariest cereal they've got. Pop-Tarts."

"See you in half an hour," he said.

"Any flavor Pringles," I said.

Two other people might have hugged each other, but by the time I thought of it, the door was slamming shut, and I was alone. I used to be the way he was; until I went to Thailand, every minute here felt like a day yanked off my own life. Or that's how I remembered it.

While he was gone, I went to all the old hiding places, the ones I'd mentioned and others, places he didn't know about, places I'd forgotten until I walked through the house. There was something in each spot, a pint with a few swallows left, unopened Tanqueray, some cheap brand in the liquor store bag. She still thought she had to hide all this.

I brought the bottles to the kitchen counter and lined them up, seven in all. I was about to pour them down the sink, but I realized I could leave the bottles there all night, all week, for a year, two years, and no one would drink them. Like the house, they'd out-lasted my mother.

Cal came through the door with a bag of groceries that he plopped on the counter. "What's that?" he asked.

"Mom's stash," I said. "I think I got it all."

"All this was hidden?"

I nodded. "Who was she trying to kid."

He grabbed the closest bottle and unscrewed the cap. Then he poured the clear liquid down the drain, raising a sharp smell—I'd once heard my mother say on the phone, "I'd sell one of my children for a good martini right now," and then laugh; which child? I wondered. Cal shook the bottle to get the last drops, then chucked it into the trash can. "Your turn," he said.

I shook my head. I would've left them all out as long as I could, through my stay in Phoenix, through the real estate agent's open house, to the closing; I wasn't the same girl who used to have to sneak around watching after my mother, trying so hard to take care of someone who didn't want to be taken care of.

He glared at me. "You're not going to drink it, are you?"

I shook my head again. "Go ahead," and he poured the next one. He was afraid to do it back when it mattered; he'd find me and whisper, "Look in the shoebox," and there'd be a new bottle, so I'd sneak it to the kitchen and pour it out, leaving the bottle on the sink where she'd be sure to see it, then wait to see if this would be the time she yelled, if this time would be something different. The empty bottles always disappeared somehow; I couldn't find them in the trash.

As Cal methodically went down the line of bottles, I remem-bered one summer at our grandmother's house in Detroit, the way we spent hours outside with our mother's cousins' children, squirt-ing each other with the hose, playing games under the sprinkler, like tag and capture the flag and red rover and what color is my birdy. When someone's yard got too waterlogged, we moved the sprinkler and hose to another yard; we played this way every day, from after lunch (waiting thirty minutes after eating so we wouldn't get stomach cramps and die), all the way up to supper (spending the thirty waiting-after-supper minutes drying the silverware with a soft dish towel my grandmother had embroidered), and on and on until it was dark and time for bed, and we'd run out of "five more minutes, please's," and everyone had to be dragged home, and sometimes they'd forget to turn off the sprinkler so I could hear the wide arc of water whoosh back and forth outside my window all night. One night I was listening to that whoosh, the moonlight so bright in my eyes it seemed wasteful to sleep, and I heard something different, giggles rippling up to my window, and I sat up in bed to see who'd snuck out of the house, who, like me, couldn't resist that moon, but it was my mother in her white nightgown standing under the sprinkler. That same deep pit opened in my stomach—she'd been so good that summer—but then she stretched out her arms, said, "Come on," and my grandmother came down the porch steps, her arms crossed and holding her bathrobe tight around her, and she murmured, "I shouldn't," but she did. She and my mother held hands and laughed and it was as if they knew exactly how they looked—under the moonlight the droplets of water fell on them like tiny silver coins—because they stood there for a long time, longer than I was able to watch, and the next morning I would've thought it was all a dream except that for the first time my grandmother wasn't wearing her robe when she fixed breakfast.

The next year when we were driving to Detroit, all Cal and I did was talk about how we were going to play games under the sprinkler for three weeks, but when we got there, it was like no one had ever played under the sprinkler in their lives, it was like that had never happened and Cal and I were the only ones who thought it had; so we spent the visit playing Monopoly with everyone instead, which was okay but not the same as the sprinkler, and our mother wore her dark glasses around the house in the morning and took drives late at night, and my grandmother and her sisters spent too many afternoons whispering around the kitchen table, dropping silent when I walked in looking for Kool-Aid, someone finally saying in a fake voice, "We were just talking about how much you've grown, Amy," when I was old enough to know who they'd been talking about and what they were saying; later, I couldn't decide whether I was the most angry at them or at my mother or at the fact that we weren't playing under the sprinklers anymore or that I wasn't good at Monopoly because I never got hotels on my property.

Cal turned on the faucet and ran the garbage disposal for a longer time than he needed to, and the smell faded. "I've got to go," he called, not looking at me. "Last chance." He turned off the disposal, the water; the house felt too quiet again.

"I'll be fine." I reached for the groceries, started to put things on the counter. As he was leaving, I called after him, "Hey." I'd been about to ask if he remembered that summer when we played under the sprinkler, but what if he didn't? "What time tomorrow?" I asked instead.

He pulled a small appointment book out of his back pocket, flipped through several pages. "I've got a ten o'clock class, then I need to meet with my professor for like fifteen minutes, so how about I pick you up, say twelve-thirty, and we'll grab a bite."

It sounded like what you say when you're going out for lunch, not like what you say when your mother died. I nodded. Maybe it was a mistake to want to be here. Things were so simple back in Thailand; all you had to do to get by when you didn't understand something was nod and smile. They knew by looking that you were a foreigner.

I'd walked through every room in the house, sat in the chair or on the floor in each and looked around. I was responsible for everything I saw. If I wanted to throw away that ugly Georgia

O'Keeffe cow skull print, I could. No one would fuss or notice it was missing. But I couldn't even take it down off the wall; I just ran my finger along the edge of the frame, collected a line of dust that I let fall onto the carpet. Sofa—mine. Tape player and all the tapes, the old records—mine. The raincoat in the closet with the used tissue in the pocket—mine. The pennies in the bowl on the dresser in the bedroom—mine. The scissors in the drawer that were never where they were supposed to be—mine. I was expected to pack up my mother's life into a bunch of cardboard boxes, donate it all to Goodwill, where a whole new set of people would buy the stuff and make their own memories with it, sort of like reincarnation.

It was me coming in to take care of everything again.

The hell. If Cal could walk away and leave this crap behind, so could I. My father could keep on with what he'd been doing all along, paying the bills from a distance, the price of staying untangled.

I went back to look at the Georgia O'Keeffe. I'd thrown a softball at it once and cracked the glass; I got grounded for a week, but that night my mother asked me to help her make popcorn balls to take to a Halloween party, and as we were molding the goopy popcorn, she told me all about how she met my father and knew that she was in love with him because he was the first person who gave her a nickname, but she wouldn't tell me what he'd called her, and I started tickling her to try to get her to tell, but she wouldn't, and she started tickling me, and we laughed and got ourselves sticky all over. She let me use her good bubble bath before I went to bed.

I closed my eyes. There was a story about everything. In Thailand it was only my stories, told exactly the way I wanted them told to people who barely understood English.

I fell asleep on the couch in front of the TV, woke up and should've been hungry but wasn't. Everywhere I looked now was something else to remember—finding an Easter egg behind the candlesticks in the hutch in July, my mother saying, "There's still one more you kids didn't get"; my mother draping her good tablecloths over the chairs and card tables the day after a bridge party so Cal and I could play jungle tents underneath, bringing us lion-and-tiger stew for lunch that tasted a lot like Beef-a-roni. A million things.

Only the kitchen was safe, because there I could think about Cal and me earlier in the day, turning it into our place, not hers. Between the jet lag and the nap, I was way screwed up, and I wasn't at all tired, though it was morning where I'd been, or afternoon, or tomorrow or yesterday, or some time that wasn't this time. I was too stubborn to call Cal to pick me up and get me out, so I decided to do some baking.

The utensils weren't where I remembered, the mixing bowls, the measuring cups, the wooden spoons—they'd all been shuffled around, making room for things I'd never seen before, a cappuccino machine, a bread machine, a pasta maker, the sorts of things I saw in American magazine ads in Thailand and thought, Who needs these? and it turns out my mother did. I imagined her mixing up squid ink fettuccine (nothing ever so simple as spaghetti), watching long dark noodles spew out of her little machine as if she'd conjured them. I could hear my grandmother exclaiming, "Black noodles! Who thinks of this nonsense?" My great-grandmother told me all anyone needed to be a good cook was a big bowl, a sharp knife, and an iron skillet.

The bowls were in what used to be the cereal cupboard, and the measuring spoons and cups were with the dirty dishes in the dishwasher, so I washed them in the sink and ran the dishwasher. How come no one had checked before now? But then who expected to die with dirty dishes at home?

I started to assemble ingredients—my favorite part of cooking, lining everything up on one side of the counter, seeing all the parts that were about to come together into the whole. Or maybe

I liked everything set out because that's not the way my mother cooked—she was always discovering she was out of something while the mixer was running, always swearing that she knew there was tarragon somewhere as she pulled everything down out of the spice shelf while something sizzled and burned in a little frying pan.

As I was searching for vanilla I found a knotted produce bag from Kroger, my grandmother's grocery store in Detroit. Inside was a lifetime's supply of poppy seeds. They still smelled okay, earthy, and I couldn't imagine why my mother had so many poppy seeds, what she would make with them, or how long they'd been there. It could've been my grandmother slipping them into a bag of food for us to take home after a summer visit to Detroit, but the last time we'd all been there was nine years ago; I was sixteen, and Alzheimer's was already starting in on my grandmother. Or maybe one of the great-aunts sent them; when my grandmother went into the nursing home, they took over as if a baton had been passed; they were always sending down food they thought couldn't be found in Arizona—rye bread, three-pound jars of sauerkraut from Poland, home-canned tomatoes. As far as I remembered, my mother threw it all away, everything but these carefully wrapped poppy seeds, and I twirled my finger through them in the bag, around and around as if I were rubbing a genie's bottle.

The phone rang, and I almost dropped the poppy seeds. It was late, eleven-thirty, so my first thought was bad news, then my next thought was Cal, then I decided wrong number—bad news for someone else.

"Hello?" I said. There was only static, bouncy jitters like the buzz of a mosquito. "Hello?"

"Ginger?"

Though it was her phone, I wasn't expecting her name. It was the same as when you're a child—maybe you understand that your mother's name is Ginger, but that's not who she really is.

"Ginger? Are you there, dear?" Each word was slower and quieter than the one before until the last almost drifted into nothing, into a word that was not thought, not said.

"Grandma?" and as soon as I said it, I knew it was her; it was impossible to imagine her calling from a nursing home at whatever time it was in Detroit, but she was.

"Ginger?"

"It's Amy, Grandma. I'm home from Thailand."

"Where's Ginger?" she said.

"This is Amy, Ginger's daughter," I said. "Remember? I visited you all those summers. We used to—"

"I call Ginger every night, but she won't answer the phone," she said. "For weeks now. Same old Ginger, stubborn as anything." She made a dry, scratchy sound that maybe was a laugh, maybe a cough.

"How are you?" I asked.

"I miss Ginger," she said. "She left."

"Grandma—"

"She thought she wasn't like the rest of us," she said. "Not one of us."

"What do you mean?"

"But she *was*," she said. "She couldn't see it, but I knew. A mother understands her daughter better than the daughter ever knows. Why is that? Why?" She sighed, not waiting for an answer, as if any answer I gave would be a disappointment.

"Tell me more about Ginger." I liked saying my mother's name this way instead of as a response to someone official asking, Name of the deceased?

"She moved far away; she's gone." There was a pause. "She visits me every summer. When she left, it was summer and before she got on the bus, she said summer was the time you wanted to get on the road and go someplace else."

There was a long silence, almost as if she'd set down the phone. "Hello?" I called, just above a whisper.

"What do I know about being someplace else?" she said. "I was never anyplace else my whole life. My mother wouldn't allow it. But I didn't tell Ginger all that when she went away, I nodded like I knew. Maybe if I didn't nod, she wouldn't have left. Maybe if I'd ever been someplace else, she wouldn't't've thought she had to go. Too late now. Good-bye is the hardest word for a mother to say, I told Ginger. Not for her—good-bye, good-bye, chirping it like a bird. I waited for her to come back to be with her family, I waited and waited." She coughed. "Can I talk to her now, please?"

I listened to her breathe for a moment, then I said, "Grandma, don't you remember me? It's Amy. I was in Thailand for almost three years, but I'm back now."

"Amy is the nurse here with red hair," she said.

I looked at the bag of poppy seeds. Clutching the plastic bag so hard was making my palm sticky with sweat. How could I make her remember me? All those postcards and letters from Thailand were nothing, were words she couldn't understand.

I asked, "How do you make poppy seed cake?" It was what they ate with their coffee, my grandmother and her sisters sitting around the table in the kitchen, the sun moving across the squares of the checkered tablecloth like a pendulum swinging one way; I never much liked that cake, just as I never liked the coffee either, but I always asked for some anyway, just so I could hear my grandmother say, "This one knows the good Polish food; remember how it was Ma's favorite?" My mother wouldn't eat the poppy seed cake, she said she was on a diet; or she'd take a piece but pick at it, either thinking no one noticed or not caring that they all noticed.

My grandmother said, "Poppy seed cake?"

"To have with coffee," I said.

"*Strucla?*" The strange word sounded like it came from somewhere far away. "I know that," she said, slow and surprised.

"How do I make one?" I opened the drawer where pens and notepads were supposed to be; it was filled with place mats. I didn't want her to stop, so I stretched the phone cord so I could reach the wipe-off memo board on the fridge.

"My mother said I made the best; of all the girls, mine was the one she liked most. Never too dry, never too sweet. This is why— because I listened to her; I watched and did what she did. Always whip your egg yolks with salt first to keep them yellow. And my Ginger . . . you know Ginger? I showed her *strucla*. Chicken fat with the butter was what I showed her to keep the cake moist. Or listen—goose fat is better."

"Goose fat!"

"But butter alone is good. A piece of soft butter as big as one finger folded over. Mix that into the sugar, about half a teacup. Two eggs out of the icebox half an hour before you start; all you need is the yolks. Put the whites aside to slip into tomorrow's scrambled eggs; salt the yolks and whip so they turn the color of lemons; mix into your sugar. Are you listening?"

"Yes," I said, writing fast on the memo board, turning her words into abbreviations to figure out later.

"Heat your milk almost to boiling, about a teacup, let it cool down to warm; why not just heat it only to warm? I don't know, but this is how you do it—almost boiling first, then cooled down. Yeast dissolved in a spoonful of warm water, and then into the bowl. You need a pinch of ground cardamom—smells like summer, Ginger said—then add some of your milk, then some flour, milk, flour, milk, flour—two big cupfuls of flour total, and knead until the dough pulls away from your fingers. Rest your dough some-where warm for a couple hours—do laundry, weed the garden, change everyone's bedsheets; there's always something to fill time with—punch down your dough, let it rise another hour." She was silent, as if she'd run out of words sooner than expected.

"What about the poppy seeds?" I asked.

"This is what Ginger didn't like," she said. "Poppy seed filling rolled inside. Mud, she called it. I rolled it up with no filling; too dry. Then I remembered Ma had another way, make the dough into four logs and braid them together; rise once more for luck, then brush egg yolk on top and sprinkle poppy seeds over. She said, 'In the old country, when there was barely sugar, this is how women found to manage. There's always a way to manage.' Did I say braid the four logs and let rise the third time for luck? Forty-five minutes in the oven. That is *strucla z makiem*. See how simple it is?"

There was a long pause as my writing finally caught up to her words. I crooked the phone between my head and shoulder and put a poppy seed on my tongue.

"Wait," she said. "There's more."

Another pause, longer than the previous one. A scrap of some-one else's conversation cut through the silence.

She said, "I prayed for the kind of daughter who would cook with me in the kitchen, but Ginger wasn't that kind, and that's why she went away and never came back."

"No, that's not why."

"Then why? How could a daughter leave?"

I had the answer ready; I thought I was waiting for my mother to ask, but she never did, and of course now she wouldn't. Because you have to. How else will you know who you really are? You think maybe you're more than the person pouring tomato juice for the hangovers, but how can you find out?

My grandmother said, "Tell her when I die is too late. It's sad to learn what too late means. Such a stubborn Polish girl." They were words you could carve into a tombstone. "She should answer the phone herself tomorrow when I call."

I thought about that distant buzz you hear when a phone isn't being answered, that rhythmic scrape against your ear and how you think each ring will be the one that's picked up, and when it isn't, you think, "Just one more," and the crushing sudden silence when you give up, twenty rings later, thirty. I said, "I'm so sorry. Ginger's dead."

"They told me that," she said. "But it can't be right. Can it?"

"It's hard to believe," I said.

"But she's my daughter."

"I know." They didn't look alike, they didn't talk alike, they didn't think the same way. Each thought the other was impossible. Did any of that matter?

She said, "I forget who you are."

"I'm Amy."

"But *who* are you?"

She meant, Are you Ginger's friend or neighbor or what? But I shouldn't have to explain who I was to her; she should know me. What did it mean to have the same memories, to be in the same family if it all came to this, to be explaining who you were? It was like looking in a mirror and seeing no reflection, like coming back from a vacation with no pictures.

She repeated her question: "Who are you?"

I tried to be patient. "I'm your granddaughter. I'm Ginger's girl. I'm Amy."

"My Amy?"

Without thinking I nodded, and it was as if she saw me because she spoke immediately: "Then you know *strucla* because it's in you, in your veins. You're a Polish girl, just like me and your mother and my mother."

"But I—"

"You know how to make *strucla*."

"I do?"

"I showed you how that summer . . . what summer was it? You mixed the egg yolks and salt with a fork in the little white bowl from the set Ma got with the green stamps. We made the braid; the poppy seeds on top were like snow, you said. Remember that? Remember that summer? Which summer . . . was it the summer we . . . ? Oh, I don't know now which summer that was. One summer." She made clicking noises with her tongue.

I slipped one hand into the bag of poppy seeds, let them trickle through my fingers, cool like sand at night.

She said, "One summer. I want to remember."

I closed my eyes. "Was it the summer—"

"I don't know."

"Was it the summer all the kids were playing games under the sprinkler?" I said. "We were running around all the time, and I wore your apron over my bathing suit in the kitchen, and you braided the four pieces of dough. There was a trick you said, a special way so the four pieces came out even. You brushed egg on the top and I started to sprinkle seeds, but you grabbed a handful and said, 'Never skimp on poppy seeds—more!' So I threw a handful, but I missed and seeds scattered on the floor, and we laughed so much my mother came into the kitchen, and she threw a handful, and you told us how Great-Grandma used to make the four-way braid and say, 'Here's Wanda and here's Joane and here's Helen and here's Marie, all my four girls,' and so she called it the four-girl cake. And you said, 'Here's Amy and here's Ginger, and here's me, and here's Ma,' and I was part of the four-girl cake. It was that summer, remember?"

"Oh, yes," she said, her voice very polite. "Of course. I remember that summer."

"That was a great summer," I said. "One of the best. We—"

"Tell me who you are again."

"Amy."

"The nurse with the red hair is Amy," she said.

"No! I'm Amy!"

Something on the phone line crackled.

"Amy"—she said it like she had a bad taste collecting in her mouth—"tell Ginger I can call again tomorrow night. They don't want me to call, but I manage. I must talk to her tomorrow," and then she was gone, the silence clicking over into a dial tone, and then into a recorded voice smugly telling me to hang up and redial if I wished to make a call, and finally that angry insistent beep, pushing my grandmother's voice out of my head.

I hung up the phone.

It was that summer, I was sure of it. I remembered throwing the seeds and missing the cake, I remembered laughing. Funny I didn't remember beating the egg yolks in a little white bowl. I wore the apron over my bathing suit, the string wrapped twice around my waist and tied in a bow. My bathing suit was wet, I remember coming in from the sprinkler; my grandmother said, "Amy, want to help me in the kitchen?" and I said, "We're playing red rover," and she closed the screen door. She closed the screen door . . . and I walked away, and the other team called, "Red rover, red rover, send Amy right over," and I broke through the line. I saw my grandmother watching at the door, smiling, smiling like there were a hundred years of red rover waiting for me, not just the three more days of that visit, and it was my mother making *strucla* in the kitchen that summer while I played under the sprinkler. I came in at the end, to throw the seeds on top. I'd heard them laughing, and I was jealous, so I tied on the apron, and I was in time only to throw the seeds and hear the story.

How could I know that was what would push through the fog of my grandmother's memories, making *strucla* that one summer?

I did exactly as she'd said—butter the size of my finger folded, eggs out of the fridge and yolks whipped with salt, dough kneaded until it peeled away from my fingers, the whole bit. I even found ground cardamom in the back of the cupboard, unopened, with a price sticker from Kroger. While the dough rose, I did other things. I still wasn't tired, so I skimmed all the magazines that were on my mother's coffee table; I unloaded the dishwasher, guessing at where some of the things went; I looked through the cupboards and threw away food I didn't think I'd be eating while I was here—half empty bags of croutons, stale crackers, and old spice bottles with a quarter inch left of the spice—three cinnamons, two basils, a dried parsley; when it was time to punch down the dough, I did, and it gasped slightly like it had expected to go on rising forever.

I still wasn't tired. I started a load of laundry with the stuff in the hamper; I stacked up the years and years worth of *National Geographics* to take to a school where the kids could cut out the pictures Cal and I were never allowed to; I made a list of cleaning supplies to buy, then ripped that up and looked through the Yellow Pages and circled cleaning companies to call for estimates.

The sky outside the window was fading from black to gray when the dough was ready to be braided. I spread handfuls of flour on the counter and plopped the dough in the middle, lifting a quick white puff, and I sneezed into my shoulder. The dough felt like soft skin. I divided it in half, then each half in half—the four girls—and rolled each piece with my palms along the floured counter. When I had four strips, equal enough in length and width, I started to braid, but right away I could see that one strand wasn't incorporated properly and was only draped over the others; my next attempt got me two separate twists; by the third try my braid was just a wad of dough, and I was crying: it just didn't seem possible to braid four strands—three were easy, two would be a twist, but I couldn't do four, no one had shown me the trick to the four-way braid that one summer in the kitchen, and I didn't even like this cake.

I punched down my dough and slopped it back into the bowl. So many tears streamed down my face, I felt like it was wearing away.

I wanted to be my grandmother, calling every night, certain that one time she'd answer, that one time she'd say, "Hello?" in her smooth voice. There were just a few things to say, a few quick questions, and if I had one more chance I'd talk fast, I'd ask everything: "What was I like when I was a baby? What was my first word? How many hot dogs did I eat that one time? What was the name of that girl who threw up when the clown kissed her at my birthday party? How hot was it that night the air conditioner broke and you let us sleep in the bathtub? What do you think is the worst way to die, really—rats, buried alive, razor blades, gored by a bull in the rodeo? Or like this, packed up in boxes and garbage bags?"

I wanted to be my mother, sure that going away was the right thing. "Do you ever miss Detroit?" I asked her in the car on the way there, "because sometimes I wish we lived there with Grandma." "There's nothing to miss," she said, each word a chopped-up-no-more-questions kind of answer.

I'd told everyone one year in Thailand, then wrote and said two, and now I was stretched into three, maybe because, like my mother, I didn't know how to go back once I'd been away.

Once I asked my great-grandmother if she missed Poland. After a minute she answered in Polish. "What'd she say?" I asked my grandmother, and she translated, "It's impossible for a good daughter to leave; it's impossible for a good daughter to stay." "That's not what I asked," I said; "Of course it is," my great-grandmother said in English, and she touched my cheek.

I dried my eyes on a dish towel, blew my nose, then dropped the towel in the trash. I had to start learning to manage. Women in my family had been braiding bread for centuries. I pulled the dough out of the bowl and divided it into four pieces, rolled the pieces out, and looped them together. Okay, it wasn't a braid, it wasn't a twist; it was four pieces of dough connected, not neat the way I remember my grandmother's *strucla*, but something you could serve to women around a kitchen table.

I set it aside to rise one more time for luck as my grandmother had said. While the *strucla* was rising, I copied the recipe from the wipe-off memo board onto a piece of paper, using my grandmother's words as exact as I could get them.

I brushed egg yolk on top and didn't skimp on poppy seeds.

While it baked, I walked around the house. It was different this time. The stories I remembered were mixed-up good and bad, streaky, hard to hold and hard to let go. Ready or not, I was responsible for them now.

When the *strucla* came out of the oven, the kitchen smelled like a house I knew, like a house I'd recognize immediately—in Thailand, in another life, anywhere. This is what I wanted to come back for, and I sat at the table and ate big pieces of my warm cake, and it was almost as if they were all there with me—I honestly think I smelled coffee, though I hadn't made any.

The day I went to see my mother's grave was unseasonably hot; the guy on the radio thought it might be the first one-hundred-degree day of the year. The whole time I was driving along the curvy cemetery roads, he kept talking about the weather, saying things like, "You know how Satan greets all the new recruits? Hot enough for ya?" He thought he was pretty funny.

I parked the car and walked through the grass to my mother's stone. She never much liked grass in Arizona—"It's a desert for God's sake," she always said—but this grass looked cool and restful, as if hundreds of sprinklers watered it all night as soon as the sun went down. She would've liked this grass, this place. It wasn't like being buried alive at all; it was like summer surrounding you.

I had decided not to return to Thailand right away. There were things to do here. Read through the thick folder of papers and letters I'd found tucked under my mother's mattress. Meet Cal's girlfriend. See my father. Visit my grandmother. Maybe she wouldn't remember me. Maybe she would. Talk to the rest of my family in Detroit, not just send letters.

When I looked at my mother's marker I didn't know what to think, if I should touch it or kneel or whisper a prayer. So I just looked at it, its smooth shiny surface, the way her name and the two dates were so perfectly centered, as if this stone had been formed eons ago for this name, these dates. I didn't touch it. Instead I took the last slice of *strucla* out of my purse, unwrapped the foil, and set the cake in the grass on top of some withered flowers. "Four-girl cake just like Grandma's," I said. But that didn't seem enough. "I've got the recipe now," I added, and that still wasn't exactly right. "We know you had it in you, Mom, in your veins. Just like it's in mine," and I knew I'd never get closer than that.

I watched cars pull up a short ways away, someone else's funeral. Sun glared off the car roofs. People stepped out, gathered, but all I heard was the slamming of car doors, coming at me as if from far away.

The mourners clustered, their arms stiff and straight at their sides, a woman holding the hands of two small children.

The sun was so bright, uncomfortable even with sunglasses. I closed my eyes. I wanted to know I'd remember something from this moment for the rest of my life—the marker, the sun, the cake, the other funeral—I wanted to be sure.

But no one could be sure of anything. Only ready. And most of us not even that.

Pears on a Willow Tree

A M Y — P r e s e n t

My daughter still doesn't believe the people in photographs are real. We've just picked up our photos at the one-hour place, we're sitting in the backseat of the car in the parking lot, and I flip through the pictures of us raking leaves last Saturday. The sky is very blue in these photos, the kind of blue that's not a color anymore but a feeling. The sky couldn't have really been that blue because I know I would have remembered, would have noticed. "See, that's Mama," I say, pointing to myself in the picture. My daughter looks, presses her finger against my tiny Kodak face, scrunches her forehead. I go on to the next photo: "That's Daddy, and that's you," but she shakes her head slow then fast, sets her mouth in that stubborn twisted-tight line that means NO—no cauliflower, no pretty pink dress, no I don't believe you. I try again, going back to the picture of me, but she pushes my hand away and turns her head to look out the window. NO.

At home, I show the pictures to my husband. One he sets aside to put in a frame to take to his office. I know he already has at least a dozen framed pictures in his office, five or six more that he carries in his wallet. This is only one of the reasons I love him so much.

My daughter sprawls on the floor looking through her picture books. She thinks these people and animals are real. She tells me she wants them to come to her birthday party; then she asks to drive by their houses, demands to call them on the phone. "Why not?" she asks when I tell her no, "Why?"

"They aren't real," I say.

"Yes, they are," and she points to the picture of three cats sitting around a table eating mice sandwiches. "See?" She turns to another page, a picture of four skunks playing "crack the whip" on ice skates. "Yes."

After we put her to bed, my husband and I sit, as we sometimes do, in the dark, watching out the back window as the moon climbs through our neighbor's trees.

"She'll outgrow it," he says, putting his hand on top of mine, sliding his fingers between my fingers, curling them under, holding tight. "It's cute."

Part of me knows that's true because she'll outgrow all sorts of things, like the way she sticks her tongue into a glass before she drinks and how she smiles and waves at the sun when she goes outside.

"She'll outgrow it," he says again. "Promise."

I nod, not to agree but to hold the silence between us. Outside the moon is big and round and perfect.

I try harder: I show her photographs of my mother, my grand-mother, my great-grandmother, explain who they were, photos of me as a little girl, photos of those summers in Detroit. She listens because she likes to sit in my lap when I'm in the big chair by the window, and I make my voice sound the way it does when I'm reading from one of her picture books. But she shakes her head when I point to my grandmother's face in a photograph. NO.

Of course she'll outgrow it.

But even then, how will I know she understands what I'm telling her when maybe I don't understand it myself?

I spend an hour alone in an art supply store one Saturday afternoon, trailing the tips of my fingers over pale expanses of drawing paper, sketch pads, crinkle-edged paper soft as rags, unbendable white squares; picking up every sample pastel crayon, streaking it along scrap paper to learn exactly the color it leaves behind, its texture, how it feels in my hand making big strokes, tiny lines, only a dot. Then I make my decisions.

It's the next day before I have a chance to take my art supplies out of the trunk of the car and bring them into the house; it's late at night, my daughter sleeps in her room, my husband sleeps in our bed, the TV chattering at him. I sit alone at the kitchen table, and this is all there is: the whir of the dishwasher behind me, the refrigerator burping on and off, the clink of ice cubes piling up in the ice maker, and me drawing pictures on my big stiff sheets of paper, coloring them in with my special crayons, choosing each color with precision. Time disappears.

I spend many long, late nights just like that first one, reaching for every detail from my mind to put on paper. As I draw, I think out the words to the story in my head, silently reciting them over and over until they come as natural as breathing, and I know they're right. Then, using my best handwriting, I put the words of the story with my pictures. *The Night the Wolves Ran Through the Snow*, I call our book, and I lace the pages together with a blue ribbon, my daughter's favorite color.

In our bedroom, both bedside lamps still glow, dropping a yellowy light on my husband's closed eyes. A folded magazine slides off his chest onto the floor as he sits up, reaching his arms for me: "I'm awake," he mumbles, "I am."

I show him the book. "How did you learn this?" he asks, "I thought I knew you." He flips through the pages, reads the story, goes back to the beginning and reads it again, and then once more, as if there are secrets he wants to understand.

We share a deep, peaceful sleep, our arms and legs and dreams entwined.

Late the next afternoon I gather my daughter into my lap and we sit in our favorite chair by the window. Outside the sky is gray and drizzly—the kind of day you expect will be forgotten and I start to read from our book. She listens like she's heard the words before, like it's one of the stories she knows and loves and mumbles to herself when she thinks she's alone. I say the words slow, let her look at the pictures as long as she likes, I read the story again and again. Outside, the drizzle turns into a sprinkle then a quiet rain; water droplets collect on the window and dribble down in quick, sudden zigzags.

I don't know this but I feel it: one day my daughter will take this story and all the other stories and make them into picture books that win awards, and she'll live in New York City and on the coast of Maine and all the other places that sound distant but that on a map are only a plane ride away from me. I'll mean, Stay, when I say, "Good-bye," the word surprising me with its suddenness each time.

But I don't know this. What I know is my daughter in my lap, my daughter here with me turning the pages of the story, looking hard at the pictures, making them real, the afternoon wearing away into evening, another day we won't have again. If we know we can't have the one thing we want most, why does our desire for it never lessen?

This is what my grandmother always said when I asked a certain kind of impossible question: "Amy, you're looking for pears on a willow tree," and then she sighed hard, like maybe there were more words to say, but she didn't know them. It's something her mother said to her, something they said back in Poland. Pears grow on pear trees, I thought, but maybe somewhere they didn't, maybe somewhere they grew on willow trees, if I could just find them.

But of course they didn't. Not in Poland or Detroit or Phoenix or Thailand or anywhere I went.

She's gone now—they're all gone—my great-grandmother, my grandmother, my mother, all the great-aunts. When I remember them, it's all of us sitting around my grandmother's kitchen table, their words and stories looping me in, holding me close:

> "I tell you, I gave that lady at the butcher's a piece of my mind."
> "Always let your dress hang overnight before hemming it up."
> "Lay down newspapers flat between corn rows to keep out weeds."
> "You got those lumps in your mashed potatoes because you boiled them too hard."
> "I know I've told you before that Arizona has dry heat."
> "More coffee?"

Then someone says, "Time for dinner," and they're gone, and the clock on the mantel chimes, and yes, it *is* time for dinner, and my daughter crawls off my lap, and together we go into the kitchen.